FANTASTIC WORLDS

FANTASTIC WORLDS

CURATED BY
MARYANN DIEDWARDO

Printed in the United States of America
First Printing: 2025

ISBN: 978-1-954102-34-7 (paperback)
ISBN: 978-1-954102-24-8 (ebook)
Library of Congress Control Number: 2025948000

Curated by Maryann DiEdwardo
Edited by Beth Rule
Cover design by Veronica Coello
Interior design by Amit Dey

Published by:
SOMETHING OR OTHER PUBLISHING LLC
Brooklyn, Wisconsin 53521
For general inquiries: Info@SOOPLLC.com
For bulk orders: Orders@SOOPLLC.com

CONTENTS

INTRODUCTION

Greetings from Cameron Lee Cowan

Hello! My name is Cameron Lee Cowan, and I'm the Director of Publications and Anthologies here at Something or Other Publishing (soon to be SOOPmedia!). I am excited for this collection because it is the first one we've put together during my time in the anthology program. This collection took about a year and a half to complete, but from the first concept, I knew we had something interesting.

We knew we wanted to explore the genres of fantasy and science fiction, and we almost immediately came up with the name *Fantastic Worlds*. It was a true pleasure to work with all the authors. From the first emails of interest to our town halls, we navigated every stage of the process—from concept to final production—together. It was a fun (if sometimes stressful) experience.

When I think of *Fantastic Worlds*, I think of literature, art, movies, and even music that not only entertain us but inspire us to see the world in a new light. These stories transport us to new heights of fantasy and reality. *Fantastic Worlds* offers us the new and novel, but always tells us something about ourselves along the way. Fantasy and science fiction together have the power to help us reevaluate our own lives and our greater society. They compel us to look through a new lens—and sometimes they reveal truths about who we truly are.

Anthologies have had an outsized effect on science fiction. Some of the great writers in this genre began their careers in collections like this one. I hope this anthology introduces some new voices as well.

I want to thank the writers for trusting us with their work—and for trusting this process.

Cameron Lee Cowan, MFA
Director of Publications and Anthologies
Something or Other Publishing

Greetings from Maryann DiEdwardo

I am Curator of *Fantastic Worlds*, the seventh anthology produced by Something or Other Publishing and the first in the genre of fantasy and science fiction. My name is Maryann DiEdwardo M.A., Ed.D. My curating emphasizes the importance of crafting an imaginative journey into new worlds through characters, setting, and plot. We apply specific genre criteria for science fiction and fantasy writing.

I am working alongside Cameron Lee Cowan, MFA, the Director of Publications and Anthologies at Something or Other Publishing. The historical significance of this collection is timely and maintains a sophisticated approach. Each writer offers a unique gift and an important contribution to this new book and shared vision.

Briefly, I want to share both my personal and professional experience and to thank the SOOP organization for this opportunity. I dedicated a full year to working with our writers on this project. My approach as curator included daily sessions to organize the anthology, craft methods of thematic grouping and story placement, address grammar and mechanics, and offer detailed editorial feedback. I also engaged in regular email communication and conversations with our writers.

I developed criteria that emphasized originality and key literary elements. The structures of our stories maintain balance with the themes and language design within the manuscripts. The dialogue supports narrative, action, suspense, and the creation of immersive imaginary worlds. For instance, many openings use narration to express thematic points to the reader—specific points such as setting and place, as well as the development of character traits. In fact, dialogue and character offer transformative insights into the messages of our stories. The criteria of originality include a superb narration, structure with orientation to a narrator voice who reaches out to the reader, and substance with an action-adventure. The quality of our stories is remarkably high.

All in all, I experienced a marvelous year of editing and communicating. My experience with these talented writers has been a journey that I will never forget.

Thanks to everyone,
Maryann DiEdwardo M.A., Ed.D.
Curator, *Fantastic Worlds*

SPACEMAN DAN
AND THE JELLIES

By

Ashley Woughter

The year is 2267. Lieutenant "Spaceman Dan" Daniel Daniels is six years into a two-year exploratory mission to locate a habitable planet for the relocation of humanity. How he came to be in this neighboring solar system and so far beyond his initial deadline are stories for another day—although I suspect you'll want to hear them all, should you ever get the opportunity.

What makes this particular adventure significant is that, on this day—or night, it's impossible to tell in the vastness of space—after years of painstakingly combing the galaxy, Spaceman Dan believes he has finally located a life-sustaining planet. With the atmosphere on Earth becoming increasingly unbreathable, such a find would be astronomical in its importance—more important still to Spaceman Dan himself, who promised his wife, children, and golden retriever that he would not return until he brought the hope of continued survival along with him.

Spaceman Dan checks his landing gear, which he has not used in nearly a year, and finds it operational. With a deep breath and a quick tap of his golden retriever bobblehead (for luck), he begins his descent to the planet below. He has steadfastly studied this unnamed planet for weeks and has chosen his landing spot with great care. Still, there are many unknown variables and—as with any first-time arrival on a new planet—the potential risks are unfathomable.

As the black vastness of space grows smaller behind him, Spaceman Dan passes through strange fluorescent clouds in every color imaginable—including colors he has never laid eyes on until now. The cotton-candy clouds puff away into colored mist as he pilots his small ship through them. Emerging out the other side, Dan gapes in awe at the magnificent alien landscape before him.

In the distance are mountains so great in size they would dwarf even the tallest of those on earth. They are a brilliant sapphire blue and appear to be snow-capped, although Spaceman Dan can't be sure snow exists here as it does on Earth. He activates his landing gear and sets down in a sprawling meadow of lavender-colored grass speckled with flowers in every shape, size, and color. At one edge of the meadow, a forest thick with towering trees wrapped in meaty vines of emerald green. Surrounding the other edges are steep cliffs with sparkling waterfalls spilling into a crystal clear river with pink pearlescent stones at the bottom.

Spaceman Dan engages the hydraulic hatch and exits his ship. He treks slowly to the edge of the river, admiring the beauty of the waterfalls and savoring the roar of the water in his ears. Dan pulls a water test kit from his pack and sets to work testing the water. As he waits for results, he peers into the water and sees schools of brilliantly colored fish. The fish here are reminiscent of those on Earth, yet somehow vastly different—bearing odd numbers of fins and eyes on stalks for maximum visibility. Dan notes that they appear to be bioluminescent, lighting the water around them as they swim. Glancing at his surroundings, Spaceman Dan observes that the butterflies and birds flitting through the meadow are also bioluminescent, and he wonders if all the creatures on this planet share the trait.

The timer on the water test kit gives an abrupt *ding,* and upon checking the results, Spaceman Dan declares with glee that the water is safe for human consumption. His glee turns to ambivalence when he realizes the time has come to remove his helmet and see, once and for all, if the air here is breathable. He suspects it is—the chemical analysis he conducted from orbit all but confirmed it—and yet he hesitates. The analysis is not always without fault, and if he happens to be wrong, any number of things could occur, not least of all the total collapse of his lungs, the bulging of his eyes, and the inevitable demise of one Lieutenant "Spaceman Dan" Daniel Daniels—may he rest in peace.

Spaceman Dan grasps his helmet—wishing for one last good-luck poke of his golden retriever bobblehead, though he knows that ship has sailed—and pulls it from his head with a quick *hiss* as the airlock seal breaks. His lungs don't collapse. His eyes don't bulge. He briefly wonders how long he can hold his breath before finding his courage and inhaling the air.

And what a breath it is…

Fresh. Clean. Hints of lavender, honey and so many beautiful scents he's never smelled before. He breathes it in—and after six years of breathing the stale, recycled air aboard his ship, he is almost certain this must be heaven.

A tear runs down his face.

He is on his knees and doesn't remember falling. He listens to the waterfalls and the strange alien chirping of the birds. Inhales the clean, fragrant, *breathable* air.

He knows his mission is finally nearing its end. He has found what he has been seeking. He has found hope for survival. A new home for humanity and for his family.

A new home for Spaceman Dan.

Dan is so elated by the discovery of this beautiful new planet that he doesn't hear the approach of its current residents from the forest behind him. Not that there is much to hear—they bob and float lazily through the air like bioluminescent helium balloons.

Maybe it's the change in air currents, maybe it's the military training, or maybe just a feeling of being watched, but finally Spaceman Dan turns—slowly—to face the approaching creatures.

Jellyfish? He asks himself. He must admit—the resemblance is uncanny. There are about twenty of them in various sizes and colors, their caps ballooning in and out as they float dreamily over the meadow, long tendrils drifting around them alight with a faint bioluminescent glow.

Spaceman Dan is not at once uneasy, though he cannot know the motives behind their approach. He has met lifeforms on previously visited planets, many of whom were surprisingly uninterested in violence—seeking only to satisfy their curiosity by investigating their peculiar visitor. He has always found it best to approach with caution and peaceful intent.

"Friend or foe, we soon will know." Dan says and chuckles to himself as he watches their approach. The jellies stop a few yards away, and Spaceman Dan raises a hand in what he hopes is a friendly and disarming manner.

"Greetings," he says, knowing the chances of being understood are almost non-existent. "I'm Lieutenant Daniels from the planet Earth. I come in peace."

The jellies float buoyantly in place, but the bioluminescence in their tendrils begins to pulse—darker, then lighter again—as they study him. *Communicating amongst themselves*, he thinks. Although it's impossible to say for sure.

After a moment's hesitation, the smallest of the jellies, yellow in color, makes its way toward him. He stands as still as he can while the creature bobs clumsily around him—its curiosity unmistakable. After a few laps, the jelly stops in front of him, floating in place. Spaceman Dan holds up a hand and the jelly lifts a tendril, mirroring him. Dan waits. The jelly reaches out tentatively and touches the very tip of his tendril to Dan's gloved hand.

ZZAP!

A quick, angry jolt zips through the glove and down his fingertips. Spaceman Dan jumps back with a yelp and gives his hand a little shake. The jelly dips back too—afraid of his outburst. Dan gives his hands a few more shakes and lets out a laugh.

"Quite the greeting, little fellow." He says to the jellyfish. Sensing his good humor, the jelly dips closer again but is careful to keep his tendrils back. Spaceman Dan reaches out slowly toward the cap of the jellyfish.

"May I?" he asks.

The jelly hesitates for only a moment before bobbing its glowing cap up under the outstretched hand. Dan nods to himself and gives the jelly a little pet.

"Just like the jellyfish on Earth—stingers on the bottom but the top is safe to touch. Interesting."

The jelly nuzzles into his hand as he strokes it, and Dan smiles to himself.

The remaining jellies begin to drift closer, encircling him. Their lighted tendrils are quite a sight to behold as they fan out around him. Spaceman Dan is so delighted by their unique beauty and friendly demeanor that he doesn't see the biggest jelly approaching from behind. At that exact moment he takes one small, unfortunate step back, and his foot comes down directly on the biggest jelly's tendrils. He feels it squish beneath his foot and springs forward, an apology on his lips. But before he can mutter a single word, the jellies abandon their previous array of bioluminescent colors in unison and turn a bright, angry red. Like the flipping of a light switch.

"Oh," Dan says.

The jellies bob around him, their movements becoming more frenzied—almost enraged. Dan holds up his gloved hands in a way he hopes is disarming.

"I don't suppose it matters that it was an accident?" he asks. "One small misstep for man?" He chuckles nervously. "That's a little astronaut humor for you..."

He drifts off, suddenly and terrifyingly aware that he is trying to reason with giant, angry blobs of space jelly who have no idea what he's saying.

Spaceman Dan hoists his pack over his shoulder and prepares to flee. But the jellies have him surrounded on all sides. The only way out is through them. Dan squares his shoulders and barrels straight toward the smallest jelly in the circle. To say he was stung on his way through the beast is an understatement. The pain is brief but excruciating. He is certain there is not a single inch of his body that doesn't feel as though high voltage electricity is coursing through it. For a moment he wishes for a swift death and then that moment passes, and he is running at top speed through the meadow, the jellies hot on his trail and surprisingly swift. Dan reaches his ship not a moment too soon. He slams the door shut behind him and unintentionally severs one of the jelly's tendrils when the airlock seals behind him.

"My apologies sir!" he yells through the airlock.

The jellies have his ship surrounded but, thankfully, do not seem to know what to do with it. They poke at the side panels with their tendrils but their jolts don't make it through.

"A small mercy," he grumbles to himself.

Spaceman Dan straps himself into the captain's seat and does a brief systems check while the angry jellies continue to circle outside. He heaves a sigh of relief, puts his ship in gear, and takes off for the great, vastness of space. It is not until he is comfortably sailing through the deep darkness that he notices a faint yellow glow at the back of the cabin. He turns in his seat to find the littlest jelly. Still yellow to his relief.

"I didn't realize I had a stowaway," he says.

The jelly drifts closer and settles itself into the seat beside him, careful to keep its tendrils to itself.

"I'm afraid you're stuck with me now my friend. I can't risk returning you."

The jelly hesitates a moment and then his colors pulse— *communicating*, Dan thinks again.

"I'm sorry, friend. I don't understand," he tells the jelly.

They ride in silence for a while, and Dan is lost in his own thoughts.

Sure, he was attacked by giant space jellyfish, but he *did* finally manage to find a habitable planet. The jellies would have to be dealt with, of course, but that is above his pay grade. He hopes for a peaceful solution for both parties. It was the jellies' planet first, after all.

Of course none of this will matter if he can't make it back to Earth.

He casts a sidelong glance at his broken navigation system and heaves the heavy sigh of a man carrying the universe on his back. He bops the golden retriever bobblehead for luck. A moment later the jelly bops it, too. Spaceman Dan laughs.

"That's a problem for another day my friend," he says.

And indeed, it is a story for another day as well. Although I suspect you'll want to hear it.

A SIREN'S TREASURE

By

Rebecca Rose

Deep beneath the waters of an uncharted island in the tropics lay a bountiful coral reef, untouched by man or otherwise. It served as an established home to many varieties of coral and plant life, as well as various fish and other sea dwellers. The vibrancy of the colors was unmatched—hues of orange, red, and green forming a rainbow across the ocean terrain. Everything thrived under the radiant beams of sunlight that traveled down beneath the clear cerulean waters, making the myriad fish all the more vivid. And when you traveled further away from the brilliance of the rays, deeper into the sea, you'd come across a civilization with a meager population of thirty-seven. Thirty-seven merfolk, to be precise.

There were two classifications of these sea humanoids: sirens and merfolk. Merfolk had adapted to simple lives in societal villages, developing a reliable and comfortable way of life within the security of their groups. They worked together to ensure everyone's needs were met, maintaining a systematic way of life based on the trade of labor and goods. Meanwhile, sirens were nomadic hunters, traveling in small packs of two or three. They used their infamous songs to their advantage, manipulating and luring prey into a false sense of security before sinking their teeth into their next meal. Despite the popular belief that these species were the same, there were distinct differences in their appearances and demeanors. Encounters between the two groups were rare—so rare, in fact, that this meeting was entirely unforeseen.

A stray creature had somehow wound up in unfamiliar territory—a vibrant reef bursting with plant life and color. He had been so drawn to the energy and hues that he now had to face an unfortunate reality: he, a siren accustomed to small groups, was now in the inner sanctum of a merfolk's civilization. He let out a fretful whine, unused to being surrounded by so many merfolk. Their language was unfamiliar to him. His lavender fins flared out—a natural reaction to stress and his body's attempt to appear larger. This siren, called Sonare by his former pack, was now alone due to unforeseen circumstances.

The temperature of the water felt pleasant against his violet scales. They extended beyond his waistline, like a mer's might, lining either side of his ribcage—a stark contrast to the pale skin of his chest. The shimmering scales encased his biceps, continuing up to the nape of his neck, where sandy blonde hair took their place. His periwinkle eyes scanned his surroundings with apprehension, painfully aware of the confused merfolk gathered nearby, whispering among themselves as if wondering what had brought a lone siren to their crowded little town. He was far from oblivious to the fact that he was an outsider; the purple iridescent tones on him were uncommon among merfolk.

Though Sonare wasn't unfriendly, he felt defensive—isolated and outnumbered. It made him uneasy, as if surrounded by a pack of wolves. His eyes darted frantically, searching for an escape route, when they locked onto a burst of color turning a corner—something he knew *had* to belong to a siren. Without hesitation, he flicked his body forward, propelling himself through the water like a torpedo after his guide.

The farther he strayed from the bustling mers, the more at ease he became. Finally, through drifting marine snow and schools of fish, he caught full sight of the figure he had been following. Contrary to his initial belief, the figure was not a siren but a young merman with a neon orange tail, marked with captivating teal streaks along the appendage. The deep tone of his complexion complemented the vivid scales, and by Poseidon, Sonare found himself unable to look away. He watched as the colorful boy spiraled happily backward through the water, studying something between his webbed fingers before tucking the object into a woven bag at his side.

The captivating stranger seemed blissful—until their eyes met. The thinner of the pair startled at first, shrinking back into the rock formation as if to hide himself. His multicolored tail tucked slightly behind him, the rounded edges of his fins shielded by most of his body. His once jovial features now held an edge, as if he were cornered by a predator. It was hard to tell what—or who—could be perceived as a threat, especially to one as sheltered as this recently independent merman. In this moment, caught between fight or flight, the tropical mer chose submission.

Sonare kept his distance, able to read the instinctual way the merman had responded to his presence. He made a noise like the soft crooning of a bird, sinking down to sit against the ocean floor, his shimmering tail stirring sand into the water. He moved with utmost caution, careful to give the other boy an abundance of space. *I'm not a danger. Don't be afraid.* Sonare was content simply to be near someone so spectacular, as if he might fall into despair at the thought of being abandoned by someone whose name he didn't even know.

It was safe to assume that this approach had eased the boy's nerves. His body relaxed—a change barely noticeable to most. He chewed on his lip, still teetering on a fine line of uncertainty about Sonare and self-conscious about his own reaction.

Then the merman spoke. "I don't think you're from around here." His voice was quiet, a smooth baritone, and Sonare was overwhelmed by a feeling of safety—similar to what he'd felt with his two companions in his pack.

Sonare's fins flattened against his body, and he offered a nonthreatening smile, which helped him appear less of a threat. His head snapped around as the sounds of other merfolk nearby rippled to his senses. *I don't like this—too many mers.* His thoughts vanished, and he refocused on the other boy, who had pried himself from the rock mound he'd previously clung to.

"Anyways… my name's Enyo." He offered a small smile, a dainty motion to himself ending with his webbed fingers tapping his chest. "And you are?" His hand fell to the strap across his body, grasping it as if holding something of utmost importance.

Sonare wished he'd keep talking. Though he had no idea what Enyo was saying due to the language barrier, he found his voice more stunning than any siren's song and never wanted it to stop. Fully aware that Enyo wouldn't understand him, Sonare replied with a string of excited clicks and trills. *I find you captivating, and I'd like to know more.* His relaxed expression and broad smile said it all more clearly than any words could. He was absolutely enthralled by the discovery of him, even if an impediment kept them from fully understanding each other. His eyes locked onto the bag at Enyo's hip, and he motioned toward it with a sharp fingernail, tilting his head in curiosity. He glided forward, yielding several feet ahead of Enyo to avoid overstepping and frightening him again.

"Oh… um." Enyo glanced down at the plain satchel at his side, pulling it open and arranging it so Sonare could peek inside at his treasures. They weren't anything special—just seashells and rocks that had caught Enyo's fancy. But he liked to give them away as gifts to those he appreciated, and sometimes he kept them to decorate his own home. "I thought they were pretty…" he whispered sheepishly, waving his hand over his head to summon a tiny current that pushed drifting curls from his face.

Sonare peered inside, his dark eyes scanning the jagged edges of broken corals, abandoned shells, and shiny rocks piled within. He emitted a quiet trill, comparable to a kitten's purr, his eyes glowing with shared excitement as they met Enyo's. Still as a statue for a split second, he gauged Enyo's reaction for any sign of dissatisfaction before moving closer. *I like you. Tell me more.*

Enyo didn't withdraw from the close proximity; instead, he shifted his bag over his hip to rest against the small of his back and beamed. "Can I show you around?" he asked, outstretching a brown hand toward him in an outgoing gesture.

The blond studied the hand before his lips formed into a grin mirroring Enyo's enthusiasm. Without hesitation, a pale webbed hand clasped Enyo's, and the pair set off in no particular direction, weaving through rainbows made by schools of fish that scattered at their rapid movements. It was the first time Sonare had heard anything as exquisite as Enyo's laugh—a bubbling sound expressing pure glee, airy and full of joy that seemed to radiate onto Sonare. The sound deepened Enyo's image as an even more divine being in the siren's eyes.

Enyo released his hand as they came across a clearing on the outskirts of town, bursting with life. Small orange fish circled burgundy- and rosy-colored corals. Coral tables lay flat, with a stray octopus's legs hugging the underside of one of the shelves. A pink-orange-hued anemone waved nearby as a pair of clownfish peeked out from the security of their home. The diversity of the reef was made all the more evident here, with the groups of fish brightening the waters. Above their heads, Sonare saw a blond mermaid making her way toward the surface, which stirred further curiosity in him.

Below them, something caught Enyo's eye, and he promptly swam downward to investigate the shimmering artifact. He pushed his hair out of his eyes once more, turning the swirling blue shell in his hand—a turbo shell, round in shape with a cream swirl at its turquoise center. These shells held significance in the culture of this homestead, so it was rare to find one simply lying in the reef. He giggled, pleased with his discovery, and tucked the shell into the contents of his bag. Glancing up, he saw Sonare's gaze still fixed on the surface. Enyo returned to his side, a brown hand resting against the forearm of purple scales which were much smoother than he had expected.

Sonare couldn't help but notice the warmth spreading from Enyo's hand to his chest, where his heartbeat quickened. Dark brown eyes met his periwinkle ones, but he quickly turned his attention back to the surface of the water, where he could almost make out the sun's face. He pointed upward with some of his siren noises, glancing at Enyo as if hoping he might translate the clicks and trills. *What is up there?*

The darker boy chewed on his lip before realizing what he was being asked. "Oh! The shore is up that way. A lot of us like to sit up there in the sun for a bit. It's warm and dry!" His rambling abruptly stopped as he decided it was pointless to explain further. Instead, he looked at the blond and took his hand once again, his striking tail beginning to sway and propel him forward. Enyo's head emerged from the surface of the water, his black hair plastered in swirls around his shoulders and neck. Sonare popped up beside him, his eyes squinting shut, indicating he had never met the sun except through the ocean's protective glass.

Sonare took a moment to take everything in: the pair of mermaids gossiping on the shore, the looming trees just beyond the beach, the waves rolling in and leaving seafoam in their wake. It was exhilarating and new, and he wanted to see more. Taking the initiative, he dove back under the water, gaining speed as he approached the shore, a wide grin spreading across his face. It was then that Enyo fully noticed the way Sonare's teeth came to sharp points—enough to remind him of a siren's nature.

"Did you hear that Enyo was seen hanging around a rogue siren?" the blond mermaid said, running her fingers through her long, half-dried hair. "He's such an idiot. Everyone knows sirens aren't to be trusted."

The other mermaid shrugged off the comment, lying beside her lazily as droplets of water dripped down her tan sides onto the sand below. "I don't see what the problem is. I saw the siren earlier, and he didn't seem to be bloodthirsty like the elders say. He looked kinda scared, poor guy."

"Amity! It's the *principle*! He's gonna end up getting killed or something because he's too trusting!" Eris snapped, before she noticed the siren making his way up to the shore with the so-called 'idiot' on his tail. "Oh gods. Speaking of..."

Amity sat up, pushing her locs off her shoulder so they tumbled behind her back. She shook her head and cupped the other mermaid's cheek fondly. "*Baby...* don't start anything. Spend time with me, alright?" she cooed, kissing Eris's nose in an attempt to capture her attention. It worked, as Eris said nothing further and instead showered Amity's face with soft, amorous kisses.

Enyo and Sonare settled a little further down the beach, Enyo plopping down and feeling the sand stick to his still-dampened scales. Sonare seemed excited, his tongue chattering nonstop. *It's warm and bright! The ocean looks so different from here, and the sand here sticks! This is spectacular!* The warmth of the sun on his fair skin was new, as was the feeling of water dripping down his face. It felt like the lightest touches from fish—only the drops disappeared onto his scales or the sand below.

And then there was Enyo. As if this mer couldn't become even more beautiful, the sun on his scales created the effect of a radiant fire—burning and impossible to ignore. His skin glistened with salted water, his curls already drying into their natural form, making his hair appear shorter than it actually was. When he turned to smile at Sonare, that was it. Sonare had to come to his own conclusions about what he felt for this mer he now considered a friend of sorts. He glanced toward the mermaids further down the shore, their soft touches and physical affections, and he crooned quietly: *I want that.*

Enyo enjoyed moments spent on the beach, although usually it was time spent alone, rummaging through treasures and considering which would suit whom. But this time was different. Now he had a companion who didn't find him odd or boring—at least to his knowledge. He felt accepted in his presence, and despite their short-lived relationship, he found himself pondering the blue treasure nestled atop the pile in his bag. He glanced over at Eris and Amity, or more particularly, at a similar shell hanging from Amity's neck. "So they're like that now..."

He whispered to himself, although the unmistakable fluttering in his chest as soon as he caught the piercing gaze of Sonare. "Hi…"

Sonare's lips curled into a bashful half smile before some unknown force caught his attention. He whipped around, his eyes darkening as he fixated on the sounds he'd heard. Golden hair fell into his eyes, but that wasn't a problem. He was quickly becoming distressed, staring past the trees. He looked over at Amity and Eris, then to Enyo, whose expression shifted to one of concern as he inquired about something Sonare didn't quite catch. *Do they not notice anything?!* He felt the soft hand of Enyo against his neck, concern shining in his brown eyes as if trying to draw him into their warmth. But this time, there was no calming his suspicion.

Especially when he heard the heavy treading of footsteps rapidly approaching from behind them, Sonare let out a feral scream unlike anything Enyo had heard from him before, just before the merman was shoved harshly toward the water. Enyo's eyes widened, uncertain of what was happening, though he saw Eris and Amity dive into the water before disappearing behind a large rock. Foreign voices rang in his ears.

"Look! A couple of sea creatures! Bet we could get a good price for them," one of them said, scratching his beard and daydreaming of the profit he could make from capturing these freaks of nature on the beach. *Oh, how lucky they must be to have discovered a new island—and never-before-seen humanoids.*

"They're on our turf, so they're our property," the other cackled as he approached with a tool Sonare wasn't completely unfamiliar with. It was a harpoon—the same tool used to take his pack away from him. *And by the gods, if I'm going to allow them to take away my newfound light…* His body tensed, fins flaring out like a betta fish might when it senses a threat to its livelihood.

As he heard the words coming from behind him, Enyo was suddenly overcome with the understanding of Sonare's rash actions. *He wants me to retreat to the water before I fall victim to this danger.* With the scuffling of feet approaching, he heard Sonare let out an aggressive hiss behind him and turned to watch the events unfold before him. As soon as one of the humans was within reach, Sonare lunged at him, fins flared out and defensive. His jaw clamped down on the man's forearm, sharp teeth embedding into flesh, a downpour of blood dripping onto the white sand as he released. That was enough to make the man retreat behind his friend wielding the harpoon, and Sonare urgently called to Enyo, *"Get to the water!"*

And despite everything, Enyo could understand what Sonare meant this time. He dragged himself back to the water, diving toward the large rock behind which Eris and Amity were tucked away. It served as a good hiding spot. Amity's turbo shell heaved against her chest as she pressed into the blond, her blue eyes meeting Enyo's before her hand settled on his shoulder in a comforting gesture. It was as if she could sense his utter fear—the wish for Sonare to join them safely.

Once Sonare could no longer see Enyo, he turned to retreat himself, before he felt the sting of the blade slicing through the side of his tail. He hissed in pain, and with no further choice of defense, he knew what he had to do. A siren's song—commonly addressed as being used to lure sailors to their deaths—was actually the clearest way of voicing intentions as well as hypnotizing one. It didn't have to be used for particularly one or the other, although for now he would be using his song for hypnotizing purposes.

And then Sonare opened his mouth, revealing his pointed teeth, and with a heaving breath began his song. It wasn't any kind of song Enyo had heard before—no, it was entirely Sonare. Wordless, it was a hauntingly beautiful sound with a register far higher than Enyo would have expected. Even without words, Enyo could tell precisely what he was saying: *Take your weapon, take yourselves. Leave the island and never return, lest you meet an unfortunate end. Forget what you've seen, forget the existence of it all. Live to tell no tales, but live nonetheless.*

The men stood dumbfounded for a moment before the bearded one stepped forward to retrieve the harpoon from the sand, his eyes glassy and dull. Then, silently, they fell into line and retreated into the forest, returning to the shore where they'd left their ship to continue their voyage elsewhere. Sonare sank against the sand with a sigh of relief, the sun blinding as it shone into his eyes. But at least Enyo was safe.

Enyo was the first to peek over the side of the rock, the stress and uncertainty of Sonare's well-being eating at him. As soon as his eyes locked onto Sonare, alone against the sand, he dived under the water to make his way back up to him. He first noticed the slit in the side of his tail—raw and bleeding, but thankfully not too deep. He felt a twinge of guilt. Perhaps if he hadn't been so useless, he would've been of more assistance. What if he'd ended up worse off? Tears pricked at his eyes, slipping down his cheeks as he gazed upon Sonare.

Sonare, now catching onto the negative emotions in Enyo, sat up with urgency. He shook his head at him, clawed fingers brushing away the tears. *That's not good. I'm okay. You're okay. We're supposed to be happy.* He tilted his head slightly, catching sight of Eris and Amity lingering in the shallow waters, but ultimately not giving it much caution. Instead, he sat up fully, wrapping his arms around Enyo and pulling him on top of himself, the pounding of his heart resonating against Enyo.

"I told you he was a good siren." Eris told Amity as they relaxed in the water, still a bit on edge from those menacing events.

Amity's lips parted to gape at her, splashing her playfully. "You *did* not! You're lucky I adore you."

Enyo chewed on his lip, his brown eyes scanning Sonare's face as he felt the heat of blood rushing to his cheeks at his own swirling thoughts. "You're magnificent," Enyo praised, pushing his now dry blond hair off his forehead. "I'm glad you're safe," he added, trying to keep his thoughts off his own wishful thinking.

The most frustrating part of being unable to understand each other was, by far, the way Sonare would never be able to fully explain how he longed for him. He wasn't capable of making sense of the words Enyo's lovely voice spoke to him, and he doubted Enyo could decode his own language. *But maybe…* he thought, *I could put in the effort. I could learn to formulate words rather than just primeval noises.*

"Sss-" His eyebrows furrowed in concentration as he tried to parrot the last word Enyo had said. "Ssss…ay…eff."

That effort didn't go unnoticed. Enyo pressed his forehead against his, uttering the word again. "Safe…"

"Ssss…ay…ffff… Sa…fe…" And that was enough for Enyo to practically jump him, knocking them both into the sand. He erupted into a fit of giggles, overjoyed with the turn out.

"Tell him you love him!" Eris called from the shore, a groan promptly following as Amity jabbed her elbow into her freckled shoulder. Enyo's face burned, and he shot a glare at Eris over his shoulder. The girls took it as their signal to leave, disappearing under the waves, likely to venture back to the village.

Sonare looked at Enyo, fingertips brushing the side of his hips in a mannerism he'd seen Eris perform on Amity during their canoodling. He was content, and that soft rumbling returned to his throat as he caressed Enyo's skin, relishing the softness that was all his. Then he sighed, pondering how long they would be able to carry on like this. He had to tell him—in the only way he was capable. And so, he began to sing once more.

This time, it was soft and less intense—vocalizations made not to manipulate, but to shatter the blockage between their hearts. Eloquent notes designed solely to expose the truths in his soul. The notes painted an image in his target's mind: an image of love and the things the siren longed to say, silenced only by the language barrier. Thus revealing the genuine power of a siren's song. *My beloved, if I had the words to say to you, I would. I sing this song to whisper what I feel. You are glory itself—the sun, the sea, it all. You are kindness. You are patience. You are the loveliest thing in existence. I adore you, I love you, I want you. This Sonare wants Enyo.*

At some point, Enyo's eyes had closed, his heartbeat quickening. He was bewitched by the sound, the melody etched deep into his being so he might never forget. As soon as it stopped, his eyes snapped open, a smile spreading across his face—laced with the essence of his aura: kindness, curiosity, simplicity. Simplicity in him. "Sonare?"

Sonare's fins flitted out in recognition of the name he hadn't yet been able to voice yet. He nodded. "Sooo…nar…ehhh," he repeated, trying to get the hang of producing sounds beyond trills and clicks. "Sooonareee."

"It's beautiful," Enyo praised, an idea suddenly coming to him. With the confirmation that his feelings were reciprocated, there was only one thing left to do. He rummaged through his bag, hoping the prize he sought wasn't damaged. And lo and behold, he was fortunate— the turbo shell was intact. The vivid blue shimmered in the sun as he handed it to Sonare, cozying back up to him. There was a moment of silence as Sonare stared at the shell, turning it between his fingers.

"It's… um…" Enyo suddenly felt flustered. Was he really going to have to explain what a courting gift was?

The blond chuckled, pressing his lips gently against Enyo's forehead in a way that made him feel like he might melt. Or perhaps it was just the sun beating down on them. Enyo motioned toward the water. "We should head back…" He made his way into the cool water, relishing the contrast against his warm skin. He waited for Sonare to follow before heading back down to the reef. He was grateful that Sonare's bleeding appeared to have stopped—not only to avoid attracting sharks but also to ease his own mind, knowing it would likely heal fine.

Just before they entered the village, Sonare caught Enyo by the arm, guiding him gently back. He tapped the shell against his heart, then kissed Enyo's cheek—just as he'd seen the girls do earlier. Pale hands rested on the small of Enyo's back, still clutching the shell in one, as if he could never let go of something so precious. Enyo set his bag aside once more, closing the space between them. His eyes flickered from Sonare's gaze to his lips, then back up to those periwinkle eyes, silently wrestling with his own desires once again.

The warmth radiating between their bodies was something only they could feel—intimate and safe. Enyo's fingertips danced over the violet scales on Sonare's shoulder before settling at the nape of his neck. "You're amazing, and I appreciate your help earlier…" he whispered, trying to steer the conversation with praise and resist the urge to pepper little smooches all over his face. Fortunately for him, Sonare took the initiative instead—first on the forehead, then his left cheek, right cheek, and finally the tip of his nose.

Enyo took the final dive, hands gently cupping the smooth skin of Sonare's face as he guided his lips to his. It was a sweet gesture, though Sonare was initially confused—physical affections like kissing weren't common among sirens. But that didn't mean he disliked it. In fact, he found peace in the feeling of Enyo's skin against his, especially savoring the way one of the smaller boy's hands wove into his blond hair.

After a moment, their eyes fluttered open, a slight parting between their lips as they laughed quietly together. It was a symphony of love and utter bliss, the feeling that they had found solace in each other. After a few more shared kisses and stolen moments, they would return to Enyo's home—ready for more life to live and certainly more adventures to come as a pair.

LADISLAO

By

Ava Wolfe

D *ie Mense van die Son*—the People of the Sun—walked on stilts wrapped around their calves with linen. They walked only on truths as level and straight as the stilts themselves, and their religion was to be honest and good to others every day the sun rose upon them. Grass skirts dyed fuchsia rustled out the dance of the men they clothed, rising above the otherwise bland sprawl of sandstone shelters, domed ovens, and thorn fences. Above the skirts of these parading souls, grass wreaths adorned arms as strong and capable as the stilts they walked on. Pearly-beaded masks smiled in contrast to skin as rich as fertile soil. A small, bristly mohawk of black horsehair completed each man's uniform, harmonizing with the uneven lengths of dreadlocks swaying in rhythm with the Sundance.

A game the young girls played was to outdo the men who had been selected to be Sundancers. The girls would copy them by wearing the same ruffles on their wrists and ankles, yet they would go a step further. Marching in single file, each would adorn herself with two or more heavily decorated wooden masks—square-eyed, pink-nosed, and bearing yellow geometric ears—stacked one atop the other. The largest mask concealed the girl's face, and each additional mask balanced above it grew progressively smaller. The best balancer would take her place at the back of the parade, lest, in the excited shuffle, her glorious headpiece fall.

Despite preemptive actions, such tragedy was common—as if, so long as the sun rose again, there would always be prideful little humans waiting to be humbled. The masked girls, full of unusually high self-esteem, persisted, though they were regularly put in their place by the Sundancers. The men, shaking their bodies in a primordial dance above the amateurs below, would chant, "For adulthood you wait; at your impatience, we laugh!"

The spunky girls would run off—after carefully and temporarily removing their pride—to drain their mothers' tea kettles into wooden cups. When the tea was gone, they would go back outdoors to make fun of the boys who dressed themselves in shells. All boys aimed to deserve the honor of dancing for the sun, but there were those who never grew out of their seashells.

In the arid center of the village, the women would mold giant earrings out of red clay that mimicked fat blood moons. Toddlers would watch in wonder and subsequently grope at anything flashy or dangly.

The families who had volunteered to devote their lives to farming adorned their heads with arrangements of fruit and flowers; they were the life-givers of the village. Over the years, their balance improved as they experimented with differing weights atop their heads. They also celebrated the beauty of their chubby children by painting red, yellow, and white patterns around their eyes and across their plump cheeks. Some farmer children, unaccustomed to the tingling sensation the earthy paint left on their faces, would wash away their mothers' masterpieces.

Shomari, the chief of the People of the Sun, did not act like a king. He humbly hunted alongside the rest, sundanced on stilts disguised as one of the other men, wept with the women in every moment of heartbreak, and played with the children. He always wore a headband with two feathers—one larger and one smaller, but both sturdy—which he said represented "the balance of man and woman."

To those unfamiliar with his nature, his narrow eyes could seem off-putting. The white skeleton painted across his torso might also have disturbed a stranger, but it was his way of reminding *Die Mense van die Son* that all living things would eventually return to the earth. The only possession Shomari took pride in was in the flying wild boar tusk he wore around his neck—a trophy from the beast he struck from the air with a single shot in his youth.

This land—one of thorns and thistles, little feats and fever trees— was where Ladislao was raised. He was washing the peeling paint from his body and massaging his feet after stilt-walking; his feet never seemed as calloused as those of the other dancers.

Lao (as the women called the dashing man) was changing out of his grass skirt and into an evening tunic, when a glint of light caught his eye. Shomari was approaching, the machete at his belt reflecting the glare of the setting sun. Lao gathered his dreadlocks back and continued washing off the paint.

"You were not meant to dance on stilts with a pearly mask and colorful skirt like the others!" Shomari boomed while beaming, greeting him with a rough pat on the shoulder.

Though Lao agreed with this statement, he hid his shock under laughter. "Yes… I'm not sure I can get used to it."

"Boy, you won't have time to get used to it." Shomari sat down as if they were simply having a cup of wine together and discussing the weather.

Lao stared at his chief. "You mean you notice I don't blend in with the other Sundancers?"

Shomari lowered his tone, but his voice was still excited. "With joy I share with you that you aren't needed here."

"With joy—?"

"Now listen, listen. You are a true son of the sun. But I have received signs from God that you are needed elsewhere."

"What do you mean?" Lao asked. He knew he hadn't accomplished anything astonishing in his lifetime. He had always just tried to fulfill what was asked of him.

"I do not understand it all," Shomari said, "but that is the best part about it. I was meditating in front of the sunrise this morning, and in the glow, I envisioned you traveling west and then south. I pondered the vision all day before deciding to tell you now. *You*, boy, have somehow been chosen to make this journey—and to follow a twisted river in a land more luscious than this."

"What journey? What am I to do there?"

Lao didn't know it was possible for Shomari's eyes to light up any more, but they did. "The sun is pulsing, Ladislao. It's calling for a new ruler."

"I hate to call you crazy, but I still don't understand. *Why*? Nobody can live on the sun."

Shomari grew desperate. "Hear me, Ladislao. I am beyond honored that you have been sought by God to play some part in our very sun. How perfect for you is this? In fact—take this."

He fumbled around his neck before handing Lao a necklace with a single red bead.

"Wear it always. Wear it all the way to the Amazon. It symbolizes the extensiveness of your human heart—wear it to remember that the God of the sun is with you."

"Okay… but where do I start?"

"Remember—west, then south until you find them. Use your resources along the way. You're a grown man. You'll be fine. Get on with it!"

"I'm going to—to find who?!"

"Leave as soon as possible and say goodbye to anyone you love— until you find the River Woman. All I can tell from my visions is that she is a gentle spirit who roams this certain part of the Amazon you must go to."

Before Lao could object any more, Shomari shook him excitedly by the shoulders and skipped away, whooping and hollering.

Lao was left to stare at the red-beaded necklace in the palm of his dusty hand. Stashing his parade attire away under the washbasin he shared with the other men, he told himself this is what he had been waiting for. He might never see that grass skirt again.

It didn't take him long to pack and he set off that very night to the west coast of Africa, where he would eventually find a boat that would take him all the way to South America.

Many asked where Ladislao had gone. Shomari insisted his body had gone to the sun.

THE STRANGE BREAKDOWN OF ARCH13

By
Jessica Russo

Memorandum

To: IT Department, Isaac Asimov Robotic Manufacturing Corporation

RE: AI System Malfunction Report

Diagnostic data indicated Robo unit ARCH13 (referred to here as Archie) had a malfunctioning articulated arm. Archie was transferred to articulated arm repair bot AR13L (referred to here as Ariel). During repair both Archie and Ariel units experienced unprecedented energy surges and blew multiple breakers, causing a temporary shutdown of the facility. Archie was returned to the line functioning at 100 percent efficiency.

Within two hours, the Archie unit sent out a failure alert, which would again involve the articulated arm function. The Ariel unit had unusual delays in repair time. However, the log file indicated no errors were ever found. Archie was again restored to the line with full function. Similar malfunction alerts were sent out four more times with no data to support defect or failure. It would appear that Archie's artificial intelligence was *intentionally* creating false error files.

Upon the next such malfunction, it was decided to deactivate Archie to diagnose and reset Archie's artificial intelligence system. Before the shutdown was complete, systems indicated Ariel was experiencing critical failure. The two Robo units were found shut down with articulated arms interlocked with one another. Central computing indicated Ariel self-terminated moments after Archie was deactivated. The Archie and Ariel units will remain in storage together, as they were unable to be separated. The last line of Ariel's final log file read, curiously: "Thus, with a kiss, I die."

End of report.

JLP, Robot Manufacturing Technician Lead

CHRONOSPHERE

By

Stephen St. Clair

Psychiatrist Dr. Monroe sat across from his newest patient—known only as John Doe—reviewing the medical records. The doctor noted that John was still unaware of how he'd arrived at the hospital.

After only a few sessions, Dr. Monroe had begun to suspect his patient was suffering from some form of dissociative disorder. He'd seen hundreds of patients over the years, but something told him he needed to ask more questions—he needed to keep digging.

"Good morning, John. How are you doing this morning?" Dr. Monroe asked.

"Fine, I guess. Have you seen my uniform? Laundry service must be running late. I'll have to talk to the captain about that," John replied.

"Can you tell me a little more about your uniform? What does it look like? Maybe I can get someone to look into why it's not ready for you," Dr. Monroe said.

"Standard military fatigues," John answered coolly.

"I'm sorry—which branch was that again?" Dr. Monroe asked, fishing for more clues.

John stared at the ceiling, his eyes fixated on something unseen.

"John, do you remember when we first met? When they brought you to me?" Dr. Monroe asked.

John continued to stare but didn't move.

"John, why were you in that field naked?" the doctor asked.

"I was... being held captive. They were going to torture me, but I escaped," John replied.

"Who was going to torture you?" Dr. Monroe asked.

"Germans. The SS were going to torture me, but I managed to get loose and run. I took several of them out along the way too."

"You aren't in Germany, though. How could you have taken on German soldiers if you were actually in the middle of the United States?" the doctor asked.

John didn't respond but began fidgeting with his fingers.

"John, are you going to talk to me?" Dr. Monroe asked. He was beginning to think the repressors he'd given his patient weren't working—or perhaps they had been too strong.

"Can I have the radio today, Doc? I could use some music," John asked.

In the first few sessions, John had kept mumbling words that sounded like nonsense. When Dr. Monroe realized he was reciting song lyrics, he decided to use the radio as a form of positive reinforcement.

"Yes, but remember what I said last time? You can have the radio if you cooperate and answer some questions. Remember?" the doctor asked.

"I remember. I can't answer those questions, though. You're not authorized," John replied, his gaze fixed on the doctor but seeming to look straight through him.

"Forgive me. I'm sorry. How about this—what can you tell me about the SS soldiers that were holding you captive? Do you know where? Or how many there were?" Dr. Monroe asked. He was changing tactics now. "Answer those two questions, and not only will you get the radio—I'll get you a special dinner tonight."

John was quiet for a second. A calculating look entered his eyes. He was deciding how much he could reveal—or whether the bribe was worth the risk.

"Okay, deal. So—radio and dinner. Can I get a beer too?" John asked, pushing for more.

"Sure. What kind?"

"I don't care. Just not any of that German beer. Anything American is fine."

"Deal. Now—how about the answers to my two questions?"

John looked around the room as if searching for something.

"What are you looking for?" Dr. Monroe asked.

"A map. Got one?"

"Sure. Just a sec." The doctor got up and pulled out a folded world map, laying it across his desk.

John stood and walked over. His eyes scanned the map until they landed near the North Pole.

"There." He pointed to a small island in the Barents Sea.

"Were you on that island?" the doctor asked.

"Yes, but only for a day or two. One of the soldiers let his guard down, and I slammed his skull against the wall. I've never seen a man's head gush so much blood," John replied casually.

"Then what did you do?" Dr. Monroe asked, intrigued yet slightly terrified.

"I took that dead son of a bitch's clothes, put them on, moved his body to my cot, grabbed his keys and gun, and headed out. I made a mess of things, though. I got pretty far before I was stopped. Someone must have realized I wasn't SS."

"Then what?"

"I shot my way out of the bunker. I made it out, but once I was out of sight, I realized I was on an island."

"Did you make it off the island?"

John stared at the map. "I killed them, Doc. All of them," he said, his eyes blank.

"You did what you had to do, soldier. Now, how about a nice steak and baked potato?" the doctor said, deciding not to push him further. He sensed that trust, once earned, would lead to deeper revelations.

"And the radio. I still get the radio, right? I can't get these damned lyrics out of my head," John said, pounding his temple.

"And the radio, yes. Why don't I get you back to your room, and I'll call in your dinner order myself. Deal?" Dr. Monroe asked.

"Don't forget about our deal."

"I won't. Let me get the nurse to take you back to your room, and then I'll order your food. I'll hand-deliver it when it gets here. Hell, I may even have the same thing. Steak sounds good tonight."

"Attaboy. A little steak and a cold beer to wash the day's troubles away!"

A male nurse—easily twice the size of either the doctor or John— entered and escorted the patient back to his room.

As soon as John left, Dr. Monroe picked up the office phone.

"Hi, Betty? I need a favor. I want to try a new tactic with the John Doe case."

"Sure. Whatcha thinkin'?" came the voice on the other end.

"Well, for starters—two steaks, medium rare. Two baked potatoes with butter and sour cream. And two beers. American. Oh—and a radio."

"Dr. Monroe, need I remind you about hospital policy on alcohol?"

"What, that we should all be imbibing more often?" he said with a hint of sarcasm. "Look—I need to try this. If it doesn't work, the board can fire me. Do whatever you have to do. And for God's sake, bring me a radio."

"I'll see what I can do. All I've got is that old MP3 player and some headphones."

"I'll take it. Bring everything to my office. I promised John Doe I'd hand-deliver it."

"Geez, I wish someone would hand-deliver *me* a steak and beer."

"Add one more to the bill then. I'll pay for everything. Make sure they know it's on me—it's probably better that way."

"Will do. I'll bring it up as soon as I can."

Dr. Monroe hung up and turned to his computer. He began an internet search for the area John had pointed to on the map. One article after another revealed images of the remains of what looked to be underground bunkers with Nazi swastikas on the walls.

Something didn't add up. Based on his physical appearance, John appeared to be in his twenties, possibly early thirties—yet everything he described matched historical records. He reviewed notes from previous sessions and found himself considering other diagnoses—perhaps not dissociative disorder as initially thought, but **chronesthesia,** the vivid mental projection of oneself into the past. John had described things as if he had actually been there.

Then he remembered something from John's medical exam when he was brought in.

Pulling up the medical records, he found what he was looking for—a photo showing a brand—or tattoo—of numbers on John's chest.

He tried cross-referencing the numbers, but hit a dead end.

There was one more path to try. He had an old military contact who specialized in special cases. It had been a long time since they had spoken.

He looked up the number and called. After three rings, a simple beep signaled the caller to leave a voicemail after the tone.

"This is Dr. Monroe. I have something that might be of interest. Call me back."

He'd just set down the phone when it rang again.

"Hello?"

"This is Captain Stockton. Is this Dr. Monroe?"

"Yes."

"What do you have for me?"

"I'm not sure how to explain. I have a John Doe who was found naked in a field outside town. During the medical exam, a tattoo was discovered on his chest."

"Why is this of interest to me?" the captain asked with a hint of impatience.

"Because my John Doe just described being held in a secret Nazi SS bunker where they tattooed him with prisoner numbers."

"Did he say anything else? Or has he asked for anything?"

"Yes. He asked for a radio. Said he has song lyrics stuck in his head."

"Don't give it to him yet. I'm on my way."

Click.

Dr. Monroe pulled the phone away, stunned. A knock at the door startled him—it was Betty.

"I've got your food. And thank you for mine. It looks delicious!"

"Ah—almost forgot. Set it there. I'll take it down in a minute," Dr. Monroe commented distractedly.

Betty looked at Dr. Monroe and noticed he was acting a little strange.

"You okay?"

"Shut the door and come here. Hurry."

Betty set the food down on the table, then shut the office door. She quickly made her way over to Dr. Monroe's desk.

"What's going on?" Betty asked.

"There might be military personnel showing up soon. I contacted a military source about John Doe."

"Oh my goodness—is he a terrorist?" Betty asked, worried.

"No. I don't think so. I guess we're going to find out, though."

"You still taking him the food?"

"I have to. I can't let him know I know something's up."

"Good idea. Want Bruno to come with?" Betty asked.

"Yeah, not a bad idea. He can stand outside the door just in case," Dr. Monroe said.

"Alright, well, let's go. I'll go finish my dinner and you go have yours with your patient. Please be careful," Betty said.

"I will, and if a Captain Stockton shows up, try to give me a heads up so I can decide if I need to be prepared for anything," Dr. Monroe replied.

"Will do. Now go enjoy your dinner," Betty said, then left the office.

Dr. Monroe gathered the food items, then headed towards his patient's room. He made sure Bruno followed.

When he arrived, John was staring out the window. His patient's room had a view of the lake that was behind the hospital. It wasn't a bad view to have.

"Well, as promised—steak and potato, and I managed to smuggle you in a beer. Two beers to be exact," the doctor said.

"I'm ready." John reached over and cleared off the side table so his dinner could be placed there.

"Did you bring the radio?" John asked anxiously.

"I'm still working on that. What song did you say you had stuck in your head?' the doctor asked.

"Something like: 'Always being here, looking out from behind these eyes… feeling more than a lifetime.'"

Bruno popped his head in. "That's Pink Floyd! 'A New Machine.' Good song."

The doctor looked to John, expecting an "ah-ha!" moment. Instead, John froze mid-bite.

"John, you okay?" Dr. Monroe asked.

The fork dropped out of his right hand and with a quick movement of his now empty hand, he double-tapped his left wrist with two fingers. "This is Agent Andrew Carmichael. I need a new machine. Code red. I repeat—code red."

Beeping followed.

The man—now known as Andrew Carmichael—looked up at Dr. Monroe and his orderly Bruno and smiled. "I gotta hitch a ride. I've been recalled," Andrew said.

"What do you mean?" Dr. Monroe asked.

"Did you contact anyone?"

"A man named Stockton. Captain Stockton. Why?" the doctor asked.

"You might as well kill yourselves now or come with me. I don't have time to answer all your questions, but let's just say that I've been around for a while and seen a few things," Andrew said vaguely.

"How about we just eat our dinner and talk about something other than what's going on right now," the doctor suggested. He sensed something more was going on but was trying to keep his cool.

"Sorry, Doc. I can't. Look, I know you think I have some sort of dissociative disorder just like the others, but I promise you I don't. I'm a time agent from the year 2304. That Captain Stockton you just mentioned? I've been after him for a very long time. Who do you think gave me this tattoo?" Andrew said, pointing to his upper chest area.

Dr. Monroe now faced something completely unordinary. There *was* something more to the story with the man in front of him—he was sure of it. Something was telling him to trust Andrew and let him do what was needed.

"Let's say I halfway believe you. I've gotta have something more to go on. Do you realize how many patients I have seen over the years that have had similar stories to yours?" the doctor asked.

"Yes—but how many of your patients can actually travel through time?" Andrew asked, smiling.

Suddenly, the room crackled with electricity. Light bulbs exploded, causing the doctor and Bruno to cover their heads.

"You got about five seconds, then you're going to want to have an escape plan of your own. Stockton is a ruthless killer, and he will end you," Andrew warned.

A strange-looking mirage formed before their eyes. Machines and shadowy figures moved inside it.

"Looks like my ride's here, Doc. I gotta go. You coming?" Andrew asked. "You'll be fine, I promise."

"Doc, what if he's right?" Bruno asked.

Dr. Monroe hesitated. He looked at Bruno, then back at the mirage.

"Two seconds, Doc, then you're on your own," Andrew warned again.

"Ah, hell with it. Come on, Bruno. You only live once!" Dr. Monroe shouted.

The sound of rushing wind now filled the air—the electrical current in the room looking more like a giant Tesla coil with every second that passed.

Dr. Monroe stood up and stepped towards Andrew. Bruno followed suit.

"Let's go, Agent Carmichael. Take me to your leaders. They have some explaining to do!" Dr. Monroe said.

"Attaboy! Come on, Bruno, I have a new job for you!" Andrew said.

Andrew led the way as all three men stepped into the electrified swirling mirage.

There was a sudden burst of energy, blowing out the window in the room. Then silence.

Moments later, shouting from the hallway could be heard, and Captain Stockton and his men burst through the door—too late. They had just missed capturing Andrew. Their plans had been ruined. For now.

Back in 2304, Andrew Carmichael, Dr. Monroe, and Bruno stood safely in the Chronosphere—a large underground black ops facility where special projects like time travel were made possible.

Agents—like Andrew Carmichael—protected the citizens of Earth from people like Captain Stockton who sought to rearrange the time continuum to their benefit and destroy anything and anyone that got in their way.

So for now, the Chronosphere and its agents stand guard at the Gates of Time keeping all that pass through in check.

Andrew Carmichael had more missions to complete to stop Captain Stockton and his minions. The time continuum still needed defending—whatever the cost.

A CHIP IN THE MASK

By

Cody Kennebeck

What is a mask? Is it what we want to be seen,
or what they wish to see?

An air of sugary temptations hung heavy. Syrup, cheese, and chocolate cooked a hue into the air. I sat back on the bench as the waitress brought my food. With a smile and nod, she walked past to tend to more customers, the smell of tobacco trailing behind her. The scent I came for soon overpowered it—though the food had no taste I could remember well enough. From my coat pocket, I pulled a small metal flask and dribbled the red fluid into my coffee. After stirring it with my finger, I picked up the fork to eat.

I glanced toward the window, only to see in its reflection the cook behind me, humming happily. I wasn't two bites into my food when I heard my pocket ringing. As I swallowed, I fumbled the phone from my coat. Marcus's name flashed on the caller ID. I flipped it open.

"Yes, Marcus?" I say

"Shun, the boss is getting everyone together."

"What is it this time?" I took a sip—and nearly spat it out when he responded.

"She thinks it's a masquerade breach."

I coughed the drink from my lungs. "Are you sure?"

"I don't know. Just get here fast."

"Hold my seat. I'll be there in five minutes."

Flipping the phone closed, I sighed and dropped my head into my hand. Why tonight?

I got up, dawned my hood, and dropped a ten dollar bill on the table before leaving to the jingle of the hanging bell. I wiped my mouth as I stepped out onto the neon-lit streets, ducking into an alley to cross to the proper block.

My curse of overthinking was getting the better of me as I asked myself what could have happened—just as a squelch of mystery fluids came from under my shoes.

Everyone in this district knows the first rule of our society: don't get caught! We've lived that way for centuries…or so I've been told. What are centuries to an immortal? Still a word I don't understand. Endless options—and pondering them too hard could drive lesser men mad.

My thoughts were interrupted by a voice calling to me. I looked over my shoulder towards the gruff sound and spotted another hooded figure behind me.

"You look hungry, friend."

I could smell the booze dripping from his beard and a lit cigarette in his fingers. I turned to him. "I don't know what you are talking about," I said, playing dumb and pulling out my flask again for a drink, to aid with the smell of humans.

The man took a puff and said, "I think you do know what I mean… vampire."

I let out a laugh. "Easy, you know the first rule of our society… thrall."

The man's eyes glowed blue as his jaw hung slightly more limp. "Perhaps then I could interest you in my wares, friend?" The thrall opened his jacket and inside were medical bags of blood labeled, "virgins' blood."

"Virgins' blood, eh? Blood and red wine. Naughty, naughty. I'd bet you don't have a reasonable source, do you?"

"The first rule, friend. Don't get caught."

I flip my flask to show the crest on the front. The crest sparked fear to all in the New York black market. "You did just get caught. We rule this district. Your master should have been more careful."

"You're a noble…" he said, clearly nervous.

"Yep. Now I'm willing to let this slide for a price. Then you tell your master to at least ask. My coven will usually say yes."

The man offered a pack to me. I took it and stowed it in my jacket pocket while smelling someone very familiar on this thrall. "Tell Amanda, Shun said hi. Good hunting. But I better not see you again, until I see her."

I wave, as I turn back to my path. I heard the thrall running off. Poor man. Robbed of the majority of his will. Not my business now.

I walked past a line in front of the door, being eyed closely by the bouncer. I dropped my hood and flashed the symbol on my flask. With a nod he pulled back the rope that was blocking the entrance. The people in line were not amused.

Shaking my head as the smoke, lights, and EDM music berated my senses, I stepped into the facility. Though I could sit and laugh at drunk college students pretending they could dance all night, I made my way to the back room. A fellow kindred stood at the door, but this one knew who I was. The man was dressed in black, juxtaposed to his pale skin. He looked down to me as I showed the flask and asked, "What do you search for?"

I smiled back at the man, "The line of light and dark."

The broad man smiled, stepped aside, and opened the door for me. "Right this way, Mr. Kurosami."

"Thank you, Phelix. Give me one second." I pulled my flask and my bag of contraband from my pocket. I poured my share and slipped the rest into the guard's hand. "Consider it a thanks for not locking me out for tardiness."

"Thank you, Mr. Kurosami. Better not keep Lady Catherine waiting any longer."

"Right," I say as I turn down the hallway, the click from the door bolt echoing behind me. The hall was dark and undecorated. But, thankfully, the bulk of the noise was behind me. How could anyone live back here?

I came upon a door and on it was a symbol—identical to the one on my flask—and under it the words "crow's nest." With a nudge, the door opened into a large room. Music played from a corner bar bubbling with human and nonhuman drinks. There was a small market to the left, filled with things that could be useful in the night life— concealable weapons, medical supplies, and other things that would be difficult to find in the human world. The stairs to personal rooms are in front, the dormitories of vampires who don't feel ready to live amongst humans again, for one reason or another.

I took the stairs on my right to the offices. I bound up the stairs and into a large meeting room. It was time for the clan leaders to meet, and I was running late. The main table was encircled by the rest of the leaders, their elder gaze upon me. Though they tried to look down, I made them see me as equals. I see out of the corner of my eye a huddled figure in the corner. That must be what we are here for—poor thing…must be scared senseless. I tried to keep my gaze away for now as I made my way to my seat between Marcus and Lady Catherine.

She commented, "Late, I see, Shun?" Lady Catherine pondered as she swirled a glass in her hand.

"Yes ma'am. It's Sunday."

"Oh yeah, your day off," she said passively. "Where did you spend it this time?"

"The diner on 22nd. This better be important for interrupting my waffles," I said with a laugh.

"You are always one to keep high spirits, Shun."

"In my line of work, you laugh or go mad."

"Then let's get to business, shall we?" Catherine said as she stood up. "Today we have potential for something far more dangerous, a masquerade breach. Though it's the risk of plain sight concealment, getting caught is still dangerous, no matter the circumstances."

She stepped away from the table and offered a hand to the mass sniffling on the ground "It's ok…like I said earlier, you're safe." The mass began to stand up—a young lady, no older than sixteen emerged and timidly took Catherine's hand. "Would you introduce yourself, Miss?"

The girl was like a newborn baby deer as she tried to stay up. She clutched onto Catherine for support. "I… I'm… Isabel," she stuttered.

Catherine talks for her, knowing to ask more of her would be foolish. "She has known a far too familiar tragedy to us—she was stripped of her humanity."

We sat silent. I contemplated how I lost my own.

"Of course, I don't blame her for what happened. And none of you should either. But the point still stands, what do we do? This happened on our watch. We can't just sit back."

The people at the table began to call out their own solutions. Before it became a witch hunt, I shouted out, "All of you shove it!" Feeling my fangs ache, I pull out my flask and take a sip before continuing. "If we are going to bicker like children, could we do it without the fledgling here? She's scared enough."

"Do you have any suggestions, Shun?"

"While all of you figure out how to track her sire, I could take her back to my apartment. As the youngest member, perhaps I could get the most information out of her and help her the best with adjustment. I'm sure we would have appreciated that when our dusk fell."

"That's smart, Shun. That's why I refused to start without my number two."

"I'm flattered ma'am." I smiled before rising to offer my hand to Isabell. "Let's get you out of here. Believe me, these meetings get really boring." She smiled a little, her fangs had hardly come in.

Fledgling babysitting. How fun.

SECOND CHANCE

By

Jamey O'Donnell

"We've been given the green light. They're going to let us proceed, but it has to be someone already sentenced to at least twenty years to life," said Dr. Phillips.

"We've got to get busy then. We have a lot of convicts in the Colorado Penal System that fit into that category," said Professor Milieu.

A new experimental drug had been invented to bring the dead back to life—under certain circumstances. To qualify, the deceased party would have to be under the age of thirty, considered a vital member of society on the verge of contributing breakthrough advancements to the human condition in physiology, psychology, or a technology critical to either field, and never convicted of a sex crime.

The physiological requirements were stringent. The subject must not have died from a foreign substance in the body, must not have died in such a way that could not be corrected with surgery within twenty-four hours of death, and must not have any underlying diseases.

Dr. Phillips had been spearheading this research at Mindspeak Laboratories for the last seven years, prompted by the Department of Defense and the National Security Agency, whereas Dr. Milieu had come into the picture later when it looked like advancements were going to be ready for clinical trials.

Dr. Milieu's interest was from a biblical and spiritual perspective—he wanted evidence of life after death in the spiritual sense. In other words, he wanted proof of heaven and hell.

Dr. Milieu was a professor of religious studies at Denver University. He had written two controversial books on the existence of life after death, taking the position that there was no evidence supporting the theory and dismissing near-death experiences as dreams.

Their test patient must first agree to be executed—a tall order in and of itself—and the execution could not be done by lethal injection, firing squad, guillotine, gas, or hanging. To fit into the physiological parameters of the clinical trial, the only permissible method was oxygen deprivation—either by suffocation or drowning, both horrific ways to die.

They would begin their search within the Colorado Penal System, and if they could not find a volunteer, they would have to look outside of the state.

Anyone willing to enter this clinical trial and risk an early death would have to believe they could not endure a full twenty-year prison sentence—let alone life—or any significant time in prison at all. In exchange, their sentence would be commuted and they would be released from prison with a $250,000 stake to start a new life for themselves, funded by Mindspeak Laboratories.

The search began. Eliminating all of the sex crime and homicide convicts left fifteen percent of those serving life sentences in Colorado as eligible. Unfortunately, none of these convicts agreed to the program. The search expanded nationwide. After months of interviewing thousands of inmates across the country, they finally found an inmate in Texas who agreed not only to be executed, but to die by drowning or suffocation. His name was Gerald Bostwich.

Gerald Bostwich was convicted in 2020 for manslaughter—he had killed a family of four while driving intoxicated, his third DUI in the state of Texas—and was serving twenty-five years to life at Huntsville State Prison in Huntsville, Texas.

Bostwich was twenty-seven years old and had already served thirteen months. He had been raped and beaten numerous times in the general population and was seriously considering taking his own life—until the opportunity presented itself to him by the warden of the prison.

After numerous interviews and physical and psychological testing, it was determined by both doctors that Gerald Bostwich fit the parameters for their test subject. Legal papers and releases were signed, and the execution date was set for January 23, 2022.

Bostwich chose to be drowned instead of suffocated, for reasons unknown.

New ground was being broken in America. This would be the first time a man not sentenced to death for his crime would be legally executed by any Department of Corrections. The only reason it was allowed to proceed was because of the new assisted suicide law that had gone into effect in Texas the year prior, even though this stretched the meaning of the law to its absolute limit.

One of the questions never asked of any of the potential volunteers was their position on faith in a higher power. Had they asked Bostwich, he would have told them he was a devout and faithful follower of Christ, even though he was considering the ultimate and unforgivable sin of suicide. He believed in heaven and hell, and that someday he would be in one or the other.

Dr. Phillips never considered the participant's faith as germane to the results he was looking for, and Dr. Milieu did not want to influence any outcome should the experiment succeed.

It was the morning of January 23, and a glass tank of water had been assembled outside of the gas chamber at the prison. The tank measured ten feet tall and six feet wide on all sides. Cameras were set up against the outside of the glass of the tank, along with two cameras inside the tank at each front corner.

Bostwich was to have his hands cuffed from behind and would be shackled to a 100-pound weight on each ankle, preventing him from moving within the tank and possibly breaking the glass. Heart and lung monitors would be attached to Bostwich's body to determine absolute death and time. In addition, neural monitoring devices would be attached to both of his temples, recording and displaying EMF emissions from his brain and optic nerve.

During U.S. Army Research and Development testing, scientists accidentally discovered a previously undetectable transmissible signal connecting the optic nerve to the temporal lobe of the brain. This signal could be recorded, transferred, and replayed on video—revealing thoughts and visions previously not accessible to researchers—potentially proving the existence of life after death. Though the body would be physically dead, the brain, in theory, would remain active long enough to provide evidence.

Once Bostwich had been fully outfitted for his death and was moments away from being submerged in the tank, he was given his last rites and a moment to speak.

Drs. Phillips and Milieu were positioned outside of the tank, ready. Over the video screen, they could see what Bostwich saw through his own eyes. Then he was dropped into the tank. The screen immediately was clouded with bubbles and the doctors could see themselves through the water and glass—just as Bostwich saw them. This was extremely hard to witness. They were watching a man die before their eyes, and they could almost feel his distress through the images on the video monitor.

Bostwich held his breath for as long as he could, then finally acquiesced to his fate and took in his first breath of water, filling his lungs and choking the air out of them. As this was happening, the video monitor started to dim, but they could still see themselves through Bostwich's eyes—until the screen went completely blank, which coincided with the heart monitor flatlining.

Gerald Bostwich was now deceased.

Then the screen lit up again. What they saw next marked the first time humanity's most enduring questions could begin to be answered.

Two of the most beautiful beings appeared on the monitor, distant at first, yet their beauty was so striking, it was undeniable, even from afar. As the beings moved closer to Bostwich, both doctors began to tear up—neither had ever seen anything so beautiful in all their lives.

Then appeared both of Bostwich's hands, which now looked more like vapor than actual flesh and bone. The beings each grabbed a hand, and Bostwich began to move forward at tremendous speed through what could only be described as a tunnel of stars and galaxies—which scientists might call a wormhole.

Everything that Dr. Milieu had believed up until the experiment began was crumbling because he was seeing the proof with his own eyes.

Suddenly, the travelers exited the wormhole and were now surrounded by white fluffy clouds. They then descended on the most majestic cityscape ever seen which seemed to go on forever.

They were now on the ground and the spiritual beings had released Bostwich's hands. Next, they saw people of all ages come up to him and embrace him, and you could feel the joy of Bostwich through the video monitor as if it were recording that as well.

The people that came to embrace Bostwich disappeared into him as if they were absorbed by him. Then appeared a glowing man that could only be Jesus, and he was absorbed as well. In the background of all of this was a bright orb of light, and suddenly Bostwich was thrust into the light. Then the screen turned white.

The doctors and prison staff, and anyone that could see the video monitor, were all in tears, as this was the most significant moment of their lives because they now had proof of the existence of God.

This display they witnessed had lasted two hours. It was now time to pull Bostwich's lifeless body from the tank of water and administer lifesaving procedures before injecting the drug into his body for resuscitation.

He was laid on a table outside of the tank, and the water was extracted from his lungs.

He was then injected with the experimental drug—now they would see the results of their experiment. Almost simultaneously with the injection, the video monitor slowly started to lose its luminescence, then suddenly went black.

Bostwich began to cough and started to move on the table. Then he opened his eyes as the video monitor now showed all the people around him standing next to the table he was on.

"Nooooo, no no no no. I want to go back. Please, please, I want to go back," screamed Bostwich, and then he began to cry like a child that had just been ripped from the arms of his mother.

The drug had worked and the experiment was a complete success.

"I saw my mother and my father. My little brother who died in childbirth. I saw Jesus, and I saw God. I want to go back," said Bostwich.

This was never anticipated. The experiment gave a man heaven and brought him back to the hell he'd always known.

THE DRAGON OF CHILKOOT PASS

By

Henrietta DuCap

The sounds of heavy-laden footsteps and pickaxes striking rang along the Chilkoot Trail where it passed by S'eik's mountain. Mining the stone, running rivers through a sieve—the strangers took and took. What were they looking for? Where were the people that S'eik had known—those who had seen him when his scales shone, who had shared the mighty myths of his deeds? Why had the Tizheruk, the water spirit, not snapped these strangers up like so many salmon on their way to the Yukon?

S'eik's scales once gleamed like the copper nuggets the Tlingit traded. Now they were tarnished greenish by his thousand-year life.

As he turned on his pile of gold, S'eik let out a sluggish sigh. The strangers would never—could never—pierce his fortress. His two heads saw everything. He had outlived all the other Sisiutl by at least a hundred years. True, they had put up a valiant fight—banding together to burn the forests where the intruders camped, and shaking the ground beneath their feet by flapping their great wings in the mountains. The Sisiutl had even turned to the Tlingit shamans for help. Still, the strangers had come with blazing metal sticks and candles that blasted the mountains away.

To all of these threats, S'eik turned a blind, golden eye. His hoard ran deeper than the roots of the old-growth spruces—this was the burrow in which he had been born a millennium ago. He slept soundly.

∽ѻ∾

Half an inch of whiskey stood in the bottom of the bottle between the two men. Low candles lit their faces from underneath, hollowing their eyes.

"Naw," said the young man. "If Kaola hasn't told me 'bout that, it ain't true."

"Think again," the old man growled from beneath his long mustache. "If it was true, why would she tell ya?" He raised a bushy gray eyebrow.

The young man grunted. "How many folks have tried to slay this fairy-tale dragon, then?"

"Without number, for sure. But if you did, you'd be the richest man in the world. Forget this camp—breaking your back searching for one nugget in miles of mud."

"I don't buy it. But if he's in there, fat old Smoky had better hustle before we blow that mountain to smithereens first thing in the morning."

"I s'pose we'll see, Will." The old man downed the whiskey.

The candle nearest the younger man snuffed itself out, its wax a pool of red.

∽ѻ∾

Kaola sat up waiting for her man as her baby and her mother's mother slept. She rubbed an antler amulet between her fingers, carved in the shape of an orca. It was one of the only things she had left of her grandfather, who had mediated between the Tlingit people and the spirit world for generations. He saw the spirit in each person and each animal, and treated them all with respect.

Kaola's mother and father entered the spirit world when she was very young, so she did not know whether her mother had inherited some of Grandfather's wisdom. No spirit had been visible to Kaola until the day her grandfather died. She was in his home, at his bedside with her grandmother, when she saw smoke rising like a candle just blown out.

The smoke swirled around her, embracing her. She thought she recognized the smell of tobacco that her grandfather had smoked before he became so sick. When the smoke dissipated, Grandmother lifted her head up from her prayers. She let out a cry and closed her husband's eyes.

Kaola and her grandmother closed their eyes on their old lives. Kaola left her grandfather's home, taking the old widow with her. No spirits had visited Kaola since then, and she didn't blame them. There was no room for their songs and their wisdom anymore—her mind crowded like the camp she now lived in. The prospectors came up the pass looking for treasure, and she mended their clothes to earn her own meager pieces of gold.

When the strangers had first arrived, she had caught a young man's eye—like a glimmer of gold in a muddy river. And with the baby, he had caught her too, like a salmon on a spear. Kaola's son had her soft nose and strong eyebrows—and Will's large ears.

"Hellooooo!" Will called out in a wavering voice as he pulled back the tent flap. The baby stirred but stayed asleep. Kaola's grandmother opened an eye and made a sound of disgust.

"Come to bed, Will." Kaola stiffly brought the small light toward their cot.

"We're blasting that mountain tomorrow," Will said as he took his hat off and lay down. "Hope we find the dragon in there."

Kaola sighed. When her grandfather had spoken of the last of the Sisiutl in the mountains, she had listened with eager ears. But now it had just become another thing for Will and the other prospectors to misunderstand.

"Good night," she whispered.

☙○❧

The boom thundered through the echo chamber of the rumpled landscape. High on another mountain, two men—one old and one young—stood in safety.

Far below, S'eik awoke.

When the dust settled, the men descended from the peak and looked down into the chasm created by their dynamite.

"I think I see something!" cried the older man.

"Come off it, Jeb," Will stood up and kicked a shattered brown stone. It clattered to the old man's feet, and he kicked it into the hole.

Clink!

"Tarnation," said Jeb. "A burial ground?"

"Or Smoky the prospectin' dragon." Will sneered and pulled his earlobe. "Come on, Jeb—we've got other mountains to blast."

He walked forward, but didn't hear any steps behind him. Looking back, he saw the old man fishing around in the hole with his hand. He brought up a fistful of something.

"Gold!" he cried. "It's gold, boy! We ain't leavin' this spot!" He leaned over the gaping hole.

The young man walked back to his partner, and sure enough, *Aani*—or Alaska—had used one of her rare beams of daylight to expose the flecks of glitter in the slag.

"I'm thinkin' we came upon somebody's stash," the young man muttered, watching as his companion tilted his hand to catch the sunlight on each piece of gold imbedded in the rock. His eyes moved up to the high place where they had stood before, scanning for whoever had discovered the hoard.

Jeb laughed. "Finders keepers—we just have to keep watch. We've got all day."

"What about our other jobs for today?"

"You kidding, boy? This here is enough to keep us cozy for the rest of our lives—even for a young 'un like you."

Will nodded, though the old man couldn't see him, and touched the gun at his side. "Mhm."

"What's the matter—you worried about Kaola and the little one? Something like this could keep them out of your hair forever. Hand her some money and start over somewhere else. It's not like you spent anything on gold or diamonds or that hogwash to start with."

Jeb handed the young man his pack of supplies and his coat. Sweat darkened his shirt underneath. "Or keep 'em—I don't care what you do. Just get down here and dig."

Will set the satchel down and drew his gun. He pointed it at the old man's back, which was turned to him as he dug. But before Will could pull the trigger, the ground under his boots quivered and a crack split off the side of the chasm.

The men scrambled to grab their gear as the earthquake intensified, but the crack widened—and an arc of tarnished green scales emerged from the mountain's remains for the first time in a hundred years.

S'eik's head rose above ground. He breathed a plume of fire on his intruders. The flames caught the dynamite in their satchels, and the blast flung debris far and wide with the detonation.

As the dragon lowered back into his home, nuggets of gold— refined by fire—rained down on the smoking earth.

Just after dawn, between waking and sleeping, Kaola caught the sour smell of whiskey. She turned over, but did not see Will. Tendrils of scented smoke swirled around the cot. Slowly, they formed an image of Will before her eyes—from his big ears down to his lanky legs. An old spirit she could not identify floated next to him. When she sat up, her heart drumming, both of them dissipated into the air around her.

Grandfather's amulets clinked together where they hung above Grandmother's sleeping place, and Kaola's vision blurred from the vibrations that now shook the ground. She stumbled as she took her son from the already-swaying cradle.

"Grandmother!" She stuck out her free hand to the old woman, who had fallen to her knees in her attempt to get out of bed.

Kaola pulled her grandmother along as they ran from the camp, past others shouting and scrambling to put on clothes amid the shaking of the earth. They lay down in the grass, the baby crying, until it was over.

"I smell a strange burning." Kaola's dark eyebrows drew together. "That's not gunpowder." She stood up, holding her son to her chest lest he breathe the settling dust and sulfur. Dark smoke rose from between two mountains in the distance.

"The breath of the Sisiutl," Grandmother whispered.

"Will was working on that mountain." Debris and emotion reddened Kaola's black eyes. "I must go. I must know what happened."

"Let the men do it." Grandmother stood and took Kaola's hand, stroking it. "Please, Kaola, think of baby Edensaw."

"Am I not my grandfather's blood?"

"Indeed—but you do not yet have his wisdom."

"I saw Will this morning." The words came out chopped and quivering, like pieces of blubber cut from a beached whale.

Kaola felt her grandmother's soft, wrinkled hand drop from the grip of her own.

"The way I saw Grandfather's spirit, I saw Will. I will go, and I will leave Edensaw with you." She put the baby in the old woman's arms and kissed first her grandmother's forehead, then her son's.

She ran back to the camp, where things lay tousled and out of place. She grabbed her grandfather's amulets and put them around her neck. She flung the clothes from her mending pile until she found a pair of pants that would stay up on her small frame and a too-large shirt. She had no spear against the dragon, but took the knife that she kept underneath the place where she and Will slept.

She dared not look at the empty cradle as she silently slipped on her moccasins and left in pursuit of the black smoke.

Kaola stepped between the two mountains and searched among the spilled blood and gold for a remnant of Will—but could find none in the charred chaos. To the beat of the drums in her memory, she stepped and chanted in a funeral song around the blasted hole in the ground. She did not care how loudly she sang or how quickly the tears fell. She wondered whether there had ever been a dragon, or whether her grandfather had simply fed her myth. The horrors of death and explosion she saw in the debris made her wonder how any greater horrors could still lurk beneath the earth.

The ground quaked once again—but this time Kaola kept low and rose to her feet, knife in hand, in tandem with the dragon's rising. He was well half as tall as the mountain he had come from, and his four copper eyes roved over her until they caught on the bright beading of her moccasins.

"Do my own people disturb me now?" The dragon's words rumbled as deep as thunder. Gray vapors came from the nostrils on both of his heads, shrouding the front of his body.

Kaola's heart jumped at the beast's words. She let the shock pass through her, jolting her arms and legs into a stiff warrior stance against the dragon. "I'm not here for your gold." She kicked away a shining nugget. "You killed my kin."

"Your man?" The dragon scoffed, releasing more gray vapor. "He was just another intruder. I should have known you were tied to the one who blew my mountain away. How do I know you are not the same?"

Kaola held up the amulet around her neck. "My grandfather wore a shaman's crown. You and I—we are the same, straddling two worlds."

S'eik chuckled deep in his throat. "If you were truly a shaman, this would be true. But I accept nothing without proof in blood or gold. Fight me to the first blood. Then I will know whether you have any right to speak to me on my mountain."

"The gold has made you forget much," Kaola said, eyes narrow, heart drumming. "I accept your challenge."

The smell of brimstone reached her nose as the dragon's chuckle turned to a gurgle. Fire was coming—sparks already escaping from between the dragon's teeth as both heads lowered towards her. Kaola stood square in front of him, just a few feet from his jaws. Though her voice trembled, she sang words to a song her grandfather had taught her, holding her knife in one hand and her grandfather's orca amulet in the other.

The plume of fire scorched the air around it, blurring the distant mountains on the horizon. Kaola felt the heat singe her black hair— but then red flame met blue smoke. Above her head, the spirit of a great killer whale swam in smoke as blue as the ocean, evaporating the fire as it came.

Kaola dropped to the ground, coughing, and crawled to the dragon's feet. The smoke of the spirit veiled what she was doing, but she could hear the roars of the dragon and the groans of the whale. She took her knife and cut off the smallest claw on the dragon's right foot. With her sharp knife it was only a little more difficult than trimming a hunting dog's claws. Still, the blood came. First blood.

S'eik lowered one of his heads beneath the cloud of smoke, trying to bite Kaola as the other head snapped at the whale with its sharp, yellow teeth. But his jaws closed on thin air as the whale dove back into the sky's ocean, and Kaola rolled away from the dragon beneath the swirling smoke that smelled of ocean salt.

"I am grateful," Kaola said to the whale as it disappeared.

S'eik tapped nine black claws on the ground, and looked down as blood dripped from his smallest toe. His sheathed chest heaved and his voice came out hoarse from the fire.

"I see you are no common prospector," he said. "Who are you?"

"I am Kaola," her ragged breaths fogged the steel of her still-drawn knife. She lowered it. "I am granddaughter of the shaman of Chilkoot."

"I see you have the wisdom of those who have gone before."

"Indeed." Kaola made her word sound hard and sure, even though she was still piecing together what she had just done.

Kaola's eyes fell to the orca amulet. It had been just a decoration—a memory of her grandfather. But now, with her doubts gone at the sight of the dragon, power had flowed through it.

S'eik coughed. "You and I both want the prospectors gone. They purpose to ruin our land, but I can wipe them out in one burst of flame."

"Look around you," said Kaola, her feet scuffing the charred earth as she rose. "Is that not what they have tried to do to you? Are you not just as greedy as they are?"

S'eik shook his heads. "This is all mine, not theirs."

"But you sleep on your hoard, leaving us to die on our own land. Surely you could help your own people in some way."

"Then take a few pieces of my gold. After I have caused you so much grief, I must offer you some token."

"No," Kaola said. "I ask only for this claw that I have cut off, to make a crown for the new shamans to come."

"Very well." S'eik nodded.

Kaola bent down to pick up the shining black claw that was as long as her hand. "I am grateful," she said.

Kaola never mended clothes for a prospector again. She traded her sewing needle for a fishing line and fed her son and grandmother with fish from the river. She taught her son Edensaw to do the same— and to respect the spirit of all life. She taught him the wisdom her grandfather had taught her and told the true tales of the dragon that still hid in the mountains.

He grew old enough to ask many questions, and she taught him Tlingit as well as the English of the town. Edensaw repeated the words, but there were some he didn't quite understand.

"Mama," he asked one day, "why did you name me Edensaw, after the glaciers?"

"Because," said Kaola, touching the claw that she wore on her headdress, "it is the glaciers that move the mountains."

QUEEN OF DESTRUCTION

By

Joseph Anderson

The world was her dominion, and the sky her birthright. She twisted, and—faster than an arrow—sped toward a small mountain range to the east as the bright sun rose above the peaks. Golden rays fell upon her, the light of dawn turning her scales to flames of gold. A flap of her gilded wings carried her higher, allowing her to gaze imperiously down at the earth below. Her lips curled into a sneer, revealing sharp dagger-like fangs as she surveyed the various settlements of the lesser races beneath her. *Let them toil and labor for their lives*, she thought. *A dragon needs only her wings and the sky.*

Her mouth opened, and with a piercing roar, she loosed a gout of white flame, gliding upon the winds from the north. Angling her body, she beat her wings faster, climbing higher. By now, the earthbound races would have perished from the thin air for lack of breath. Dragons had no such weakness. At last, just as she reached her limits, she tucked her limbs close and dove like a comet, her body straight as a spear. Down she sped, gaining speed and momentum, until she suddenly spread her wings out, halting her descent.

Forth she glided, eyes half-lidded as her thoughts turned to other matters. Idly, she recalled the days of her youth, flying through the skies upon her mighty wings alongside her brothers and sisters. A bitter feeling filled her before being banished; all her sisters hatched in the likeness of their sire, Temujin, the grandson of the mighty Dragon God Ryunosuke—serpentine in body and tranquil in mind. Yet, she, Jarnasaxa, hatched in the image of her dame, the she-dragon Scramasaxa of the Blazing Fang, Bane of the Dwarves, who held descent from Jormünder himself, he who was prophesied at hatching as the World Eater Reborn.

No, Jarnasaxa was not like her sire or sisters. Where they were prone to japes and witticisms, she was quick to take offense; where they meditated and reviewed before making a choice, she allowed instinct to rule above reason. Where her sisters adored their sire and spent much of their youth with him, swimming in the wide rivers of their home, she preferred to spend her days with her mother and brothers. Vivid images of nights spent coiled amidst her mother's treasure hoard danced in her mind, as did remembered tales of Scramasaxa's deeds and exploits against the Dwarves and her wars against the Goblins of the North.

As she soared through the sky, her mind turned to her own deeds of adolescence. She let out a snort, recalling the many human kings and lords who trembled in fear at her glory, each one granting her their entire treasury as tribute. By now, the riches she had accumulated rivaled that of Scramasaxa. But all the gold and silver in the world could not replace the greatest of her treasures.

She snapped to attention as a sharp horn blow rang out. Her eyes narrowed in suspicion. *That was a human horn. Why are humans near our nest?* A snap of her wings sped her toward a lone peak standing a few leagues from the rest of the range proper. While the eyes of most other races could not possibly penetrate the fierce woods covering the mountainside, her sharp eyes sliced through the leafy canopy to scan the ravine leading to her nest. Shock jolted down her spine, followed soon by a deep pit forming in her stomach. With a lurch, Jarnasaxa realized that for the first time, she had felt the cruel touch of fear.

Fear was soon replaced by a familiar fire blazing in her heart, and heat began to race in her blood as her wings beat faster, the air itself being rent by the force of her fury. From the back of her throat, a low rumbling echoed out. The familiar scent of brimstone flew out as Jarnasaxa shook her head, seeking out the interlopers of her home. With practiced motions, she dodged through the trees on the mountain and reached the ravine leading to her nest. There, over a dozen humans stood, clad in steel and armed for war, bearing the insignia of a red boar's head on a green field. Beside them sat a ballista, a weapon used by many would-be dragon slayers. One of them looked up at her and paled.

"Dragon!" he cried, hurriedly setting an arrow in his bow. His compatriots looked up and panicked, three rushing to the ballista. Her rage born of fury could be halted no longer. Descending upon them like eagles upon doves, she let forth her deadly flame-roar—bright and bold and devastating. The sound echoed across the mountain, repeating her displeasure for all the mountain to hear. Her golden flames set everything in her path aflame, blackening the earth and incinerating the unrighteous. The screams of the mongrels beneath her were music to her ears, and it was with vindictive pleasure she pulled up and noted she had slain half their party with a single pass.

With distaste, she saw she had missed the ballista, however. With another beat of her wings, she unleashed a stream of fire just as the crew launched a bolt. Contemptuously, she moved to the side, the bolt sailing past as her fire ignited the siege weapon and turned the barbarians before her into carrion food. She touched down on the burned ground, crouching low. Teeth bared, she scanned the area, tilting her head to and fro. The scent of humans near her home irritated her—wait.

They didn't.

She whipped her body around, her tail smacking into a tree and shaking it. On pensive legs, she advanced toward the cave where her nest was located. The closer she came, the stronger the stench of human became. Once more, the taste of fear clogged her mind, growing with each step.

Finally, she came before the entrance to her nest, the mouth of a cave. The moment she stepped into the cavern she knew something was wrong. The scent of humans mingled with that of hers and her mate's, as did the overwhelming smell of iron and fire. Yet, there was an underlying smell as well—almost like copper mixed with brimstone. Dread pooled in her heart.

She advanced into what should have been her family's sanctuary, her keen senses detecting the charred remains of the invaders. Through the cave she went, apprehensive, until at last she entered the cavern where her nest and hoard were. Except there was nothing but ruin and devastation.

She had been only a few years into adulthood when she had met Farranav, grandson of Favreg Bloodbane. Himself still a few months from adulthood, they had both clashed—him to demonstrate his prowess and vigor, and her to deter him from encroaching on her hunting grounds. Chasing him off, Jarnasaxa did not think of him again until he approached her many moons ago, fully grown and bringing with him piles of gold, silver, and precious stones.

The sheer amount of wealth was enough to gain her interest, but Farranav himself—his demeanor, his vitality, and his battle-scarred appearance—won her over. Not long after she mated with him, she allowed him into her nest, adding his hoard to hers and marking their union as one. Humans, dwarves, even elves might fall out of love and stray from their mates, but a dragon's love burns hotter than the sun itself.

The sight of her beloved mate lying dead, skewered with ballista bolts and long spears, brought steaming tears to her eyes.

"My love," she crooned, horror and grief pooling together as one. She stepped forward and nuzzled her mate's fallen body. His death was days ago it seemed, for his body had turned cold, and his blood had congealed and dried on the bare stone, bereft of their treasure. Heart breaking, she finally turned to their nest and peered into it.

Her heart shattered.

When she had left, Farranav had been curled around three beautiful eggs—ruby, emerald, and sapphire—each of which had carried a treasure more valuable than all the jewels beneath the earth. Now, to add to the tragedy of her fallen love, his last remnants lay broken and dead, dispatched to the afterlife before they even had a chance at life.

All of this was too much for the she-dragon. Her mate killed, her babies murdered, her wealth stolen, all she could feel was a tidal wave of grief and despair. She raised her head and let out a scream of anguish, her soul in tatters. Her legs folded beneath her, and she dropped to the ground next to Farranav's body. Time seemed to stand still as she mourned the loss of her family. Her soul was empty, her spirit drained.

Yet it is not in a dragon's nature to let sorrow bind them in its chains for long. Sadness and grief soon gave way to hate and loathing, and the familiar rage that was her inheritance flared into fury. As slowly as she had returned, she now turned and left, speed and bloodlust lending her strength and energy. The moment she cleared the cave entrance, she was in the air, and as the midday sun shone down, she sped away, into the west.

Over forest, fell, and fen, over stream and river and lake, over mountain and over hill, above the kingdoms of Men and Elves and Dwarves and more she flew, casting the world below into shadow for brief moments. No doubt tales would spread. She did not care. Passing by the coast, she endured the aroma of salt, crossing the channel into frozen wastelands of the Land of the Great North Waters by the time day became twilight. By the time the crescent moon began to rise into the sky, Jarnasaxa had spied the mountain range she sought, capped with naught but ice and snow.

By now her treasure would have been dispersed across the continent, and the killers of her mate and babies as well. She would need aid to ensure justice was done.

Circling above it, she let out a great roar, filled with rage and sorrow and promises of vengeance. Thrice she circled the mountain peaks; thrice she roared her pain for all the world to hear. Finally, just as she prepared to land, a mighty roar sounded from below, and several shapes took flight to join her.

One of them pulled up next to her, vermillion eyes gleaming in the darkness.

"Why do you come to my domain, sister, filled with such pain?" The voice of her broodmate was filled with brotherly concern, his scent and that of his own family a comfort in this hour.

"I come seeking the comfort of my kin, Ravanak, for the loss of my mate and children," her response could not hide her distress.

Ravanak reared his head back, letting loose a burst of sparks and smoke.

"Who dares to wrong you in this way? Tell me, and I shall join you in rending them apart," he snarled.

Jarnasaxa shook her head.

"The lesser races have long held envy and jealousy for us. No doubt some of the ones nearest my domain have plotted for long to dispose of me and mine, to slay us and seize our hoard." Jarnasaxa sneered at the thought of the lesser races. "It is only by luck they did not catch me in their assault."

Ravanak let loose a roar.

"Then we shall join you in enacting retribution upon those thieves and murderers." He turned to the other dragons in the air with them. "Kolkissa, will you join us in this endeavor?" Ravanak called out to his mate.

"Of course, my love!" Jarnasaxa's fellow she-dragon declared.

Ravanak's two dragonets roared out as well, and as one the five soon wheeled out in formation away from the mountain range and toward the Great North Waters.

Once more, they soared above the lesser races earthbound below, as the endless wall of night turned to the enlightening blanket of day.

Midmorning had come when they finally set down on a small bay to rest. Ravanak's get and their dame dove into the water, returning with mouthfuls of fish and several seals clamped in Kolkissa's claws. Jarnasaxa and Ravanak leapt into the water for their own food. The cool water hissed and bubbled against the two dragons, although Jarnasaxa found it most refreshing to her tired limbs.

A tired part of her wondered why no one had set up any dwellings in the bay, for there was open access to both land and sea, and there were plenty of fish as well. The rest of her did not care, for she was focused only on feasting upon the bounties of the sea.

The two siblings returned to shore, where they all sunbathed upon some rocks nearby. Twilight was once more upon them when they finally came across a hollowed-out hill, scorched and crumbling. Crouched upon the crown of the hill were the lithe appearances of her last two brothers, who leapt into the air and spread their wings, neatly sliding into their formation.

"Our condolences for your loss, dear sister," his bronze scales blazing in the light, Anzak inclined his head in solemnity.

"We grieve with you, for your mate and eggs," his eggmate chimed in, viridian scales reflecting light in all directions. "News of the death of the grandson of the Bloodbane along with the destruction of his eggs has spread far and wide. Many amongst the lesser races rejoice at the death of your family, sister."

Disdain and indignation bloomed to life in her chest at Midori's words.

"Filthy mongrels," Jarnasaxa growled.

She swiveled her head around, taking one last look at her kin gathered around her: Ravanak, his mate Kolkissa, and their two offspring; Anzak; and Midori. Fury empowering her, Jarnasaxa surged forward into the distance, her kin adjusting the formation to give her the lead.

Once more night had fallen when they at last returned to where her nest used to be, now ransacked and desolate. Their presence comforted her as they set aflame the bodies of her family, their combined fire igniting the trees upon the mountainside and reaching high into the night. There, gathered in a circle, they held a silent vigil as the mountainside burned.

After an eternity, dawn came at last. And with the dawn came a renewed desire for revenge on those who had wronged her.

Into the sky she and her kin ascended, climbing above the world of men. Her pain and sorrow transformed into fury, and with a flame-roar that put all others to shame, she fell upon the first human settlement she spied. It appeared to be a farming village; farms surrounded it for leagues around, and there were very few people there. Still, their very presence fueled Jarnasaxa's wrath, and from her maw she unleashed golden death upon the hapless villagers, setting their wooden huts ablaze and leaving naught but charred corpses in her wake.

Her kin fanned out, setting fire to the nearby farms and slaughtering all in their path. After three passes, the village was destroyed—nothing but ashes and cinders left of the people who once lived there.

Beating her wings, Jarnasaxa sought out her next target—another village not far from her first. Her kinsfolk continued to fan out, setting every town, farm, and village they came across afire, leaving nothing but destruction and devastation.

Three days and three nights passed in this manner—days and nights of fiery conflagration and mayhem, the doom of man and beast alike.

As a bloody dawn broke on the fourth day of her vengeance, an agonized roar sounded out, filled with pain. Immediately she banked in that direction, dashing high above the smoking landscape bearing the charred remains of a lost nation. By midmorning she had come to where the roar had come from. Anger surged through her.

Sprawled by the bank of a rushing river was Midori—his body unmoving, a curtain of steam rising from where his body touched the water. His once emerald scales were stained and scarred, his corpse stuffed with ballista bolts and showing signs of crash landing. His wings were ripped and broken, the delicate membranes shredded. His legs were bent at unnatural angles, as was his neck. An ebony bolt impaled through one eye socket declared once and for all he was slain.

The death of more of her kin was like adding wood to an inferno. With a screech and increased wing beats, she soared to the seat of her brother's bane.

When she had first made this region hers, the land was wild and untamed, with only wandering barbarians there to call it home. In her years of inactivity, humans came and settled the region, and nowhere was that more clear than by the great city sitting beneath her.

The river where Midori had landed was but one of many that crisscrossed the land, and the city the humans had built was surrounded by no less than five artificial channels being dug to create what was in essence one giant moat.

Upon the makeshift island, three circular walls had been built, each one taller than the last and built of brick and stone. Built into the walls were round, coned-roofed towers, each tower bearing three ballistae. Behind the inner wall was a squat keep that towered above the rest of the city, the banner of a red boar's head on a green field still standing despite being singed along the edges.

Between the three layers were various buildings belonging to the people inside. To complete the picture were several stone bridges built over the rivers onto the other banks—one for each of the four directions and packed with fleeing refugees. However, the bridge built for the eastern side was little more than ruins, for it was plain to see the remains in the wake of now Anzak's fall. His projectile-ridden body could still be seen beneath the rushing, steaming waters.

Jarnasaxa knew what had to be done.

With wings of death, she swooped down over the inner wall, strafing the exposed battlements with her fire breath. The few archers that weren't killed or routed by her brothers died swiftly, although some managed to leap from the walls before they could be incinerated. The towers would be an issue.

Legs out and braced, she landed upon the tiled roofs, the roofs groaning with her weight. Bracing herself, she stretched her neck out and under, her mouth opened wide and sprayed flame at the men within, torching them and their weapons in moments.

That done, she leapt from the tower into the inner level of the city, head down and letting loose with her fire. She crouched down low in the streets, wings folded close to her. Again and again she unleashed her devastating fire, torching every building and person before her without mercy or hesitation.

All the rage she felt—the heartbreak, the despair, the grief—she expelled in the form of infernal retribution, sending the humans unlucky enough to be in her path on a one-way journey to their gods. Over the crackling of her flames, she distantly heard Ravanak and Kolkissa join in setting this city of humans ablaze.

For Farranav, for her eggs, for Anzak and Midori, she would have her revenge.

And then—the flaming hellscape vanished. In an instant, the sector before her lay shrouded in smoke and steam as all her golden fire was snuffed out in a heartbeat.

"I apologize, Great Queen, but I am afraid I cannot let this continue."

The sheer arrogance in those words caused Jarnasaxa's blood to boil once more.

"And who are you, human, to deny me my retribution?" the she-dragon hissed.

Her mind raced, trying to conjure the reason why her flames had been extinguished. Her keen eyes picked out a figure standing in the shadows of one house, shrouded in a cloud of smoke. Jarnasaxa presumed it to be a female human, late adolescence or early adulthood, hunched down low.

Quick as lightning, she turned her head and spat a glob of fiery death toward the human; however, the woman sprinted away, the fire splashing harmlessly against the building.

Unfolding her wings, Jarnasaxa beat the air once, twice, and thrice, blasting smoke and debris away and revealing the unwelcome meddler. Her clothes were form-fitting and dark, with red trimmings. Long, dark hair was held back in a hempen braid, revealing a bronzed face. Eyes as black as obsidian stared up at her.

Standing in the middle of the street, the woman took up what Jarnasaxa recalled to be a human martial arts stance. The sheer gall of that girl! To think she could last even a moment against a dragon! The she-dragon would not let this continue.

From Jarnasaxa's maw came a river of golden fire, rushing toward the girl. For several seconds, Jarnasaxa bathed the street in dragonfire, the stone blocks appearing to melt and warp from the heat. At length, Jarnasaxa ceased, a satisfied rumble sounding from her throat. The sight of the woman standing there unharmed and in a different pose sent shock through the she-dragon.

Once more she let loose flame, and again the human remained unfazed and serene.

When Jarnasaxa launched a blazing fireball toward a column of fleeing citizens, the woman slid a leg to the side and brought both arms down. The fireball swerved and burst onto the stone streets, leaving scorch marks on the cobblestone—and sparing the humans.

Suspicion reared its head at the display. Jarnasaxa took a step toward the human, head cocked. "Tell me, human," Jarnasaxa dug deep into her memories, internally channeling her father, "by what art or craft are you able to defy and wield the fire of a dragon?"

Her disdain for the mongrel aside, she found herself genuinely curious. Very few people were able to cast shield spells that could withstand dragonflame, and of that number even fewer could actually take control of the fire she unleashed. To her knowledge, only elves had such powerful magic; if humans had magical abilities of that level, she would have learned long ago.

The human's answer left only more questions.

"I am a Meta-Human, oh Great Queen. My meta-ability is pyrokinesis." The woman tilted her head in confusion. "I would have thought someone as old and experienced as yourself would have known this."

That little—!

"DIE!!!" With a bestial roar of rage, Jarnasaxa tensed her legs and sprang, front claws sweeping in great slashes. The mongrel spun to the side, beginning a sequence of evasive maneuvers that would have left the she-dragon impressed had it not been for the fact that she was trying to kill the human.

While Jarnasaxa allowed her instincts to take over, her thoughts turned to the little information she had learned. The human said her power was pyrokinesis. Logically, based on her previous displays, Jarnasaxa presumed that she was able to manipulate and control fire. However, when combined with the term "Meta-Human," Jarnasaxa suspected there were likely more humans like her with similar abilities. Yet, if that were the case, she would have learned of this by now through her years of traveling. Furthermore, the human had taken the time to specify what her ability was. If all "Meta-Humans" could control fire, then she likely would not have specified. As such, Jarnasaxa could only conclude that "Meta-Humans" were a group with diverse skill sets. From the sounds of it, these meta-abilities were not spells as she had previously thought, but were likely some form of genetic anomaly, no doubt created from the mutagenic alchemy utilized by humans.

Mentally, Jarnasaxa shrugged. Her curiosity over Meta-Humans could wait: she had a human to slay and a city to burn. She could pursue her inquiries at a later date.

"Eat rock!"

Slam! Pain exploded in her flank as a massive stone block slammed into her flank, sending her sprawling. Her wings—folded—were spared, but a deep ache throbbed in her side. If not for her scaled hide, she would have taken even greater hurt. Jarnasaxa felt her eyes narrow. Whoever had managed to shoot her with a glob of stone had better—Start. Running.

Clambering to her feet, the she-dragon whipped her head in the direction of the projectile attack. Standing in the middle of the street in a battle stance, a male human of a similar size, appearance, and age to the fire wielder stared her down with a wild grin. His grin widened.

"How do you like that, you stupid lizard?"

Jarnasaxa stilled. *How dare he? HOW DARE HE?!!!!!*

All the air in the area was suddenly consumed by the fire blast she unleashed in her newfound rage. She was a scion of gods and god killers. How dare that mongrel refer to her as a lizard!

Once more, her pyronic fury was halted and snuffed out, revealing a district of ash and rubble. The absence of the male human, nevertheless, filled Jarnasaxa with vindictive pleasure. She held her head up, at last determined to sniff the woman out... until the male human suddenly popped up out of the ground like a deranged weasel.

"Hah! Can't touch this boy, lizard!" He raised his arms and clenched his fists.

Immediately, Jarnasaxa leapt forward as the ground on either side of her rose up then collapsed. Jarnasaxa's injury made her bare her teeth.

"Of course there are more of you," she growled.

From her observation, it appeared the male could control the earth. Coupled with his ally still alive, things were not looking in her favor. If more Meta-Humans arrived, she would likely have no choice but to retreat and come back another day. Her thoughts came to a screeching halt when what could only be described as a humongous bolt of lightning shot up straight into the sky, briefly making the day feel darker. Jarnasaxa could not help but marvel at such a display, nor could she ignore the growing sense of apprehension that lurked in the back of her mind.

Just within the reach of her eyes, she spied Ravanak and his family winging away from the city at high speeds, no doubt spooked by yet another meta-ability conjured forth from the Æther.

Jarnasaxa considered her options.

Farranav, their eggs, and her brothers deserved justice. She could not let the loss of her hoard stand. However, by means borne of both meta-abilities and human technological prowess, two dragons were slain in one day and several more driven off. When compared to the tens of thousands of humans killed over the course of her rampage, the numerous farms and villages destroyed, and the damages inflicted upon this city, it would take this nation decades to recover in population, wealth, and prestige.

The she-dragon gazed at the devastation she had caused. Her lust for revenge still pounded in her heart, but she would be a fool to continue her assault. Her family had fled the battle. Albeit, considering her nephews were still far from being adults, she could understand and respect that course of action.

As well, she had lost the element of surprise.

Now that Jarnasaxa was by herself, the garrison could rally and produce a more concentrated defense against her judgment. With the inclusion of Meta-Humans and their near-magical abilities, there was a possibility that she could be defeated and killed if she pressed her attack.

No, neither her sire nor her dame were known for being foolish.

Nowhere in Jarnasaxa's breeding was there any tendency for rampant stupidity.

No, Jarnasaxa would do the intelligent thing.

Unfurling her wings, she stood up on her back legs and jumped into the air, strongly beating against the air. Swiftly she climbed into the sky, passing the wells of the city. Once clear, she turned and flew southward. She gasped as her side strained, height dipping for a moment before she readjusted her flight. She stared ahead, plots and plans running through her thoughts. While defeat was a bitter drink to stomach, nevertheless she had gained valuable knowledge from it, in addition to some experience facing Meta-Humans for the first time.

Jarnasaxa let out a smoke-filled snort.

Yes, for now she would establish another nest—her old one was now too well known, and she could not bear to remain there after what had happened with her own family.

She must go someplace new to recover her strength. Then—she would plan.

This time, she had gathered only those of her kin that were within a short distance of her. Next time, she would gather more.

It would take time, but eventually, her mate and unborn babies would finally be avenged. She would have justice at last.

Oh Geoffry, the face of the human king she had coerced into officially giving her an entire mountain range to her crossed through Jarnasaxa's mind, *it is truly a pity you aren't here to watch your kingdom burn.*

Into the south she flew—away from the memories that would haunt her, away from the burning wasteland she and her kin had wrought.

WOOD AND GOLD

By
C. S. Bennett

The wind blew strongly that dusk, driving specks of snow through the air, but the thick furs the man wore shielded him against the harshness. His back was to the forest from which he had just emerged. He stood staring down the snowy mountain at the remnants of a place he had once known. At the sight, his hand tightened instinctively around the handle of his axe from the pain he felt in his heart. His free hand reached up and clutched a small wooden talisman hanging on his neck. He traced its strange design with his fingers, able to recognize it even through his heavy gloves.

Soon, other eyes emerged from the trees. More of the large, barbaric people stepped forward, moving with a tired grace—like injured dancers—gazing silently at the land spread far below. None of them spoke. The quiet was disconcerting. Nerves and emotional pain strangled their voices.

Then one more stepped out of the forest—a man wearing a proud headdress made from the carcass of a bear. The animal's teeth hung from a necklace he wore close to his throat—a powerful chieftain for a powerful people. This man lifted a knotted and gnarled hand, removed his glove, and placed his palm against the rough, hearty bark of the nearest tree.

"Thank you, ancient ones, for concealing our approach, defending us against unwanted eyes. May you seed a thousand young, and may your forest live on for all of time."

The chieftain's voice was harsh and brutal, a sound shaped by survival and age—but he spoke from a place of love and reverence. He gave the tree a genuine and uncommon smile, one that remained on his face even as he withdrew his hand and slipped it back into his glove. He slowly walked forward, passing in front of the others, whose tired, haunted eyes met his. He looked back at them with a sad, triumphant gaze.

"We're finally going to do it," he murmured, his voice low and rough, barely audible to all but those nearest. He placed a firm hand on the shoulder of the first man who was still clutching his axe, his mind burning with anger. The man's eyes flickered upward, instantly recognizing the bear headdress, and his gaze softened slightly—from both fear and admiration.

Suddenly the chief had his arms wrapped around him—not in a strangle, a choke, a wrestle, or anything unkind, but rather a true and honest embrace. The hug was met with a slow but then intense hug back, as the man realized what was happening.

"We're finally going home," the chieftain murmured, the bear teeth at his throat vibrating as he spoke. His hardened, scarred face contorted from the emotional intensity, tears nearly spilling from his eyes.

When the men broke apart, their faces were normal, betraying nothing of what they felt. When the man with the headdress turned to face his people, he saw all their eyes fixed on him—each holding a weapon, more arriving by the moment, and still even more approaching through the trees.

"Bring me a seer," the chief called out, his eyes—along with the hollow sockets of the bear—staring into the encroaching blackness.

One of the nearest warriors bowed his head, revealing tightly braided hair, and slipped into the crowd. They parted to let him through, the seashells tied around his neck and wrists clattering faintly as he moved.

The wind picked up again as the great warriors waited in silence. The rage building among them had grown more intense, stoked by what they witnessed below—a place that sparked a terrible feeling in those who saw it. But they didn't have to wait long. Soon the warrior returned holding something which was unseen, obscured by the crowd, revealed only when he stepped forward. Cradled carefully in both hands was a masterfully crafted glass sphere, larger than the man's head. The chieftain with the bear headdress bowed his head when he saw what was within. The shadows inside the sphere twisted and contorted, as some pure form of darkness revealed itself in an unusual tentacled form.

"Is everything in order?" the chief asked solemnly, his smile wiped from his face momentarily.

The creature within remained still for a moment before a strange luminescent pattern spread over its shifting skin, portraying bright yellow triangular shapes along with touches of green slashes along the borders before it returned to visual silence. The chief understood the message he had received. He bowed again, and the seer was taken away, back into the crowd.

"Everyone," the man with the headdress began, not needing to speak loudly in the silence. The warriors—all prepared for combat—paused and looked at him, listening.

"Thirteen years. It has been thirteen years.

"I remember when it happened clear as day. I remember what they did to us—as do many of you. I remember the sights that day. I watched my child die, crushed by an unthinking imperial automaton. I watched another stab my wife through her stomach. I watched my friends and family die around me. My sword was sharp that day.

"But today it is sharper.

"I remember the sounds. I can still hear the cries of my baby—the raw, howling fear. I remember the gurgled screams of my love. The screams of my friends. The sobs of our elders. The crack of bones. The splatter of blood.

"All of it—I remember. The day they came to us.

"I remember the smell. The fire they brought. The bodies burning. The vomit in our streets. Our homes in flames. The stench of oil on their terrible metal bodies.

"I know, all too well, the evil they are capable of.

"You all have your stories—your own horrors you have seen. You all remember. You all suffered the misfortune of surviving. You carry the loss, the regret, the guilt. I know what you feel. I feel it every day. My family was stolen from me, and that emptiness is a wound that will never heal—a hole that can never be filled.

"And yet—here we are. Thirteen years later. Ready to descend the very mountain we were forced to flee up on that fateful day. That is why I am happy."

The man paused then. His face still held the shape of a tired smile, but for a moment he closed his eyes and felt the people around him. In that moment, he was keenly aware of the unity they shared, of his connection and unbreakable bond with each and every one of his people.

Then he turned once more and looked down the mountain— down to the place where it had all occurred. What had once been a thriving, beautiful community was now something entirely different, unrecognizable from what it had once been. As he stared at the remnants of wooden buildings, memories returned. He recalled what each had been used for, who had owned them—most of whom were now dead. Many of the buildings he had known were no longer present. In their place, thin golden towers had sprouted out of the ground like weeds— ugly, gleaming things, each being anywhere from three to seven stories tall, built of metal, supposedly impossible to siege.

"When I stare at those vile imperial dwellings, housing those deceitful, thieving people, I smile. I grow only more joyful the more I look. Because the more they have built, the more fun it is going to be to knock it all down," the barbarian chuckled, and a few others nodded along in approval, agreeing strongly with his sentiment. "Many of us now live knowing someone who was lost that day, or someone who succumbed to their injuries in the following days. We all have suffered. Even the children born in the last decade suffer, as they have never lived in our greatness but instead been forced to survive in our hopeless squander.

"We lost many that winter, forced to travel in hopes of finding somewhere to stay, some place to go. And we suffered in the following years, plagued by starvation, infections and disease, freezing, and more. Yet you all know that. You all lived through the suffering that they brought upon you.

"And you know that had we not stumbled toward the shores of the North Sea, then never would we have been able to survive. On our last leg we made it to those faithful shores and collapsed. That was when the seers found us. Were it not for them, none of this would be possible. I would not be here now. But they nurtured us, they fed us. The seers showed us the secrets of their underwater lands. Those strange cephalopods showed us more kindness than any humans we met. And we persisted as we always have, now preparing the greatest secrets they ever learned, right here. Thirteen years later, after everything we have been through, we have returned to reclaim our homeland," he called out with his hands raised at the end, emphasizing just how important that was not only to him but to all those around him.

There was no cheer that he received, only the glares of a few thousand bloodthirsty warriors all in strong and terrifying agreement, either around him or back in the forest, seemingly prepared to take over not just their former village but the rest of the world with it. But the man had not finished his speech yet; he knew now it was time for a pause, preparing what he needed to say as the wind rushed through them once more.

"Those imperial savages thought of us as nothing more than hopeless, dumb barbarians, with nothing but our physical strength, something they thought their automatons could best. And they were right. We are barbarians, and their war machines slaughtered hundreds of us, even going after the women and children ruthlessly," he began, and the crowd of warriors seemed to grow only steadily angrier, with a few hissing softly beneath their breath, angered by the truth, frustrated by their catastrophic failure.

"But thirteen years later, we have returned to show them that they were wrong to underestimate us. We have returned wiser now, knowing secrets that no simple-minded machine can best, knowing things that no imperial scum could ever dream of. They were right to assume that they could defeat us and set up some imperial city. They made us retreat like cowards; they butchered and tortured our people. And we could do nothing to stop them.

"And yet still they were wrong to underestimate us. We are supposedly simple-minded barbarians, strong folk that live in the forest. But if they had truly understood barbarians, then they would have hunted all of us down and killed every last one of us. But they only know themselves. They know that if an imperial scum is attacked, they'll just retreat and accept the loss. They would never dream of fighting back, with only their machines to save them."

"But we are not them!" the chief was now roaring loudly, his voice not angered but instead reflecting a level of excitement that had previously not been shown. "We are not lowly, writhing scum! We are barbarians! And we will fight back! We have studied them! We have trained! We have learned! They thought we would never come back! They thought we would never dare attack them after they brutally ruined us! They expected no further resistance. For thirteen years, they have lived comfortably, in our former beds, in our former houses, building their golden towers while sleeping peacefully as if nothing had ever happened, knowing that nothing will ever happen.

"Well, men, who's ready to show them they're wrong? Who is ready to make them regret every decision they have ever made? Who is ready to make them wish they had never underestimated us? Who is ready to retake our homeland and destroy the imperials?" he roared out at them, shouting in a tone that would have frightened even the great beasts of the north. Yet his unflinching army stood now almost perfectly still, inspired and enraged beyond normal comprehension as many readied for combat. There was a raising of weapons but no cheer then, as they felt as though they couldn't speak—the situation at hand was too important.

"Dress in your war paint, sharpen your blades, and ready the seers. The fighting starts soon," the chief instructed before he stepped into the army, moving through it easily as they parted for him. They respected him greatly, but none of the others spoke a single word to him. He drifted among the trees for a while, passing by many ranks of warriors, then into more muddled clumps of them until he escaped from the main army to the far back, where he stopped—a place where a group of women sat in a small circle in the snow, robed in impressively dazzling blue garments with seashells strung around their necks. Near them a circle of spheres sat on the ground as well, each one carrying an unusual tentacled creature.

"Hail to the great seers and the wise muses. Are we ready to begin the ceremony?" the man with the bear headdress asked quietly, not wanting to sound foolish in front of them, only able to guess the remarkable power they held.

"S'thras Utrumasha tat at al s'romrasus asinval," one of the muses hummed quietly as she placed her left hand on one of the glass spheres, revealing it to be heavily tattooed with great swirling designs—marks of a strange language. A tentacle gripped the frame, greeting her palm with a hand of its own as the being lit up with a cascade of warm blue lights.

"All is prepared," she nodded to the chief, looking up at him with her strange purple eyes, something all the muses had in common as each of them made eye contact with him in that moment. An uncomfortable position, even for a great warrior.

"Very good, please begin. We are all nearly ready for the attack."
He bowed again politely and then departed, moving back to the more
crowded areas.

As he gathered his thoughts, he paused next to a few men who were
speaking quietly, leaning against a magnificently intricate contraption.

"Is everything in order with the sea cannons?" the man asked, his
headdress tilting down slightly, requiring him to lift it back up.

"All of ours are ready. We can move into position anytime," one
of the men said with a nod. As he shifted, the shadows receded from
his face, revealing a long gash slashed down his temple. The chief's
eyes, however, remained fixed on the contraption—a strange metal
device the seers had taught them to craft from objects out of the sea.
It resembled a massive crossbow, built to launch bolts said to pierce
even the automatons and the grotesque golden towers.

"Good then. Now will be the time to move. The battle will be
starting soon," he informed them, clapping the most nervous-looking
one on the shoulder as encouragement. With a shout from the scarred
man, people who had been hidden by the trees suddenly began to
appear, revealing an entire line of sea cannons, each pushed on sleds,
moved by the undying might of the barbarians.

As the chief neared the front of his army, he saw his warriors nearly
finished with their war paint, marking themselves with symbols of red
and blue from the small pouches at their belts. Each family had its own
symbol, its own way of doing it—something that bonded siblings and
generations together as they stood unified in their uniqueness, holding
onto both their heritage and their bloodline while uniformly wearing
war paint to show readiness for battle.

Had someone stopped and listened, they might have noticed that
after everything they had been through, the entire army was now
breathing in unison—a slow and steady rhythm as each warrior grew
more connected to one another. They were all prepared to die, all
prepared to fight, and ready to do anything to reclaim their homeland.

At the very front ranks, the man with the headdress finally made his way to where he had once been and stared down, recognizing that a small force of automatons had arrived at the base of the mountain, watching them with their dead metal eyes. The strange, golden, insect-like machines flexed their many thin arms, some carrying swords while others just had claws sharp and strong enough to rip humans apart. Their heads were elongated, and from their mouths, hideous palps constantly rubbed together, prepared to shred something should anyone near them—though not one of them tried to move up the mountain. Instead, they waited, only programmed to defend what they had conquered.

"More are gathering, sir," one man warned the chief, his worry finally bringing him to speak.

"Let them gather. The more that come in the beginning, the more we can slay all at once. Those that linger—the stragglers—will be the most difficult to deal with," the man with the headdress explained, speaking louder than the others as still more of the insect-like machines sprawled out beneath them, gathering slowly but surely into an alarming horde. Not a single human could be found.

"I need to kill them," another person snarled, staring down at the machines that filled him and many others with such intense hatred that they struggled to control themselves.

"Wait. You know what the signal is. We will wait until we get it. The sun has now fully sunk below the horizon. I do not doubt that we will receive it soon," the chief growled back as he reached into the pouches on his belt and applied his own war paint—swirling curled lines, one red and one blue on either side of his face that mimicked the appearance of bear teeth.

To the back of the army, the muses all stood around a large clearing in the forest, a place that was entirely detached from the rest of the forces. They each rested a seer down in the snow in a large circle, seven in total. The muses' blue robes billowed in the wind, but their stony eyes never strayed from their purpose, and their cold hearts remained uncaring for what was to come.

"Tarton, bring the prisoners!" one of the muses called out, and with only the briefest moment of silence, a man stepped forward—a tall barbarian with a chunk of his face missing: an eye and his cheek, revealing half of his teeth. His broken, limping body was fueled by anger as he pulled on a heavy rusted chain previously concealed by the thick trees, leading to moans and gasps of pain from those hidden in the forest.

Slowly, one by one, a line of naked and pale men and women began to march through the snow to the center of the clearing. Their eyes were haunted, and many had purple or reddened bare feet, undoubtedly frostbitten, with some clearly almost unable to walk. Gashes and other wounds decorated their bodies. Some along the line had stopped moving some time ago—now just dead weight that the other weak ones had to deal with as they hopelessly groaned and marched into the clearing. Only a few had any strength left to cry; the other tortured victims were too pained or tired to follow suit. Altogether, twenty of them came with three already dead before Tarton returned to the forest.

On his way there, he struck one of the prisoners who looked at him, knocking her to the ground and causing those on either side of her to fight to remain standing, choking as their collars suddenly forced them down.

But not long after, the man began to pull another chain forward, carrying yet another string of prisoners with him—this one holding twenty-seven. These were in as rough a shape as the others, yet a few seemed to be in better condition and screamed, trying to escape to no avail. Their whining and screaming were met with Tarton approaching them and swiftly stabbing them with a short knife somewhere in their abdomens, instantly shutting them up as they observed the last moments of their freezing existence.

The forty-seven victims, some alive, some not, stood in the clearing as Tarton returned to the forest and gathered a clothed corpse—not like the others—a barbarian woman. Calmly, near the chains of corpses, Tarton knelt down and held her to his chest, making forty-nine people or bodies gathered in the center of the clearing, surrounded by the women and the seers.

The muses seemed particularly disgusted by the prisoners, each regarding the imperial scum for what they were—some even recognizing those they had been put in charge of kidnapping, one of the duties they most enjoyed.

By now the prisoners had all either collapsed or sat down in the snow, some crying to one another, a few resting against each other, their diminishing body heat the last comfort they would ever know. A few mourned those already dead, while more sobbed for their own fate or the inevitable fate of those around them.

Without a hint of mercy or sympathy, the muses began to chant, lifting their arms into the night sky, revealing their intricate tattoos, watching the stars as they spoke. The seers lit up in their glass containers, flashing series of green numbers, then golden shapes, and then lines of red—ropes of information splayed out on their tentacles before they all, in unison, started to sing their colors in a valiant array of blue while the muses chanted more feverishly.

The prisoners were suddenly jolted from their stupor, their sorrow replaced entirely by pure, raw fear as sharp, searing pains stabbed deep into their brains—worse than any torture they had endured since capture. They screamed and writhed violently, desperate as they tugged and choked against the chains binding them. Only Tarton and the lifeless corpses remained motionless. The prisoners tried to flee the clearing, but swiftly could no longer move. One man nearly reached the edge before excruciating heat surged through his eyes, causing them to boil and drip from their sockets while his tongue writhed grotesquely within his throat. The others suffered much the same. As their agony peaked, their screams and writhing abruptly ceased.

All were motionless before long, their bodies darkened from blood soaking through as if hemorrhaged from within. Then they slowly but carefully dissolved into nothing but blood—their carcasses no longer present—as all forty-nine sank into nothing but liquid, a substance that crashed and shook like the sea, with small ripples and even minuscule waves moving throughout it as it spread and shaped around the clearing into a perfect circle.

Sudden, piercing lights flared from the abyss that had formed. Thunder rolled, joined by the shuddering crack—not of the sky, but of the earth itself—as something strange writhed within. The muses chanted louder, their voices rising over the chaos, while the seers blazed in bioluminescent splendor, glowing like surface stars. From the liquid around them they summoned something radiant, casting back dazzling blues and greens that shot into the heavens—visible to all who could glimpse the mountain, no matter how far away.

A deep, churning hum rose next, swelling through the night as the liquid's surface hardened into jagged motion, surging like waves against unseen shores—shores that existed only in the minds of the muses who summoned the thing below, the very one the seers urged so eagerly to rise.

The surface of the liquid shifted again, twisting into impossible, intricate patterns that spun and wove endlessly. Then, at last, a sleek, dark shape emerged—muscular yet unreal, so black it seemed forged from pure nothingness. It was long, like a serpentine tail reaching ever higher into the sky, until it coiled and revealed a thousand, thousand eyes, each opening in a different, dazzling color.

It was an impossible tentacle, belonging to something never meant to exist. Slowly, it began to pull itself from the depths of the liquid—the portal that had been made for it—dragging its beautiful and hideous colossal form from the waves with effortless grace. It welcomed the new world, feeling the powerful wind against its body, reaching out to touch the reality it now inhabited, acknowledging it.

Then, from neither throat nor horn—nothing that should exist— merely from the emptiness within, a fragment of the great beyond, the thing roared. The sound was unlike any beast, any instrument, any noise at all. It was every sound at once, a clash of all possible noises, a perfect replacement for the oppressive silence that had once dominated.

Every barbarian froze, jolted as if their flesh itself wanted to tear from their bones. Minutes passed before any semblance of normalcy returned. When it did, the man with the bear headdress smiled again— this time, sincere and fierce. He drew a sword from his belt, the blade gleaming as he readied it for combat.

"That was the signal! Leave none alive. Smash the machines and tear down their towers! Today we will take back our home!" the chief screamed shrilly into the stars. His voice sounded small against the roar of the thing behind them—yet it lit a fire in every warrior. With a deafening cheer, they surged down the mountain, howling with rage, weapons raised and ready for battle.

The sea cannons roared to life, firing relentlessly at the towers and the automatons. The insect-like machines stared back, expressionless and unthinking, though some seemed to recognize human faces among the attackers. They now formed a formidable army, a writhing, unstoppable swarm. In their homes, the imperial people shuddered, clutching one another or breaking into sobs, knowing what was coming—and knowing there was no escaping it.

And the dark god looked down with all the eyes that had ever existed, watching the mortal conflict unfold. Its countless eyes saw the physical world, yet as it drew closer to human lands, it already knew the outcome of the battle—and the fate of the rest of the world.

CLANCY'S LAST PARTY

By

David Lastinger

Clancy stepped off the scale and, a moment later, stepped back on. Yep—it still says 190 pounds. He didn't weigh himself very often as his size and weight hadn't changed much in the last fifteen years. However, in the previous twelve months, he had noticed that his clothes seemed a little baggier. His wife even told him that she had been buying slightly smaller shirts for him, so that they fit nicer—he just hadn't noticed.

His highest weight had been 215 during the ten years he worked a desk job. He had been stick-thin for most of his life and felt both happy and sad when he reached that peak weight. He was delighted to have finally broken 200 but saddened that it was not his fighting weight—rather, his sitting-around weight.

He didn't like going to the doctor. However, he liked his current one. She was really nice and listened to him—not like the male doctors he had experienced in the past. At his wife's request, he went for a visit.

"I haven't seen you for a while. What brings you in today?" Dr. Sally asked while tugging at her glasses.

"Doc, I can't quite put my finger on it, and I haven't said anything to Carrie about this. She has enough to worry about, and I didn't want to pile this on unless it had merit." Clancy began to tell his story.

"Oh, tell me more and take off your shirt. I'd like to get a look and listen to your chest." She pulled out her stethoscope and placed it on his chest. Dr. Sally warmed it up a bit before putting the typically cold metal on him—a tip she had learned from her mentor.

"Well, you see, I am a lot lighter now, and I haven't done a thing to my diet. As a matter of fact, I sort of abuse my skinny privilege and eat a bunch of crap. Sorry, ladies—don't hate me." Clancy smiled.

Dr. Sally laughed and put the warm stethoscope right on his chest. Clancy yelped, thinking it would be cold. He started laughing when he realized that he had been tricked.

"Yeah, I deserved that one, Doc!"

"Clancy, your chest looks and sounds good. So, what else is happening?"

"The other day, for no good reason, my nose bled all day long. It was kinda dark and weird. Then, just last night, I had a weird headache and was seeing double all night."

"Since it has been a while since I've seen you, I want to do a full workup, including blood and urine samples. Right now, I don't know what the answer will be, and we will figure it out together. My nurse will be right back to get those from you. So, try not to worry about it—I will call you as soon as I hear something."

When he got home, Carrie asked about his visit. He didn't say much as there wasn't much to say just yet. No sense in raising alarms until he needed to.

"Oh, you know—all the usual 'haven't seen you in a while stuff.' Dr. Sally took some samples and will let me know if she finds out anything odd."

Quietly though, his mind was racing. So many things could be wrong: cancer, some blood-sucking virus, microscopic leeches, or maybe even some crazy brain worm. How much time do I have left? Is it gonna hurt? Will I become some crazy future prognosticator?

He told himself to shut up and sack up. *You made it through the first fifty years, ol' boy—you'll be just fine.*

Later that evening, he took the dogs on a walk. Finally, the dogs would get some sniffing time, and he would feel better too. But he couldn't help thinking about it now. *How many days do I have left? What will I feel like? Will I die in my sleep, or will it be agonizing?*

He felt a few tears welling up in his eyes—something that hadn't happened in quite a while. He was glad it was dark outside. Since no one could see, he just let them fall. As quiet as he tried to make it, it was still an ugly cry. So many thoughts about life events that have not happened yet. So many things that he should have done with Carrie. Maybe he could have been a better dog dad.

He rounded the corner to his street and pulled himself together before walking in the door. He knew Carrie would ask about his red eyes. Some excuse about allergies and rubbing them—that's what he'd say.

"The puppies did great, and I'm tired. Gonna go to bed."

"But it's only 8:00 p.m. Oh—what's wrong with your eyes? They look all red. Are you okay?"

"Yeah, just some dust got in there, and I rubbed them a little too hard. I'll be fine." *See? Told ya she'd ask,* he thought to himself. At least she bought it. He took some Benadryl and soon faded off to sleep.

When Clancy woke up, Dr. Sally was sitting next to him in his hospital room. Carrie was in a chair right next to his bed, looking like she had cried all night.

"What the hell am I doing here? I don't remember coming here at all. Oh, shit." His eyes were open wide now as he sat straight up in bed.

Dr. Sally took his hands in hers. He wasn't sure why, but the softness in her hand and the concerned look on her face told him he needed to settle down and listen carefully.

"I've only heard about this in med school and have not seen it for real until now. I am glad you are sitting down because this will be a lot to take in. Your tests have come in, and the other doctors in the office have confirmed what I am seeing. You have a rare disease called Cometatisis. It's very rare and, unfortunately, not treatable. It's in a very deep part of the brain that is difficult to access. There have been only thirty confirmed cases in the world in the last ten years. Those patients all passed in thirty days or less."

She handed him a shot of tequila, one to Carrie, and poured one for herself.

"Clancy, this isn't the news I wanted to give you today. You've had a great life, and I want to celebrate that with you. I would also like for you to document or journal about the next thirty days so we can study this more."

They clinked shot glasses and downed the tequila like champs. Clancy sat in silence for a few moments, processing the crazy news he'd just received. After a few moments, he finally spoke.

"Does it hurt? Are there drugs? How will it progress?" Those were the first questions which came to mind.

Dr. Sally looked at both him and Carrie. "We don't know much about this disease process, but one thing we do know is that it will wake up the right side of your brain—the creative side. You might start painting, writing, or drawing, even if you've never done those things before. In the last week, you will get tired quickly. But the best we know, it's painless. You'll simply drift off to your final sleep."

They were quiet on the ride home with only the radio filling the silence. That night, they changed into pajamas and sat on the backyard patio. Clancy brought out the bottle of single malt scotch and poured a glass for each of them.

Carrie gazed upon his face and spoke up first. "Clancy, you have been the love of my life, and nobody can or will ever replace you. I don't regret a moment with you—even when you leave your socks everywhere and mix the whites with the colors on laundry day."

Clancy snorted a laugh as a big smirk spread across his face.

"This is a crazy thing you are facing," she continued, "Whatever you decide, I will support you. I have thirty days of PTO saved up, or I could just take a sabbatical from work. Either way, I will be spending that time with you. I'll talk to our lawyer and financial advisor to see what options I have once you are gone."

"Carrie, I have loved you from the first day I met you and am so humbled that you said yes to marrying me. I have not regretted a moment either—except maybe when you dirty every dish in the kitchen just to boil water."

She burst out laughing and punched his arm.

"You have always been the brains behind us, and I know you will be fine."

Clancy poured two more rounds for them and held up his glass to her.

"Let's get to having fun. There will be no sadness between us, only happiness and laughter till the end."

"Sláinte!"

"Sláinte!"

His biggest worry now was how to tell their family and friends. And more importantly, which ones to tell. It would be a shocker no matter what. The next morning—a Saturday—after coffee and a banana, they got to work planning his celebration of life.

They decided on a backyard BBQ—catered so they could spend time with their friends and family—with an open bar and even a chocolate fountain. Carrie insisted on printed invitations—no impersonal, digital shortcuts for this event. This was a big deal and the event needed the personal touch it deserved. They also agreed on who they did and did not want at the party.

The invitations went out. RSVPs came in fast. Clancy took a few more naps than usual but still reported no pain or any other symptoms they had read about online.

On the day of the party, his favorite friends and family gathered. Soon they were drinking, eating, and having a good time.

Then Harry showed up.

Harry was Clancy's brother-in-law and not on the guest list. Both Carrie and Clancy had quit speaking to him five years before when he had tried to steal money from them in a money-laundering scheme. He was caught, convicted, and had spent the last three years in jail for his crimes.

At the door stood Nate, Clancy's best friend and a police officer, serving as the greeter. He had a list complete with pics to make sure that non-guests were not allowed in. Nate was the nicest guy in the world until he put on his 'don't mess with me face.'

Harry ambled up like a long-lost friend, only to be stopped by the big man at the door.

"Sorry, sir, you are not allowed in. This is a private party, and you are not on the guest list," Nate said firmly in his best police officer voice.

"Bullshit. I'm his brother-in-law. Let me pass!" Harry was annoyed that he wasn't getting past the front door.

"No, sir, you have to leave." Nate was now standing up and filling out the door frame.

"Who the hell are you to tell me when to leave? Get out of my way, or you will be sorry." Harry growled through his reddening face.

Clancy had filled in his friend about his BIL, what Harry had done to them years ago.

Nate looked him in the eye, "You're Harry McConnell, right?"

"Yea, what of it?" Harry sneered back.

Nate rechecked his list. Harry was the only one on it.

"You're the one that tried to scam them out of their life savings with your fraudulent bank scheme?"

"That's not the way it was." Harry tried to argue.

"You were caught, convicted, and spent three years in jail, right?" Nate continued in his cop voice.

"Yeah, but I'm out now. I did my time."

"Yes, I see that. Anyway, they don't like you and never have. They say that you are a downright splintery piece of toilet paper and need to be flushed down a pipe somewhere."

Nate was enjoying this part as he could never say this to someone professionally. Clancy had given him permission to have some fun with it. While he was trying to keep his serious face going, he was about to burst out laughing inside.

In the meantime, this was being captured on the security camera—complete with audio—and broadcasted to the backyard on a big TV screen for the guests to watch. Many of the guests knew about this part of Clancy's story and were delighted to see this drama unfold.

Nate continued, "I would like for you to peacefully move along, or you will be arrested for trespassing. In addition, your Parole Officer will be notified."

Harry stiffened up a little and took a big swing at Nate. In one quick move, Nate dodged the haymaker and body-slammed Harry on to the grass. Then, just to have a little more fun, he not only handcuffed him but also hog-tied him and left him face down on the turf while they waited for a patrol car to arrive.

Clancy came to the front door to see what the commotion was all about. He giggled when he saw Harry.

"You were always a hardheaded dumb ass, and now you've made a fool of yourself too."

They turned to head back into the house. As the front door shut, they could hear the sprinklers start up.

This seemed like as good a time as any to let the guests know the real reason why they were here.

Clancy clinked his glass a few times to get everyone's attention. Then, they all got quiet as Clancy began his speech.

"Well folks, now that the drama portion of the evening is over, let me tell you why I brought you here today. You may have noticed that I look a lot thinner than you are used to seeing, and Carrie reminded me that I seem to get tired more quickly now. As much as I hate doctors, I went to see Dr. Sally the other day. She ran blood work and a few other tests, then called us last week with the news. It turns out I have a very rare disease called Cometatisis. The good news is that it doesn't hurt, and it will turn on my creative side like crazy. The bad news is that it is terminal in thirty days."

Gasps went up from the crowd.

Clancy continued, "Carrie and I thought it would be best to be upfront with those we love and not let this be a surprise. Plus, you know I love a good party, and it would suck to miss my own wake!"

Laughs and cheers went up from the crowd.

"Furthermore, there are some rules for tonight. Rule One: No crying. Anyone caught crying will be given a shot of fireball. Rule Two: I only want to hear funny stories about any adventures that you and I may have had over the years. Rule Three: See Rule Two."

Carrie stepped up with a glass of champagne. "A toast to my husband, best friend, lover, and comedian who always made me laugh. I can't wait to see what comes out of your brain in the next thirty days!"

Over the next thirty days, Clancy wrote poetry and drew pictures that had been locked in his head all this time. Carrie took those thirty days off work, and they had a lifetime of fun in those days. They drank Bloody Marys for breakfast and enjoyed nooners every day.

In the fourth week, Clancy had taken to imbibing peppermint schnapps, which seemed to really awaken the artist in him. Moonlight scenes, brilliant sunrises, and snowcapped mountains were showing up on the canvases now. He finished his fourth painting and showed it to his wife.

"Oh Clancy, you have earned that beret because you have arrived as the artist, no longer just the painter."

"I would like this one to go to Dr. Sally. I want you to deliver it after my last breath." He wrapped it in brown packing paper with a note inside that said:

Dr. Sally and Staff,

I can only hope that this painting tells you how much Carrie and I loved, respected, and admired your grace and patience through all these years.

Love, Clancy

On the 29th day—while napping after their nooner—Carrie felt him squeeze her hand tightly and whisper, "I love you." She felt his hand release and knew that it was over. She kissed him on the lips and said goodbye one last time.

That afternoon, the package was delivered to Dr. Sally's office. Her staff gathered around her while she opened the package. As she slowly ripped the paper off, nobody could speak as tears rolled down their faces.

The painting showed a full moon illuminating a high desert trail lined with cacti, creosote, and manzanita bushes. In the middle of the trail were two mountain lions walking shoulder to shoulder with their tails crossing at the tips, intertwined.

MR. POMIKIN'S PUPPY

By

Richard McFarlin

M r. Pomikin handled dogs professionally. He showed all kinds of dogs and had shown all kinds of dogs over his career as a dog handler. His last dog, which he had shown for the Tomson Ranch—and specifically for Grace Tomson, who always won *any* dog show she entered with *any* dog she entered because that's what very wealthy people can do—was a Rottweiler named Boris Von Badisbad. Boris was the pup of two previous champions and had sailed through the competition at quite a number of smaller shows across the Northeast until they reached the Northeast Regional Kennel Club Invitationals, where he beat the previous year's champion, a Golden Retriever named Reginald Rickhauser, aka "Reggie." Mr. Pomikin had received a rather hefty check from Mrs. Tomson for that win, along with a pretty nice bonus.

"Mrs. Tomson, thank you so much. This is more than generous, but I wanted to ask you a favor, if I might?"

Grace Tomson was standing behind her right-hand man, who had handed Mr. Pomikin his earnings. She was gazing about the back area where handlers, owners, and their charges were packing up all the stuff that it took to enter a dog show. Dogs yipped at each other while handlers gathered brushes, lotions, leashes, blankets, and small padded beds for their charges to rest on, packing them into any number of packs or crates. Some of the dogs were in small cages, extremely well padded on the floors, often with warming lamps attached to the tops to make the puppies inside more comfortable. Grace turned toward Mr. Pomikin, fixing him with her iron gaze.

"You know I am loath to grant favors, Peter. Favors given lead those who receive them to believe somehow that I favor them over others, and you know that I do not."

"I understand that, Mrs. Tomson. I would simply ask that you allow me to purchase a puppy of my own, from any litter of any breed you choose, although you know I am partial to the toy breeds." He lowered his gaze in deference to this lady who had given him a chance when he was nothing but a dog groomer, recommended to her by a friend. He had proven his worth, but she was the one who allowed his foot to slide inside a very exclusive door. He would still be shaving Yorkies at The Pampered Pet Salon outside Wappingers Falls had she not heeded her friend's advice and walked through the door of that salon and asked to speak to "Mr. P, please" in her stiff and regal way.

"You realize that would put you in competition with my puppies? And why would I put you in direct competition with the puppies I own by giving you a competitor from my puppies?" She looked down at him, waiting for the correct answer. Peter Pomikin knew the trap that was laid, like cheese in a mousetrap awaiting the oh-too-curious mouse who wanders to the trap, the smell of the delectable cheese wafting through its nostrils—never imagining that something so glorious could turn out to be so very deadly. He had imagined this part of the conversation any number of times, rehearsing what he would say, how he would answer the challenge, and after discussing it with Raul, he had come up with the perfect solution.

"Any pup that you allow me to purchase will either continue to be shown under the covering of Tomson Ranch, or—if that is unacceptable—any competition that any Tomson Ranch pup is entered in, within the category the pup you allow me to purchase competes, we would not enter. Simple as that. You have been so very good to me, so very kind, that I will never seek to harm you in any way, shape, or form. You may have hired me for my ability to handle dogs, but along with that came my loyalty." Mr. Pomikin stopped talking, knowing now it was up to her. Grace Tomson eyed Mr. Pomikin, pursed her lips for a second, then turned and walked away, her right-hand man scurrying behind her. Mr. Pomikin smiled and then busied himself, gathering up all the puppy stuff he had yet to pack in his station wagon.

Three weeks later, Mr. Pomikin was sitting in his living room, scouring an annual breeder's publication—following the genealogy of certain puppies, hoping to find one of a breed he admired and could afford—when his phone rang. He picked it up on the second ring.

"Pomikin residence," he intoned, his eyes still perusing pictures of cute little puppies staring out at him in black and white from the page.

"Peter? It's Grace. I have a puppy for you. Reginald is bringing her by now. You're welcome. Don't forget our arrangement, you understand?" With that, Grace Tomson hung up, leaving Mr. Pomikin staring at the receiver, his heart suddenly beating like a trip-hammer inside his chest, his breath coming in small gasps. He put the magazine down, set the phone in its cradle, and stood up, clapping his hands together in what Raul called "golf claps." At that moment the doorbell rang, and Mr. Pomikin's life was forever altered.

Her name was Princess Penelope Sparklepants, and she came from a very long line of not just prize-winning but award-winning Pomeranians. She was from a line of Poms who had won numerous blue rosettes in all-breed shows around the world, including a Best of Show winner at the prestigious Westminster Kennel Club show in New York's Madison Square Garden three years ago. In other words, she truly was a princess—and now she belonged to Mr. Pomikin. She was presented to him in a puppy carrier without a word by Mrs. Tomson's assistant when Mr. Pomikin opened his door, along with her AKC paperwork and her bloodline. Mr. Pomikin brought her inside, his nerves simply jumping. He opened the door latch, and she came stepping out of her carrier, her little unsteady legs doing nothing to diminish her air of taking over his apartment. She wandered around, sniffing everything in her path, finally stopping on his throw rug under the coffee table and rolling herself around on it, her fluffy reddish-tan coat wafting back and forth as she rolled from side to side, marking the room as her own. For Mr. Pomikin, there was nothing more important in the world than her, now or forever. He got down on his knees and put his face near hers so she could get a good look and the scent of him. She immediately came up to him and started licking his face, her tongue wetting his cheeks, nose, and lips, lapping him ferociously. Mr. Pomikin returned her kisses, picking her up as gently as he could, kissing her face and the top of her head. It seemed to be mutual love, which was just what Mr. Pomikin was looking for, especially since he and Raul had ended things so very badly just a few days after the last dog show, which broke Mr. Pomikin's heart. And the car—the car still had him shaken to his core.

"Tony and I are moving to San Francisco. We didn't mean for it to happen, but it just did. I'm sorry. The climate out there is much more accepting than here, much more open. The culture is changing, Peter, and we think we'd like to be on the cutting edge of that change. Again, I'm sorry. It just happened. It's honestly not you—it's me. I'm at fault here, and I—"

"Goddamned right you're at fault, you lying, cheating bastard!" Mr. Pomikin's heart had shattered into pieces and rage had replaced it quicker than you could bat an eye. "I took you in, gave you a home, gave you love! And this—this fucking betrayal—is how you fucking pay me back after all I've done for you!" Mr. Pomikin stood without realizing that he had stood, pushing his chair backward, causing it to tumble over onto the tile floor, clattering in a little rat-tat-tat sound. His rage was fully encompassing now—fury at the betrayal but more so at the callous way Raul had simply discarded him and his feelings, as people had been doing his entire life. He picked up his plate—half-eaten meatloaf with a dollop of gravy, mashed potatoes, and green beans off to the side because he didn't like his food to touch while he ate it—and threw it at Raul's head, missing badly. The plate hit the wall behind him, splintering into a million pieces of white Pfaltzgraff Heritage dishware.

"Just like my heart and my life," Mr. Pomikin thought as he watched pieces of the round plate explode all over the kitchen, almost in a surreal slow-motion ordeal. Raul moved out that night; Mr. Pomikin refused to allow him to spend one more moment than was absolutely necessary in his home—the home he had opened wide for this man, who he had imagined at one time in the too-near past was the love of his life. Tony came by to help him move out, taking boxes to the old Jeep he owned, avoiding Mr. Pomikin's glare as they shuffled Raul's belongings out the door. When he was finally done, he brought the key, dangling the key ring with the stuffed puppy from his finger, holding it out to Mr. Pomikin.

"I am sorry, Peter. I know you don't believe it right now, but hopefully, one day in the future, you can forgive me and see the opportunity we have to be free in a very closed world."

"The only thing closed to you, Raul," Mr. Pomikin said, snatching the key ring off Raul's finger, "is my heart. Now get out of my house."

Mr. Pomikin's heart had shattered into a million tiny pieces, each one more painful than the last. He went to bed that night, the ache in his chest causing him to toss and turn most of the night and into the wee hours of the morning. Just past five, Mr. Pomikin finally tossed off the covers. For a moment, he stared at the other side of the bed—untouched, where Raul had once lain, now empty, bereft of warmth, love, and companionship—before heading downstairs to start his day. His eyes were red and itchy from having spent the night staring at the ceiling, and he made himself a whole pot of coffee, meaning to jump-start his day by any means, including artificially.

As he sat in the kitchen and sipped coffee from his mug—which Raul had purchased for him last summer when they vacationed in Massachusetts—he reflected on what had gone wrong. They had gone exploring: visiting Plymouth Rock, going on a whale-watching cruise where they saw whales breaching, taking walking tours of famous spots throughout the city, and ending each day in the Faneuil Hall Marketplace. The market, filled with shops and booths offering knickknacks and fun little trinkets, also featured famous sandwich shops where they tried a new sandwich each day: lobster rolls, hoagies, and Italian subs—all of which passed the Mr. Pomikin taste test. On the last day of the trip, as they wandered the market, Raul suddenly darted off, disappearing in the crowd. He came back a short time later with two coffee mugs, both with "I Love Boston" emblazoned on them with a little red heart off to the side. He presented them to Mr. Pomikin and said, "Just a little something so when we drink our coffee in the morning, we'll remember how much we loved spending our moments in Boston together." It was the most romantic gesture anyone had ever made to Mr. Pomikin. Raul dropped his mug a month later, and when Mr. Pomikin wanted to call the shop to order another one for him, he replied, "It's just a mug, Peter. No big deal." Mr. Pomikin should have known right then and there that it was almost over.

"What's done is done," Mr. Pomikin said to himself, setting his mug down on the table. "I can't wallow in self-pity the rest of my life. I have things to do, and they will have to be done without Raul. That's all." Mr. Pomikin got up, rinsed his mug, set it on the dish rack next to the sink, and headed out the door—sad, but ready to greet the day.

Mr. Pomikin's apartment was located one street off Main Street in downtown Fishkill; he lived above a bike shop that was busy all day long. He had his own separate entrance at the back of the building and was able to come down the stairs and head out on Broad Street, walk up a block, and find himself on Main Street of what he considered Small Town, USA. Fishkill was a busy little burg where people were friendly to one another, stuck their noses in your business occasionally, but would give you the shirt off their backs if you had a need. It was a lovely place to live.

Although, to be honest, lately there was a certain pall over the town, almost as if something was wrong with everyone and everything collectively. People were unusually pensive, forgoing greeting each other on the street, instead hurrying by with eyes downwardly cast. Mr. Pomikin noticed but chalked it up to the chilly weather they'd been experiencing the past few weeks. Fall normally snuck in just around the first week of October, but this year it had come in with a roaring "how do you do" the second week of September, turning the summer breezes downright cold, drizzling rain wetting the town every other day, and the skies a menacing grey for the last couple of weeks, virtually ending any sunshine they should have had. It was unusual weather, to say the least, and it had put everyone in a somber mood.

Mr. Pomikin had a few errands to run, which living just off Main Street made them that much easier to do. He grabbed his umbrella, having seen the grey skies out his window and anticipating at least a shower—maybe more. He started out walking up Broad until he hit Main Street, swinging by the chocolate shop that had recently opened, peering in the window as he sauntered by, promising himself a treat after his errands were done. He went into the post office to drop off a package to his brother—some toys for his two little kids—then went into the bank to deposit his check. He exchanged pleasantries with Matilda behind the counter, handed her the check and deposit slip, and got back his receipt with his balance. Depositing the check plus bonus for winning certainly helped the low number he had started with. He walked out of the bank and turned west, heading toward Mays department store. He wanted to pick up a few things, including a new pair of slacks for the shows he had upcoming. "If one was to continue to win, then one must look like a winner," he thought to himself.

Mr. Pomikin decided to cut through the back streets running parallel to Main Street, which would empty him out right at the plaza next to Mays, where Giuseppe's House of Slices was—best pizza in town. Mr. Pomikin had decided that he would get two slices, both with sausage, and a Yahoo—living dangerously. He knew that his delicate constitution would probably revolt later, but he felt very naughty for some reason, particularly since Raul had flown the nest with Tony.

He was wondering if they had left for San Francisco yet when a small dog passed by him, walking almost in the street. As it passed, Mr. Pomikin took a look and thought the dog must be homeless but had been a pet at one point in its life; it just had an air about it that said, *"I'm a good puppy who just wants to be loved."* It was a smaller dog, obviously a mixed breed of the short-haired persuasion, with a face and tail like a Labrador. It sauntered by Mr. Pomikin, tail wagging as it bounced past, its tiny little rump swinging back and forth.

Mr. Pomikin suddenly felt something behind him—sensed something approaching—and the hair on the back of his neck stood up. A chilly wind blew, wrapping around him like an icy embrace, freezing his hands and slipping its way up his pant leg to chill his ankles. He shuddered, catching movement from the corner of his eye—something sliding past him stealthily. A low, a rumbling murmur came from it. It was a car of some kind—long and black—that slunk past, forcing Mr. Pomikin to wrap his arms around himself in search of warmth.

The dog slowed down in front of him and started to whine and whimper, its legs barely able to support its own weight. It had started to pee, hunched over as it stumbled forward, now turning its head to see the mechanical beast sliding up to it.

"There's something terribly wrong with this car, something absolutely wicked—quite possibly actually evil," thought Mr. Pomikin as he watched the long wagon approach the dog, its taillights brightening and almost winking in a weirdly staccato pattern as the driver touched the brakes to slow down. The puppy now had its tail between its legs, almost sitting down, whimpering and whining, while at the same time trying to growl at the vehicle now next to it.

Mr. Pomikin watched as the car slowed, almost stopping next to the dog. He wanted to run and grab it—save it from the car—but he was suddenly terrified, rooted to the spot. The sides of the car started to waver, like it wasn't made of metal but of some kind of liquid substance. The running board began to quiver as if an electric current were running through it. Suddenly, it sprouted what looked like an arm, with a small hand attached. The hand flexed itself, testing the air around it, while the arm it sat on waved and undulated, like a pond would ripple when you threw a rock in it.

The poor puppy was acting the same way Mr. Pomikin was—terrified and rooted to the ground, unable to move, run, scream, or cry, helpless to do anything but watch what fate had in store for him. The hand quickly stretched out, grabbing the dog by the back of the neck, by its scruff, picking it up off its feet as it yelped in horror and surprise. Mr. Pomikin could hear someone whining in a high-pitched tone—almost crying out—but when he looked around for the source, he realized it was coming from him.

The running board hand pulled the dog toward the car, stuffing it—not through an open door, but through *the door itself*, which had pooled in the center, creating an opening large enough for the hand to shove the dog through. Mr. Pomikin, shaking with fear and frozen in its grip, watched as the running board shook and quivered and slowly returned to its original form, seemingly melting back into shape. The door snapped shut, once again just a door.

The car picked up speed, its engine not rumbling but rather snickering as it moved down the street. At the corner, the car didn't simply turn—it twisted and bent in the center, slinking around the corner, as if it were a large black snake slithering around an obstacle in its path.

As it passed down the block, so did the terrible fear that had held Mr. Pomikin in its grip. He felt a release and almost sat down with joy, finding his limbs able to move once again.

"What the hell was that?" Mr. Pomikin asked, almost shouting out loud to no one in particular. He looked around, up and down the street, hoping he wasn't the only one to have seen—well, exactly what he wasn't quite sure. *A large black car eating a dog? Or did it not eat it but kidnap it? And how, exactly, did it accomplish that task—with a hand that it made from a part of itself?* Mr. Pomikin asked himself, still too shaken by the event to actually want the answers. He turned away from the plaza, his appetite for both pizza and new pants gone as quickly as the tiny Lab had disappeared. As he headed home, his mind racing with possibilities, it began to rain ferociously.

All of that—both Raul and the mysterious car abduction—had been put on hold, relegated to the back of Mr. Pomikin's mind with the arrival of Penny, which was what Mr. Pomikin had decided to call Princess Penelope Sparklepants after he saw her.

They spent the next few days getting to know one another—discovering Penny's likes and dislikes, observing her disposition, and testing how quickly she could be trained. She learned remarkably fast—thanks to her championship heritage. She came from a long line of not just smart dogs, but brilliant ones. She quickly mastered the art of pawing or yipping at the front door when she had to pee—or, if Mr. Pomikin was not handy, of relieving herself on the little puppy pee pads he spread in the bathroom when he was out. After the first few small missteps, she never again wet inside the house; she was too smart for that.

They also discovered that Penny loved Mr. Pomikin ferociously, unwilling to leave his side for anything other than food or the tiny red ball he would bounce down the hallway. She loved chasing the red rubber ball—open like a cage so she could grip it with her teeth—pouncing on it as it piddle-paddled down the hall, then dragging it back and dropping it at Mr. Pomikin's feet, yipping as if to say, "*Throw it again, Daddy! Throw it again!*"

She was very insistent and could play with the ball for what seemed like hours until, finally exhausted, she would throw herself onto the tiny pink dog bed with white daisies that Mr. Pomikin had bought her, scratch at the small pink throw blanket until it was just right, crawl underneath, and fall asleep with a faint sigh. Mr. Pomikin would sit and watch her tiny five-pound inert form lying under the pink blanket for hours—until she awakened, crawled out, and came to sit quietly in his lap until fully awake while he stroked her tiny head.

Mr. Pomikin walked Penny twice a day—sometimes three—hooking her pink collar to a woven pink leash and strolling with her along Main Street. They greeted people along the way, letting Penny get used to being petted and fawned over. People loved her, and she loved them right back. The only real issue she had was other dogs. She was terrified of them and would try to run away, wrestling with her collar and struggling to break free so she could flee the menace of another dog—one who usually just wanted to sniff her and find out what the tiny ball of fur was made of. It was that fear that led to what happened that fateful evening.

Mr. Pomikin had walked Penny around town during the afternoon—stopping at the deli where she got a piece of turkey from Mr. Bill, then at the pet store where she got a new sweater for the upcoming winter. They had eaten lunch at Friendly's, Mr. Pomikin breaking off pieces of his double cheeseburger (no cheese, just the burger) for Penny as she sat in the kids' chair like a little lady, getting made over by customers and waitstaff alike. She ate up not only the pieces of burger but the attention as well. The problem came when Mr. Pomikin tried to mail a letter.

Mr. Pomikin was walking down Main Street, having spent an absolutely lovely day showing Penny off to his friends in town. He held a letter to be dropped in the post office box at the corner of Main and Broad, while Penny trotted slightly ahead of him at the end of her pink leash. She looked regal as she pranced before him, surveying her surroundings.

Mr. Pomikin had nearly reached the mailbox when a shepherd jumped out from behind it and snapped at Penny, causing her to yelp and bolt—slipping out of her collar. The shepherd was tied to a tree, likely by its owner who must have been shopping in one of the nearby stores. Penny had simply startled the dog, causing it to snap.

"Penny! No!" Mr. Pomikin yelled, running after the terrified pup.

Penny took off down Broad Street, weaving her way through a fence and dashing through someone's backyard, before emerging farther down the street. Mr. Pomikin gave chase, running as fast as his little legs would take him. He was about thirty yards behind her when he heard the low thrumming of a car.

The same black car he had seen before—long and sleek—hummed past him, gliding silently on the road. Its tires made no sound and the engine emitted only a strange metallic sound that made the fillings in Mr. Pomikin's teeth ache. He saw Penny stopped in the middle of the road, staring at the car, her ears pinned back, a stream of pee puddling beneath her. The fear in her eyes matched the pounding fear in his chest: sharp, palpable, paralyzing.

The car rolled slowly up to her, its skin seeming to pulse as it came to a stop beside his baby. This time it was the side mirror that transformed—morphed, actually—twisting and shuddering into a hand-like appendage with three claws. It grabbed Penny by the scruff of her neck, pulling her through the glass which undulated and puckered open just enough to receive her tiny figure, then sealed with a pop much like a pricked party balloon. Then the car moved forward, its prize somewhere deep inside its bowels.

"Nooooooooooo!" Mr. Pomikin screamed, wrenching himself free from the grip of fear that had nearly paralyzed him. He bolted forward, stumbling after the car as it glided down the street, turning at the end of Broad and sliding through an alley near the corner between two buildings. Mr. Pomikin was confused as to where the car was heading, knowing that behind those buildings was only a field.

He raced after the car, his shoes causing him to nearly slip and fall in his pursuit. He turned the corner into the alley and caught a glimpse of the car as it warbled past the buildings and bumped over the edge of the blacktop, making its way into the field.

Mr. Pomikin raced down the street, calling for Penny, tears streaming from his eyes. When he reached the field, he stopped cold: the car had transformed into some kind of humanoid shape—dark blue and black—with several appendages protruding from its body. It held Penny in its grasp, staring skyward. She was whining and crying, trembling but very still, obviously terrified.

"Penny! Penny! I'm here, baby! Daddy's here!" Mr. Pomikin cried, moving toward the figure holding his baby. The figure slowly turned its head toward him, registering his approach.

Suddenly, a bright aqua-blue beam shot down from above, striking both the figure and Penny. Mr. Pomikin watched in horror as both Penny and the humanoid began to dissolve in front of him—but not completely. Their forms elongated and shimmered, stretched unnaturally as the beam pulled them skyward.

"Noooooo!" he screamed again, dashing toward the beam, but before he could get there, Penny, her abductor, and the beam were whisked away with a whooshing sound—and Mr. Pomikin was alone, standing in the field. He fell to his knees and began to weep, torrents of tears falling from his eyes. His baby had been taken from him, and his heart was broken.

Suddenly he felt a strange warmth, followed by an insistent humming that sounded machine-like. When he opened his eyes, he was bathed in an aqua-blue light made of sparkly twinkling particles of matter. The beam began to pull him apart, drawing his atoms and molecules skyward. Mr. Pomikin could feel his body separating at a molecular level.

He looked upward toward the origin of the beam and saw what appeared to be a very bright, almost circular light. He smiled.

"Hang on, baby. Daddy's coming," he said—and he was gone.

ALLY

By

F. L. Havey

Aaargh! Nooooo! I groaned, flipping my pillow over to reach for the alarm blaring on the night stand—set for 7 a.m. *Beep! Beep! Beep! Beep!*

My mom suddenly barges in my room. "Ally, time to get up. Don't forget your jacket and raincoat. It's supposed to rain today".

"Okay Mom."

"Breakfast is ready".

I thought to myself, not without sarcasm, that I didn't really need an alarm clock—not when I had her.

As I sat up, I tried to recall my dream. The same one again. There was a woman, from another time—nineteenth century, maybe, based on her looks. She wore a half ponytail, teased and pinned up with long side bangs framing her face. She's definitely a red head, with fair skin and rosy cheeks. I would say that maybe she's in her thirties. She wore one of those laced high-neck white cotton shirtwaist with a long khaki or brown skirt and a brown belt sash—fashionable during the late nineteenth century.

And always, the house. A Victorian home perched on a rocky shore by the water. They seem to be connected. I've dreamed of the house so often that I know its every nook and cranny—as if I've lived there before. In reality, I've never seen that house ever in my life or met anyone like her. *Who is she? Why do I dream about that woman and that house all the time?*

Scurrying around my room to get ready for school, I grabbed a shirt and jeans from my closet and dressed quickly—before Mom could call for me again. While brushing my hair and teeth, I heard her voice.

"Ally!" Come on!"

Oops! Too late—

"Okay Mom, Coming!"

I ran down the stairs quickly. "Mom, do you believe in past lives? Do you think that our dreams have meanings—like they're trying to tell us something?"

Mom and I have a close relationship, and I can usually ask her just about anything. My mother is in her late fifties, and she grew up in the '80s with a carefree spirit that hasn't stopped. She's actually a lot of fun. When you look at her, the Irish in her is obvious—fiery red curls, freckles, and ivory skin. Mom has the most beautiful blue eyes, clear and bright like glass. It's the one thing I inherited from her that I'm most proud of. Quite often, people mistake us for sisters. She always laughs and soaks up the compliments.

"What? Why do you ask? Did you have those dreams again? I'm telling you, you need to get that book and read that doctor's theory on reincarnation—the one I told you about. I saw him on the morning show one day. He talked about hypnosis and dreams. It was incredible."

"What's the name of that doctor—or the book?"

"Oh gosh, I can't remember… let me see. Oh yes, the book is titled *Signs of Past Lives*, by Dr. Brandon Weir. Just look it up."

"Thanks, Mom. I'm really interested in what he has to say. I'm gonna look into it for sure."

I grabbed two pieces of bacon from the plate, cramming them into my mouth as I hurried, waiting for my friend to pick me up. "These are really good, Mom. I love bacon!"

"You're really curious, huh?"

"Yes. Okay, I have to go—Sylvia's mom is driving us to school today. She's coming to pick me up."

Beep! Beep!

"Oh, I guess that's her. Bye, Mom. Love you."

I grabbed my backpack and ran out the door, then stopped and rushed back inside. "Mom, I need my lunch money."

"Oh, here's five dollars."

"Thanks, Mom." I kissed her cheek and hurried out again.

"Bye, honey. Have a good day. Love you."

I ran up to my friend Sylvia's car. She opened the back passenger door.

"Hi, Ms. Cartwright."

"Hi, honey."

Sylvia was sitting in the front seat with her mom. I climbed into the back and tapped Sylvia's shoulder. We giggled together. She'd been my best friend since third grade. I could tell her anything, and we'd always had a sisterhood bond, even though we weren't really sisters.

Sylvia was half Spanish—her mom was Castilian, her dad American. She had long black curls that tumbled down to her waist, thick dark eyebrows, and deep-set brown eyes that could stare right through you. She wore glasses that made her look like a librarian, and her laugh was the weirdest I'd ever heard—squeaky, high-pitched, almost like a mouse. I teased her about it constantly.

Her mom, Elena Cartwright, spoke with a noticeable Spanish accent. When she got angry, she rattled off words so quickly it was hard to tell if she was speaking English or Spanish. Sylvia looked nothing like her, though. Mrs. Cartwright was short, about five feet tall, and a little on the heavy side. Sylvia was tall and thin—five eleven at least. She must have taken after her dad.

"Sorry, girls," Mrs. Cartwright said, pulling out of the driveway. "I have to drop you off early today. I've got a job interview at the hospital."

"It's okay," Sylvia replied. "We'll just have more time to hang out before class starts."

As she drove, I couldn't help myself. I leaned forward and tried to sniff Sylvia's hair without her noticing. But too late—she caught me in the rearview mirror and turned.

"What are you doing?"

I jerked back, rolled down the window, and stuck my head out, letting the wind blow against my face. I didn't know what came over me or why I suddenly had the urge to smell her hair. Sylvia looked stunned with my peculiar behavior, her mom puzzled.

When we arrived at school, Sylvia and I headed to the playground in back and sat on one of the benches.

"I had that dream again last night," I told her. "I dreamt of that lady again and that house. I feel like the dream is trying to tell me something. Do you ever have the feeling you've lived another life? Every time that I have that dream, I feel like I've been there before. And that lady that appears in my dream—I seem to know her and have a strong connection to her."

"Wow, that's weird. You know, I read somewhere before that some people really do remember their past lives. They can remember certain events from their past and event recall names and places from before."

"There's this doctor my mom watched on TV who is an expert in that— Ummm. Dr. Weir. That's it! Let's look him up."

"Maybe you'll find some answers about your dreams."

"Yeah, sounds like a plan."

Sylvia grinned. "Hey, are you going to the Sadie Hawkins dance?"

"No, I don't think so. My mom's taking me to see my grandma at the old folks' home in Providence this weekend."

"Oh, okay. Your grandma's in an old folks' home?"

"Yeah. I haven't seen her since my grandpa passed away. I guess it's been really hard on her since he died. Mom says she's been forgetting things—a lot—so they moved her where she'd be better taken care of. So who are you going to the dance with?"

"I haven't decided if I'm gonna go yet." I was hoping to go with you, but since you're not going to be here, maybe I won't go."

"Aww, I'm sorry. We'll go skating when I come back."

"Yeah, that sounds fun."

We high-fived and walked toward the main entrance before the bell rang.

After school, we met up at the front of the school yard to walk home together.

"What's wrong Ally?"

"I'm fine—just thinking. I wish I could get in contact with that doctor my mom mentioned.

"Hey, let's stop by the library and look him up. Maybe we can find something on past lives or reincarnation."

"That would be cool. I just have to be home by five—my mom wants me to get ready for the weekend to see my grandma, remember?"

"Yeah, I need to be home early too. My mom's going to some fortune teller. Isn't that funny? A couple of weeks ago, she went to some lady that her friend recommended—and now she's hooked. She said—no kidding—this lady was pretty accurate about her. The woman did tarot cards, read her palms, and told her things about her that no one could have ever known. Pretty neat, huh?!"

"I don't know, it's kind of spooky if you ask me".

We both laughed at the same time. As we reached the corner near the library, we noticed something odd—four or five stray dogs trailing behind us.

"What the heck? Where did they come from?" exclaimed Sylvia.

Whenever we stopped, the dogs stopped. When we walked, they followed, always keeping about ten feet away.

I couldn't resist. I turned and called to them. They whimpered as I stepped closer. Soon they sniffed my hands. One even jumped on me playfully, tail wagging.

Sylvia hung back, watching with wide eyes. "Weird. I've never seen anything like that. You're freaking me out, Ally. You're like a dog whisperer or something."

"C'mon Ally, let's go!"

Laughing, I joined her. She still gave me a suspicious look, one eyebrow raised like the principal about to interrogate me.

When we reached the library, we went straight to the reference guide. I finally found the book Mom talked about—*Signs of Past Lives* by Dr. Brandon Weir.

"Look, here it is."

Sylvia and I crouched on the floor, reading the preface. I flipped through a few pages until one passage caught my eye. Dr. Weir wrote that in Hindu belief, it's possible to reincarnate between human and animal forms, depending on how one lived. He said some people have heightened intuition, a gift tied to a divine purpose, as human or animal. That's why they return again and again. In some cases, he claimed, traces of past lives show up in present behavior—animal traits carried into human form.

"Wow, this book is very interesting," I whispered. "I'm gonna check it out. Come on, let's see if they have anything on dreams."

I found another that caught my eye—*Dreams and What They Mean* by Robert Payne, a dream analyst. "Maybe he can explain some of mine." Excited, I hurried down the aisle to search for more books on dreams.

"I just really need to find answers. I can't explain it. I get this feeling that I've been somewhere else before, in another time, and I've always felt like I was meant to do something special. It's rooted deep in my gut—I can't seem to let it go. Even in my dreams, it haunts me."

"Yes, I believe you, Ally. Maybe you are meant to do something great, and you need to find answers. Maybe you can go see that psychic reader my mom goes to. Maybe she can give you a reading, and just maybe, she might have some answers for you."

"I really don't believe in all that stuff—but I don't know anymore. Still, that's a great idea. I'd love to go, but I want you to come with me."

"Of course. I'll go with my mom tonight and ask her to set up a time for you. I'll call you later and let you know what she says."

"Yes, I'm so curious. Let's give her a try. Well, I've got all the books I wanted, so let's go."

We grabbed our backpacks, and Sylvia and I walked out together. As soon as we stepped outside, more dogs were waiting. They sat there as if they'd been expecting us. Sylvia looked on in amazement.

I walked closer and spoke softly, almost in a kind of dog language. I petted each one, then shooed them away. Instantly, the dogs scattered, and Sylvia stood stunned at what she'd just seen.

"I can't believe what you just did. How did you make them go? That was amazing!"

"I just told them to go, and they obeyed. I don't know what it is, but ever since I was little, I've always had a way with dogs. Every time I saw one, I've always been able to communicate with them, like they understood me. My mom always teased that I was a dog whisperer." I laughed. "Don't think that I'm a freak, I just understand them."

"That's not freaky," Sylvia said with a smile. "I think it's kind of cool, actually."

"Well, here I am. I'll see you after we get back this weekend. Tell me about your mom's visit with the psychic—I really want to know."

"Okay, see you later, Ally Gator!" Sylvia laughed, and I laughed with her.

The next morning, Mom and I got ready to drive to Providence.

"It's agonizing waking up so early on a Saturday," I groaned. "How long has it been since we've seen Grandma?"

"Well, your grandma's been sick a lot. Every time I tried to go, she came down with something. Believe me, I've felt guilty not visiting. I think she'll be glad to see us today."

"Where is this place again?"

"It's a little outside Providence, in the countryside by the bay. It's an old Victorian home that was turned into a private nursing home. It's been here since the late 1800s. We'd better get going. Are you ready?"

"Yeah, coming. I brought one of our photo albums to show Grandma."

"Oh, good thinking."

Mom kept talking the whole ride, but I tuned her out and listened to the radio. About half a mile from the house, everything began to look familiar. My mouth dropped open in disbelief. I knew this house! It was the house from my dream—the white Victorian on a hillside, a meadow nearby, overlooking the ocean. We pulled up to the front entrance and went inside. Immediately to the right was the information desk, where a tall, thin Asian man in green scrubs greeted us.

"Welcome to Victorian Village."

"Hi, we're here to see my mother, Ofelia Madden. She's one of the residents."

"Yes, ma'am. You're on the visitor's list. Just sign in here, and I'll show you to your mother's room."

As soon as I saw the hallway leading to the stairway, I bolted up the stairs. I recognized the attic room from my dream. I knew there was a steeple-shaped window overlooking a path to the ocean.

"This is incredible!" I gasped.

Mom had followed me upstairs, bewildered.

"What are you doing, Ally?"

A heavyset woman in uniform hurried over. "I'm the lead supervisor here, and you can't be up here. This room is reserved for new residents."

"Mom, this may sound crazy, but this is the house from my dream."

"What?" Mom's face was stunned.

"Please, ladies, come downstairs," the supervisor insisted.

"Yes, of course. Sorry." Mom tugged at my arm.

I cast one last glance at the window before following them down.

"Can you show me my mother's room, please?" Mom asked.

"Right this way."

We were led down a narrow hallway, past the living room, into one of the first rooms on the left—a cozy room with blue-and-pink floral wallpaper. White lace curtains framed a wide window where sunlight slipped through. A dark wooden canopy bed sat to the right, and in a recliner chair beside it was Grandma, surprised by our arrival.

"Hi, Grandma!"

"Hi, Mom! How are you doing?"

"Oh my, I'm glad to see you. I'm doing fine—I just had breakfast. How's my Ally doing?"

"I'm good, Grandma. Miss you." I walked over to Grandma and gave her a quick hug.

"You're growing fast. I think you've gotten taller since the last time I saw you."

"Mom, are you still going on your walks? Do you like it here?" Mom wandered over to the window and pulled back the curtain to peek out. "It's so pretty. Wow, I can see the ocean from here."

I walked over to where Mom was standing and saw the view from the window. "Mom, I've been here before. I know how to get to that beach—there's a path that leads right to the ocean. Let's go. I'll show you."

"What are you talking about We've never been here. This is our first visit."

Mom and Grandma exchanged puzzled looks. Grandma, full of life even at seventy-eight, smiled at me. She used to tell me stories when I was a little girl. When I looked into her eyes—just like Mom's beautiful blue ones—and listened to her soft, almost-whispering voice, her stories became magical. They drew you in, and you couldn't help but listen to every word.

"You know," she began, "they told me a story about this place. There was a fire here back in 1863. This whole place nearly burned down if not for a dog that saved this house. A young woman owned the house—her family was wealthy and owned half of some small town near Portland, Maine. She spent her summers here with her dog. One stormy night, while they were sleeping, a fire broke out in the living room. To this day, no one knows how it started. Anyways, the dog alerted her of the fire, and she immediately got out and was able to call the servants for help. One of the servants was able to run and call the fire department. Thanks to the dog, the servants summoned the fire department in time. They credited the dog for saving both the girl and the house."

"What was the name of the lady and what kind of dog was it?"

"Wait—I think the story's in an old newspaper clipping, framed in the front hall as you enter the house. I am pretty sure that it's still there. That's where I saw it. Let's go look. It's a really neat story"

I was enthralled by Grandma's story and couldn't wait to see the article. Excited, I dashed ahead. On the wall in the entrance, to the right of the door, hung a 16" x 10" glass frame, showcasing the article, commemorating the heroic dog that saved the Victorian home and the lady of the house. I stared at the picture, entranced. I recognized the woman in the picture immediately—the red-haired lady from my dream. Right before my eyes, my vision of this person became reality.

"Is this just a dream of mine, or did I live this event before?"

Mom marveled at my question. "Are you okay, honey?"

"Yeah. I think so," I answered softly, still gazing at the photo, mesmerized.

Her name? Emilia Ellison. *Yes—Emilia!* For some bizarre reason, her name felt familiar, as though I'd known it before. I couldn't ignore the next picture. Right next to Emilia's was a photograph of a beagle—the hero of the story. But then I read on. The dog's name was Alice, and she had died in the fire trying to save her owner. The article explained that the owner escaped, but Alice never made it out. Part of the wall collapsed on her, trapping her. By the time the fire department arrived, it was too late.

"Oh no. That's terrible." A heavy sadness swept over me, deeper than anything I'd ever felt. I couldn't look away from that picture. It was as if I had been part of it all—like déjà vu. A powerful sense of recognition gripped me, pulling me back to that time and place. While still marveling at the picture, I suddenly had a flashback. I could see the fire raging at the bottom of the stairs, spreading fast. The curtains in the living room burst into flames, whipping likes sails in the wind. I heard the ceiling boards crackle and break, the sound sharp and violent. Heavy smoke filled the room, and I felt the heat as if I were inside that burning room.

"ALLY! ALLY! ALLY!" Mom's voice cut through the vision as she shook me. "Are you all right...? What's the matter with you?"

I blinked and jerked back, arms raised as though I were falling. "Ohhh, I don't know what came over me. I felt like I was in a dream."

"We noticed," Mom said. "Your grandma and I saw you go pale and sway back a little, almost as if you were gonna faint."

I couldn't explain what had just happened. I was as lost as anyone. I shrugged my shoulders. "I don't know. I just felt... weird."

"Are you sick?"

"No. I meant, I felt spooked."

"Well, let's go and walk Grandma out in the yard. We can all use some fresh air."

We headed down the hallway toward the side door, which opened into a small garden and patio. Pots of colorful flowers lined the patio, their fragrance drifting in the breeze. Beyond the horizon, the blue ocean stretched wide, the sand dunes rolling down to meet it. I glanced at the steps leading to the pathway that wound toward the beach. I thought to myself: *I know this path. I've walked here before. Many times.*

Just then, a staff member—an older woman, perhaps in her fifties or sixties—hurried toward us with Grandma's wheelchair.

"Hello," she said, slightly breathless but smiling. "My name's Kate. I've worked here many years. If you need anything, just ask—I'll do what I can to help."

"Oh, thank you so much," Mom replied warmly.

I hesitated only a moment before my curiosity got the better of me. "So, you've been here a while. You must know the story of this house."

Kate nodded. "Yes, of course. What would you like to know?"

"The woman who owned the house—the one during the fire in 1863—what happened to her?"

Kate looked at me with mild surprise. "Oh… you don't know?"

"What do you mean?" I asked.

"The story goes that when her dog was trapped inside during the fire, she panicked and ran back in to save it. She loved that dog so much she couldn't bear to leave it behind. Sadly, the smoke overtook her before she could reach it. By the time the fire department arrived, it was too late. They managed to save most of the house, but not the woman or the dog."

Her voice softened. "Her name was Emilia Ellison. She was very young—in her late twenties, I believe. She came from a wealthy family and vacationed every summer here with her beloved dog."

Kate sighed. "It was tragic, really. The dog was considered a hero for saving the house from burning down completely. After the fire, Emilia's father had the house renovated and later donated it, turning it into the nursing home you see today. Of course, there are stories… Some say they've seen Emilia's ghost wandering the path to the beach, calling for her dog. Eerie, perhaps—but true, if you believe the tales."

I stared at Kate, my eyes widening with astonishment. Her story struck something deep inside me. Suddenly, it all made sense—I believed every word. I felt the grief of it as though Emilia herself had whispered it to me. My heart broke at the thought of her desperation to save her dog.

And then it hit me. That dog… was me.

I couldn't speak. They'd never believe me if I told them. They'd laugh. But I knew, deep in my soul, that it was true. I had been here before. I had been Emilia's dog, the one she loved so dearly. No wonder that in every dream I'd had of her, I'd felt such aching devotion. She came to me in my dreams because she still longed for me in another realm. I could feel her presence even as Kate spoke.

After we finished our walk with Grandma, we said goodbye, and Mom and I headed home. I was quiet the entire drive, anticipation building inside me. I needed to tell Sylvia what I'd discovered, though I wasn't sure how to explain it without sounding crazy. Still, I felt a strange relief—I finally understood who the woman in my dreams had been.

That night, I struggled to sleep. My thoughts circled endlessly around Emilia, around the catastrophic fire that night in 1863, around my death and rebirth. Why had I come back as a human? Deep down, I knew I had to search for answers.

When sleep finally came, so did she.

I heard her calling me: "Aaaalice, Aaaalice." Her voice was soft, drawn out, almost a whisper. I saw her silhouette moving ahead of me, pausing to turn back and wave before disappearing into a hallway. I followed, but the air filled with white smoke. The closer I got, the thicker it became until I couldn't see a thing.

Then I heard it—coughing, desperate and ragged. I looked down and saw her lying on the floor, helpless. "Emilia!" I dropped to my knees, trying to wake her, but she would not stir. She was gone—lifeless.

The smoke began to clear, and I stumbled toward the stairway. Suddenly, a beam crashed down on me. I tried to push it away, but I didn't have the strength. I could not get myself out. Another fell. Darkness swallowed me.

I was pulled through a long, dark tunnel, though I never touched its sides. At the end was a brilliant light, but it didn't hurt my eyes. It was warm and so full of love that it wrapped around me like an embrace. A voice spoke to me and knew who I was. It was a gentle voice of heaven. The greatest feeling of love was upon me. Without words, I understood everything it said.

You have to go back.

In a flash, I woke up and was back in my room again. It was clear now. I had died with Emilia that night—as her dog. And I had come back as a human for a reason.

As I lay there, my thoughts turned to my mother and grandmother. The idea of losing them was unbearable. If my purpose now was to protect the ones I loved, then I would. Just as I had with Emilia.

The next morning, I woke up anxious to see Sylvia and tell her everything I had discovered. I ran downstairs as soon as I was ready for school. Mom called me for breakfast, but I skipped it and hurried out the door. As I reached the sidewalk, I spotted Sylvia walking toward me.

"Hey! So—how did the visit with your grandmother go?" she asked.

"It was good. Sylvia, I have so *much* to tell you." I kept a smile plastered on my face as we fell into step together.

"What's the matter? Why do you have such a weird look on your face? What happened?"

"Oh—I don't even know where to start. But you have to promise me… you can't tell anybody what I say."

"What? Why?"

"Promise me. You're my best friend… and I can trust you, right?"

"Of course! What a stupid thing to say. Now tell me—you're starting to freak me out. Is it bad?"

"No, it's not bad. But you might freak out a little. You might even think I'm crazy—but I'm going to tell you anyway."

"Okay—tell me, *please*! I'm in suspense… You're giving me the creeps now. Ha, ha, ha." She giggled nervously.

"You know about my dreams—the lady and the house?"

"Yeah… and?"

"Well, when we went to visit my grandma at the nursing home, I figured it out. It's the house in my dream. I mean—as soon as we arrived, I knew every turn, every corner. Everything felt familiar—like I'd been there before."

"What? For real?" Sylvia's eyes widened, her face frozen in disbelief.

"That's not all. My grandmother showed us some old newspaper clippings that were posted near the entrance. And there she was—the lady from my dreams. Her name was Emilia Ellison. As soon as I saw her picture—I knew. It was her. It was like… she was looking right at me. The article said her dog died trying to save the house from the fire—and so did she."

Sylvia just stared, puzzled and silent. I went on, my voice low and serious, explained the whole story to her and then gave her the most shocking conclusion.

"Sylvia, I believe—with all my heart and soul—that dog was *me*."

I searched her face for a reaction, but nothing. She stopped walking and stood still for a moment, with her mouth slightly open. For a moment, it was like time had stopped.

"Sylvia! Sylvia! Did you hear me?" I finally yelled.

She squinted, shook her head, and muttered, "No way. I think that dream of yours is really getting to you. You're going cuckoo!"

"Sylvia—listen to me. I know it sounds crazy, but it's true. That's why I dream about her all the time. I'm connected to her somehow. I know it. That dog—it was me. I lived a past life... as a dog. You have to believe me—please!" I pleaded, my voice cracking. At that moment, she looked into my eyes and saw the sincerity there. Finally, she gave in.

"I can't believe this is really happening. I mean... my best friend is a dog—was a dog! What am I even saying? Oh my God—that explains everything! Why you act so weird with dogs... why they follow you around. Oh my God, Ally—what are we gonna do now?"

"We need to calm down. Think this through. There has to be a reason I was reincarnated as a human *now*, right?"

"Right..." She pressed her lips together, then suddenly brightened. "I know! Let's go see that psychic woman my mom went to. Maybe she has some answers for you."

"Yes! That's a great idea. Let's go after school today."

"Perfect. We'll meet up at the bus stop after class and take the bus to Madame Hilda's. I think I've got enough for both fares. Do you have twenty bucks? I think that's what she charges."

"Don't worry—I've got it covered. Thanks, Sylvia. And... thank you for believing in me." I grinned, relief flooding through me.

When we arrived at school, we went straight to class, but my mind was *anywhere* else. I was anxious—restless. I couldn't wait for the day to end. The bell finally rang, and I bolted out, running to the bus stop where Sylvia was already waiting.

We got on the bus, rode into Town Center, and hopped off near Madame Hilda's place. Across the street stood a little white cottage house. An "OPEN" sign hung in the window. Sylvia opened the door, and a bell jingled overhead as we stepped inside.

At once, we were greeted by a dark-haired woman with a red bandana tied around her head. Her eyebrows were sharp, her eyes deep and unreadable, with a single mole on her right cheek. She barked something in Hungarian toward the back, then turned to us with a slow smile.

"Welcome. Come in. Have a seat, girls."

Sylvia and I froze, entranced by her presence, her mystical air.

"Are you... Madame Hilda?" Sylvia asked.

"Yes of course. How may I help you?"

"My friend needs your help. We wanted to see if you can do a reading for her."

She gave me a quick stare and smiled.

"Yesss… Yesss…" She said softly as she continued to stare at me with curiosity. "Come and sit down, please. What is your name?"

"Ally."

"Okay, please shuffle cards okay? I want your energy on cards."

I shuffled the cards again and again—until Madame Hilda suddenly lifted her hand.

"Stop... now cut," she said softly.

I obeyed, splitting the deck. She gathered the stacks with a deliberate slowness, piling them on top of each other. She then drew the top card and laid it flat on the table. The deck was worn, ancient almost, her *old hand Tarot*. She set one card, then another—one by one. To the side, she placed an astrological chart.

Her eyes widened and she fixed them on me—intrigued.

"You have lived in past life before. You have great purpose and gift of intuition. I feel strong energy around you. Someone—a woman from the past—her spirit not rest. She very close to you. You know her. You must help her cross over. She stuck, looking for you."

I was blown away.

She raised her hands and grasped mine in hers. She held on to my hands for a good second and gave me a deep stare—long enough to get frightened. Then she spoke in a deep, calm voice.

"BEWARE. There is danger and you must be careful. You have gift of intuition, but you put life at risk. I see vision of you—in past life—and you try to save someone, a woman, but you die for her. That is why you come back in life now. You become you now. The Universe is happy with you. You did good thing."

Even as she spoke with her broken English, I understood every word she said. I couldn't move. She finally let go of my hands and stood up. "Everything okay? You believe? Okay, you come back next time and we talk more. Okay, you pay Olga in front."

"Thank you."

As I stood up, trying to collect my thoughts, I looked at Sylvia across the room. She looked puzzled... confused. I explained everything to her—everything Madame Hilda said. While we made our way back home, I couldn't stop thinking about her warning... the danger ahead. What did she mean? And the woman I had to help cross over... it had to be Emilia.

That night, I must have been exhausted—I went straight to bed and crashed. But the dreams came anyway. I dreamt of the night of the fire at the Victorian home. I was curled up in a blanket in the corner of a bed... sound asleep. I felt something... someone's feet near me. A loud thunderstorm raged, windows rattling downstairs, wind howling, rain pounding the roof. I bolted from the bed at the sound of shattering glass.

And then I realized... I was a dog. A beagle—brown, black, and white, with floppy ears. I saw the curtains catch fire, lit by a candle toppled from a glass holder on the curio cabinet. "Oh no!" I panicked... and ran upstairs to Emilia's room. I nudged her face with my nose, barked, but she wouldn't wake... until finally, she sat up. I bit the corner of her gown, tugging her—leading her downstairs, away from the flames.

She ran... I followed. But a piece of wood fell from the ceiling—trapping me. I struggled... heavy... defeated. Darkness swallowed everything. I heard a voice calling: *Alice! Alice! Alice!* Emilia was calling me. Emilia... coughing, frantic, crackling of burning wood around us... then silence.

A light appeared. And there she was—Emilia—brilliant, smiling at me. *There you are... I've been looking for you everywhere.* Her face glowed with life, contentment, happiness. *Come, Alice.* I followed her as she walked toward the garden... the path to the beach... toward the light. Warmth... welcoming... love... enveloped me. Then a voice whispered: *You must go back, Alice.*

I woke up—back in my bed. It had been so real... so vivid. I knew—Emilia was finally at peace. Madame Hilda's words clicked into place. I had helped her cross over.

Then I heard Mom calling me to come downstairs immediately. "Look! There's supposed to be a bad thunderstorm today. It's coming in as a Category 1 hurricane on the East Coast—headed for us! I'm calling your grandma to see what they're doing about evacuation."

Chaos filled the air, anxiety gnawing at me. Mom was frantic—tuning in to every news update, waiting for the evacuation order. After dinner, the emergency radio announced the hurricane had become Category 3. Mom ran upstairs—packed... called the nursing home. They were already preparing buses for evacuation and boarding their residents.

I felt it... wrong. Something was stirring in the air. I had an intuition that something has gone awry. "Mom! Mom!" I called—but no answer. I ran downstairs. She stood by the door, phone in hand, face ghostly pale.

"What's wrong, Mom?" I asked.

She hung up, turned to me. "We need to go to Grandma's... they were loading the buses, but when they went to your grandmother's room, she wasn't there. They can't find her! Hurry! We need to find her before the storm hits!"

"Oh my God! Let's go. Where would grandma go?"

"I don't know... but lately, they've been telling me she's been taking off a lot... running away to the beach. They've looked for her before, but this time... they can't find her."

Mom drove like a woman possessed, her worry etched across her face. I kept thinking—where could she have gone? As soon as we pulled in, one of the nurses ran up to us.

"We sent a dispatch to the sheriff's office—they've sent a crew to look for her."

I didn't waste a second. "Mom, I'm going to the beach! I can find her!"

"Ally, wait! Be careful! The wind is strong, the tide is high—"

Before she could finish, I bolted down the pathway. The wind pushed against me with every step, but I pressed on, calling out. The beach stretched for miles—sand dunes, huge waves... it would be almost impossible to find her. But I wouldn't give up.

"Grandma! Grandma!" I yelled, running for what felt like hours. Then I saw it—a drop-off at the shoreline—and there she was. Sitting by a massive boulder, clinging to it, crying, screaming.

"Grandma! It's me, Ally! I'm coming!"

The tide had risen high, waves pounding the rock. She was terrified, holding on for dear life. I had to swim around to reach her. The waves slammed me as I approached, but I kept going. I convinced her to hold on to me, to let go of the rock. With her arms wrapped around my shoulders, I paddled with all my strength, pushing toward shore.

Shallow water came at last, and I managed to push Grandma safely onto the sand—but the current grabbed me. I was caught in the undertow, dragged under—couldn't break free. I stopped fighting, and darkness swallowed everything. No sight... no sound... just silence. Death... again.

Then, a sphere of light appeared from above. Emilia's face—bright, beautiful—smiled at me. Her touch brought life back into me. Consciousness returned just as the emergency medical team pulled me from the water. They had arrived in time, performing CPR... saving me. I know that Emilia was the one that came—supernaturally—to save me from death. For whatever reason why I was spared this time. So thankful for her love... everlasting.

I heard Mom's frantic voice running toward me. "Ally! Honey, are you okay? Oh my God! You should never have taken off like that—you put your life in danger! I love you. I don't want to lose you or my mother. Thank God you're alright... Grandma's okay too. They're taking you both to the hospital. I'll meet you there! I'll follow the ambulance to the hospital."

"Love you too, Mom," I said, smiling, knowing everything would be okay. No matter what, I would protect my loved ones.

The hurricane passed, and we remained safe at the hospital. Grandma returned to the nursing home, now watched closely to prevent any more escapes.

Months later, winter arrived. Sylvia and I were walking home from school when a dog began following us—a Jack Russell Terrier, white with brown spots. I stopped... looked closer. Those gleaming eyes... just like Emilia's.

"Could it be? Where did you come from?" I whispered.

The dog jumped up, tail wagging, happily. Somehow... I just knew. It was Emilia. She had returned, reincarnated, to be with me. And I knew, from that moment, we would always be connected.

CONFLUENCE

By

TW Embry

The sun was setting as I stood in the short line at the Amoco by the Fort Pierce I-95 interchange, a twelve-pack of beer under my arm. I started fidgeting from the wait. My friends call me Bon. I've lived in Fort Pierce, on the east coast of sunny south Florida, all my life. That's when I felt the first warning tingles from the knot on the back of my head—the knot I never told anyone about.

The hot new girl who worked the register on Friday nights must have noticed my change in demeanor when the first reminder came. My involuntary look of fear betrayed me. *If I dared disobey my unseen masters, the pain would come—even if I merely dallied along the way.*

Tossing her long strawberry-blond hair to make sure she had my attention, she smiled sympathetically. "Headache?"

"I have a migraine, unfortunately. Thank you for asking, my sweet," I answered with a shy smile. *I have to keep her from asking any more questions.*

"We have packs of pain relievers on aisle three. They help mine," she said helpfully.

"No thank you, gorgeous. I have my prescription meds in the car. Just the beer—and the rest in 100 octane, please," I said as I handed her my last twenty bucks.

"Feel better, lover," she cooed as she handed me my receipt, our fingers brushing, pausing, her cheeks flushing red with the forbidden excitement of being romantic strangers.

Now is not the time for flirting. I gotta git and damn quick too. I will, however, be back, I thought. I was being commanded to go to my alone place, far away from any prying eyes. Regretfully tearing my gaze from her bottomless green eyes, I headed out the double doors.

This shit sure is a drag on my love life, I thought, hurrying across the parking lot to where my girl waited at the 100-octane pump. After I finished pumping, I reached down to put the gas cap back on when a not-so-gentle reminder hit me with a blinding stab of pain, causing me to drop the cap and watch it roll underneath my girl. After the indignity of retrieving it, I banged my head on the rear bumper as I stood up.

Pissed off, mumbling curses at my clumsiness, and rubbing the back of my head, I slid behind the steering wheel, depressed the clutch, shifted into neutral, and bumped the starter.

My girl woke with a loud snort. I smiled, waiting until she settled into her perfect symphony of lumpy idle and rumbling exhaust, the sound echoing off the storefront.

As I swung my girl off Okeechobee Road and onto the dirt of Carlton Road, another not so gentle reminder ripped through the back of my skull, causing me to spasm in pain.

Instantly infuriated, I saw everything through a murderous red haze, craving that tonight be the night I lost—and death won.

Was it too much to hope that this would be my last ride? Was this my final daring of death to take me?

"Death… please… take me!" I screamed, stomping my girl's throttle to the floor, my rage now a full-blown possession. I popped the clutch and my girl came alive. Twin rooster tails of dirt exploded as she lunged forward like the beast she was.

With the rear end constantly trying to torque-drift to the right, the tachometer shift light flashed. I shifted into second, steering out of her fishtail. Ninety-nine, then 119. The light flashed again.

With a bark, the rear tires finally got a firm grip on the paved end of Carlton Road, catapulting forward—139... 154... 161. My girl's tri-power carbs snarled, begging me to leave the leash off. This road dead-ended into Rim Ditch and certain death. *At least I would be rid of this demon*, I thought. *At last, I would be free of my unseen masters.*

Just not tonight, it would seem, for I had beaten death to 160 on a dirt road.

The thrill of spitting in death's face and living to tell about it surged through my body, coursing from head to toe. I backed off the throttle. I had to. I had won—and condemned myself to live yet one more wretched day as my unseen master's slave.

I was fast running out of road. Rim Ditch was coming up fast! I braked hard, bumping the throttle into a power slide. Downshifting, I hung the rear out while steering right, another tap on the accelerator, screeching to a stop sideways in the road, facing the entrance to the construction turn-in.

I nosed my girl around the rusted, drooping cable guarding the entrance of the abandoned housing development. Subconsciously dreading what was coming, I idled slowly around just to make sure I was alone, finally coming to a stop at my alone place.

Lost forever were the Florida swamps of my youth, once filled with ancient cypress and live oaks. Now they were drained and covered with concrete and asphalt. My alone place was a silent testament to that ferocious greed—the ancient trees sold for lumber, the wildlife gone, their homes destroyed.

I shut down my girl and waited. I set about making myself comfortable—starting a small fire and rolling out the blanket I kept in the back seat.

Boredom quickly set in. *Well, here I am. Another lonely Friday night. No girlfriend, no job, no money*, I thought, lying by the small fire, sipping my now-warm beer. I stabbed at the fire in frustration, sending a shower of sparks skyward. *I was such a loser. I always came here when the urges came. It was like I was supposed to meet the love of my life—yet she never shows.*

Look at me. Here I am, sitting by myself in the middle of nowhere, alone and miserable, waiting for who knows what. Why am I here? What the hell do they want with me? I wondered.

I rousted myself, heading for the cooler and another beer. I could feel my anger and resentment building to a slow boil. My girlfriend Deena had dumped me over two months ago—or that's what I told everybody, with a forced smile. *Who was I fooling? It had been nine weeks, three days, and thirteen hours.* Deena left me the same day I lost my job at the machine shop.

I grimaced as I lifted my girl's rusted trunk lid. Dad and I had never gotten to the bodywork. Exposed to the salt air, she was a little rough on the outside. Kind of like me—a wolf in sheep's clothing, disguised in rags. But she would burn rubber in all four gears. She could run tens down at Moroso's drag strip and still drive home. She was one bad bitch. The drivetrain was as far as Dad and I had gotten before he and Mom divorced. Then he moved out and forgot about me.

I grabbed another beer from the cooler and tended the dying fire, stirring the embers into a burst of sparks as I added wood.

I lay back down by the fire, listening to the flames lick hungrily at the new wood, watching the full pale-gray moon rise above the interstate light pollution. Sleep wasn't coming—only loneliness welling up inside as my thoughts drifted to Deena.

I felt like dying inside. Sobbing, I pounded my fists on the hard, uncaring ground.

Now I was back to living under my mother's roof. I knew my mom wouldn't miss me tonight. It was Friday, and she'd be out partying with her recently divorced friends. The sport of man-trolling, they called it.

The feelings of abandonment—by Deena, by Mom, by Dad—welled up inside me as I lay curled in the back seat of my car. Eyes squeezed shut, hands clamped over my ears, I rocked gently in the dark, sobbing to the sound of rain spattering on the roof and windshield of my girl—a sudden thunder squall having ended the night's outdoor activity.

I woke up sweating from the heat of the morning sun shining through my girl's back window. I rubbed my bleary eyes and slowly stretched, trying to work the kinks from my neck and back. My watch said 11:39 a.m.

Time to head home. With a single bump on the ignition, my girl roared to life, then settled into her perfect lumpy idle. I grinned—that sound always thrilled me. Pulling onto Okeechobee Road, I let her run wild for just a little bit, backing off after I hit eighty.

As luck would have it, Mom was up and waiting for me when I got home. From her body language, I knew another fight was brewing.

To head her off, I blurted the first thing I could think of—I told her I had a job interview that afternoon. She seemed surprised, then pleased. She smiled and made me breakfast, my night out now a thing of the past.

As I stepped into the shower, I wondered where I'd go to find a job. I'd spent my last twenty bucks on gas and the twelve-pack, so I really needed a job. As I soaped up, a sharp pain radiated from my best friend George and his two brothers. Straightening up, I took a couple of deep breaths and the pain dulled. Something was definitely wrong.

When I tried to remember why George hurt so much, the knot on the back of my head began to buzz and tingle. My memories of last night went vague, hazy, hard to recall. The harder I tried to remember, the worse George ached, until the pain drove me to my knees in the shower. The pain was so bad that I heaved up my breakfast.

Finally, the retching subsided, as did the pain.

I was NOT going to the doctor until I could remember what the hell had happened last night.

Just thinking about it set the knot on the back of my head buzzing again. In near panic, I desperately tried not to think about my problem with George. *JOB!* I thought. *Where am I going to find a job?*

That made the buzzing stop. My knees quit shaking.

As I slowly got dressed, I remembered the ad for security guards in the *News Tribune* yesterday. They were holding a job fair today. I figured

I'd fire up my girl, take a ride, and check it out—if only to get Mom off my back. Three hours later, I put my new uniform in my girl's back seat. They'd hired me on the spot. My first shift was tonight, eleven to seven. *At least Mom would be happy I finally got another job,* or so I thought.

I was wrong. Mom was not happy.

"You can do so much better," she said in her quiet, angry, passive-aggressive voice.

"I'll find something better. This is just temporary," I explained, placating her.

"All right then—it had better be." Still angry, she added, "You better get some sleep. I'll fix your lunch. Who knows what you'll find to eat at that time of night?" She fussed, but I let her.

At 3:00 a.m., the knot at the back of my head began to tingle. I was standing watch over the entrance to a construction site. The site sergeant was out on his golf cart patrolling the area.

I tried ignoring it, but it worsened, turning into a sharp throb. I knew there was nothing I could do about it now—the site sergeant would be back any minute. It wouldn't stop while someone else was around. I had to be alone.

Soon stabbing lights ripped through my mind. Suddenly I had an uncontrollable urge to pee. I bolted toward the woods to relieve myself before I pissed my new uniform.

When I stepped back out of the woods, two sheriff's deputies were parked at the gate, talking to the site sergeant. All three turned and looked at me.

"Where have you been?" shouted the site sergeant.

"I went to take a pee!" I shouted back.

"For three hours?" he bellowed as I got closer.

"What do you mean, three hours? I just left five minutes ago!"

"You've been gone three hours. I called the deputies because I thought something happened to you—here you were just off sleeping in the woods!"

With disapproving shakes of their heads, the deputies got back in their patrol cars and left.

"You're just lucky I know those guys, or you'd be in a lot more trouble than just losing your job," the sergeant said.

"Lose my job for taking a pee? Are you kidding me?"

"No. Losing your job for taking a three-hour nap," he snarled, jaw clenched. "What's that blood all over your face?" he asked as I got closer. "Did you fall in the dark and hurt yourself?"

I quickly brought my sweaty hand to my face, my arm strangely weak. My face was smeared with sticky, half-dried blood.

"I don't know. I swear I don't know," I answered, shaken by my discovery. "I just went to take a pee five minutes ago. See? My watch says 3:05. I just signed the watch log at three, like you said." I flexed my arms, trying to get my strength back.

"Then you must've broken your watch when you fell, because it's 6:05, not 3:05," the sergeant said, amused now. "They're gonna love this one back at the office. I'm gonna enjoy watching you explain it to the shift commander," he said with a thin, cruel grin. "Now go get cleaned up. The shift commander is on his way. You can explain everything to him."

In the bathroom mirror, I saw blood on my face and shirt. To make matters worse my friend George was throbbing with pain, making it hard to stand up straight. A closer look revealed bruises on my thighs. George and his two brothers were beet-red, painful to the touch.

What the fuck is going on?

Suddenly there was no more time. The shift commander had arrived.

I got lucky. He didn't fire me after hearing my side of the story and seeing the blood stains on my shirt.

"Sergeant," he barked, "is all of the equipment accounted for and the warehouse secure?"

"Yes, Sir, it was on my last patrol," answered the site sergeant.

"And what time was that?" he barked, glaring at the sergeant who visibly wilted from its ferocity.

"0300, SIR," said the sergeant.

"That was three hours ago! You've got a wounded man and an unsecured site. I suggest you find out if anything is missing or broken into that might explain this man's injuries."

"YES, SIR," the site sergeant stammered, tripping over himself in his haste to leave.

Turning his fierce gaze on me, the commander softened just a little. "Sit until your relief arrives. Then I'm taking you to the ER to get you checked out. If something's missing, you may have been attacked, and the sheriff will want to talk to you."

"I really don't need to go to the emergency room, Sir. It was just a nosebleed, I think. I don't remember being attacked. In fact, I don't remember anything except needing to pee—really badly. I was only gone five minutes, and my watch proves it."

I showed him my watch. It was exactly three hours slow.

The shift commander's face hardened, and he gave me a long, piercing stare. "That is a strange thing, young man—very strange indeed. Is there anything you want to tell me, son? Has this ever happened before?"

"No, Sir. I swear to you I was not sleeping," I answered in a panic.

"Relax, son, I believe you," said the shift commander, his face softening again. "However, if I get a report of you sleeping again, I will fire you on the spot. Is that clear? I may still fire you; it depends on what Sergeant Shultz finds out. If anything is missing or broken into, we have a real problem, and I won't be able to help you, son. Are you absolutely sure there is nothing you want to tell me?" He studied my face intently.

"No, Sir. I already told you everything," I said as earnestly as I could.

That seemed to satisfy the shift commander—for the moment, at least.

The shift commander's line of questioning was interrupted by the return of the site sergeant. "SIR," he said, panting heavily, "all of the equipment is accounted for and the supply depot is secure."

"Then I suggest you get started on that incident report, mister. I expect it on my desk by the beginning of your next shift. IS THAT CLEAR, CORPORAL TIMSON?" thundered the shift commander.

"It's Sergeant Timpson, Sir," sputtered the site sergeant.

"If you ever fuck up like this again, it won't be sergeant anymore. Do I make myself clear?"

"Crystal clear, Sir," moaned the much-subdued site sergeant, who was quite proud of his stripes, being the petty tyrant that he was.

After I got home, I stripped off my uniform, threw it in the washer, and showered before getting ready for bed. As I lay on the bed tossing and turning, I started wondering what really happened in the woods last night.

Immediately the knot on the back of my head began tingling again; the buzzing and stabbing pains would not be far behind. I quickly thought about something else—anything but what had happened last night. Once the tingling quit, I fell into a fitful sleep.

As the world around me spun into focus, I realized I was lying flat on a cold metal table, shivering, with painfully bright lights shining in my eyes. I could feel my body but could only move my eyes. Three dark figures with huge, bulbous eyes looked down at me, watching me. Somewhere in the distance, someone was screaming.

With a start, I woke up covered in sweat—I knew I had been the one screaming. A stab from the knot in the back of my head made my body spasm, doubling me over in pain.

The pain grew worse as I tried to remember why I had been screaming and who was watching me. Then my nose began to trickle blood, and I stumbled into the bathroom to grab a washcloth.

Once the bleeding stopped, I dragged myself into the shower. I had to be at work in a couple of hours, and I still needed to dry my uniform and wash my bed sheets. I knew I could not go to the doctor. With that thought, the pain receded to the familiar tingling from the knot.

I was alone, confused, and very scared. Angry and frustrated, I pounded my fists on the bathroom sink, bruising my hands. *I will find out what is going on!*

That thought doubled me up in pain, and I collapsed on the bathroom floor, hitting my head on the john on the way down. When I finally came to, I glanced at my watch. I barely had enough time to dry my uniform and make it to work on time. Slowly and painfully, I got to my feet.

My second shift at the construction site passed as quietly as the darkness that surrounded me while I manned the gate—broken only by the beam of my Maglite and the occasional scurrying rat. Sergeant Schultz, as the shift commander called him, avoided me all night, never speaking a word to me.

I was exhausted when I got home, so I went straight to bed and fell into a deep, dreamless sleep until my alarm went off ten hours later. I felt like a new man once I stepped out of the shower.

Mom had made me a plate of leftovers and packed my lunch. I was famished, so I wolfed down the leftovers before leaving. With an hour to kill, I decided to take my girl for a run on the interstate.

As I passed the only all-night diner near I-95, I saw all four state troopers assigned to patrol that stretch of interstate parked in the parking lot. It was shift change. They were all inside, chasing hot coffee and fresh doughnuts—leaving my favorite stretch of interstate unpatrolled, much to my delight.

I hit 120 as I exited the southbound ramp, the exhaust echoing off the concrete walls. Then 130. Then 140. The tri-power carbs began to really snarl before I backed off the gas. *I love this car! Even at 140 mph, she was begging to be let off the leash.*

I was tempted—all I had to do was shift into fourth gear. Speeds like that always made my troubles go away, if only for a short while. I was still grinning when I idled up to my new post.

Tonight's assignment was a solitary guard shack with an hourly patrol of the fence surrounding a new Chevrolet dealership. When I returned from my fourth patrol, I found the shift commander waiting at the gate, eyeing my girl.

"You think you can beat that new Vette?" he asked with a grin.

"Yes, Sir, I can. That Vette only runs high elevens—and that's on slicks. My girl runs ten fives on street tires," I boasted quietly.

"No shit, low tens? What the hell have you got under that hood?" His disbelief was plain.

I grinned and popped my girl's hood.

He let out a whistle, "Damn, that's pretty! Is that the original Rocket 350?"

"Yes and no," I answered. "Dad and I started building her before the divorce. We took the original stock Rocket 350 block, had it relieved and blueprinted, line-bored the crankshaft journals, and decked the block.

"We started the engine mods with a set of aluminum 77cc chamber heads, CNC ported, polished and flowed," I explained. "Then we fitted the heads with 2.07 intake and 1.90 exhaust valves. We matched the intake ports to the flowed Offenhauser tri-power manifold and topped it with three tricked-out Holley 500 cfm two-barrel carbs.

"We put in a custom .600/.580 roller cam that we matched with powder-coated triple springs. Then we installed billet flat-top pistons with valve reliefs milled out, billet connecting rods, and a billet crank. After that, we had it all balanced to 10,000 rpm.

"For the suspension," I continued, "we installed a Chassis Engineering front suspension and put Wildwood disc brakes all the way around. Then we back-halved the body and welded in a ten-point chrome-moly roll cage. We bulletproofed the Muncie four-speed and hung a Chassis Engineering four-link suspension with a narrowed Trac-Lok Dana 60 rear end, set with a 3.72 axle ratio and fitted with Strange 35-spline axles," I said proudly.

"I've seen you around town. Fire it up for me—I've never heard it up close!" the shift commander requested with a broad grin. "My name is Pete, by the way," he added, thrusting out his right hand. "Just don't call me that in front of the men."

"No, Sir, I won't. I'm Bon," I answered, shaking his hand. I slipped behind the wheel and just bumped the ignition. My girl roared to life, then settled into her perfect lumpy idle, much to the delight of my new friend Pete.

The knot on the back of my head suddenly began to tingle. I felt that familiar urge to be alone. *Not now,* I thought. I was making a friend. The tingling quickly turned to buzzing, then sharpened into a bolt of pain down my neck. Still, I resisted. The pain hit harder until I doubled over, falling out of the driver's seat and hitting the rough pavement face-first. My nose gushed blood.

Pete stood over me, concern etched on his face, calling someone on the radio. *No!* I thought as that familiar spinning darkness claimed me.

I woke up in the ER surrounded by doctors, wearing only a hospital gown. A nurse saw my eyes open. "Relax, Bon. You're going to be fine. Your mom is on the way."

"What happened?" I croaked.

"We don't know for sure," said one of the doctors as they pored over test results. "We do know that you're severely dehydrated and have lost some blood. Not enough for a transfusion, but enough to keep you off your feet for a day or two."

"What concerns me," said the youngest doctor, "is the bruising on and around your genitals. You're a lucky young man—that must be one rambunctious girlfriend you've got." He leered and winked.

"I don't have a girlfriend anymore," I mumbled, shame washing over me. *They knew.*

One of the older doctors gave me a stern look. "Then I suggest you stop doing whatever it is you're doing before you cause permanent damage—damage you'll regret when you get to be my age."

I didn't know what to say. Fortunately, Mom hurried in, saving me from further explanation.

"Are you all right, son?" she asked, tears in her eyes. Ignoring the crowd of doctors, she kissed me gently on the forehead, brushed back my hair, and placed her hands on either side of my face.

"You probably should ask them, Mom," I answered, even more upset after seeing how shaken up she was.

"What's wrong with him?" she demanded of the group of doctors, her hands on her hips, her feathers clearly ruffled. "Well? Speak up," she pressed after an awkward silence.

"Ms. Scott," began the doctor in charge of the group, "I am Dr. Jones, and I am in charge of emergency room admissions."

"Good for you, Dr. Jones, your mother must be very proud. I will ask you again: What is wrong with my son?" she demanded sternly, already out of patience.

"To be honest, Ms. Scott, other than a severe nosebleed and moderate dehydration, we can find nothing wrong with your son," answered Dr. Jones.

I breathed a sigh of relief—he had not mentioned George's injuries, sparing me that embarrassment at least.

Completely undeterred, Mom said in her quiet, angry voice—the one she only used when she was truly mad—"Just what do you mean, nothing is wrong with him? What caused the nosebleed?"

"At first we thought it was heavy cocaine use," said the youngest of the doctors, "because of the chronic damage to his nasal passages. However, the drug screen came back negative. It would appear that something quite large was forced up his nose and into his sinus cavities at a young age, and repeatedly afterward."

Oh no, I thought. *Here comes the news about George.* I was going over in my mind just how I was going to explain that to Mom. I need not have worried, though—the mere mention of drug use sent her into a rage, and she gave the doctors the tongue-lashing she thought they all deserved.

Finally, Dr. Jones held up his hands to stop her tirade. "He is fine, Ms. Scott. Why don't you take your son home and discuss the matter in private? We all have patients to see who really need our help. I strongly advise drug counseling," he added, handing her a business card for a drug rehab program.

It was a long, quiet, and extremely uncomfortable ride to go and retrieve my girl, with Mom simmering in the driver's seat.

"Mom, I don't do drugs. You heard the doctor say the drug test was clean," I said, trying to defuse the explosion I knew wasn't far off.

She turned and looked at me with fury in her eyes. I didn't know what else to say. But as suddenly as the anger had appeared, it left, and Mom's face softened.

"I believe you, son. I won't tell your dad this time, but if this happens again you will have to find someplace else to live. Is that clear, son?"

The arrival at my girl's location prevented any more conversation as I beat a hasty retreat.

"You had better go straight home. Is that clear, young man?" Mom said through her open window.

"Yes, Mom," I answered hurriedly—the tingling had started again, and it quickly turned to a sharp pain.

Seeing my face go suddenly white, she asked, "Are you all right, son?"

"I just have a bit of a headache. If you don't mind, I'd like to take my girl for a ride to clear my head."

"Okay," she said. "But you come straight home after and don't be out too late. And no racing. Is that clear?" she scolded.

"Yes, Mom," I answered.

I pulled out of the parking lot onto US1 northbound, careful not to stomp on the gas in front of Mom—no matter how badly I wanted to—and headed for Okeechobee Road and the outskirts of town.

Once I cleared the city traffic, I opened up my girl's three carbs and listened with pleasure as her low moan quickly became a vicious howl. When I let my girl run for a bit, it always made me grin like a crazy man. The only thing I loved more was showing some new hot rod in town my girl's taillights. Now THAT made me happy—though it also got me into trouble on a regular basis.

I soon found myself at my alone spot, having forgone my usual power-slide approach. I shut down my girl and just sat there, waiting for something—I had no idea what. My eyes quickly grew heavy, and I nodded off.

I woke with a start and looked at my watch. *SHIT! It was 6:38 a.m.*—I had slept three hours! Mom was going to be pissed, because she told me to go straight home after my ride. I bumped the starter and my girl roared to life. Then I hauled ass home.

Mom was not up waiting for me, which shocked me. I winced inwardly, knowing she would really let me have it later. I was exhausted, so I crawled straight into bed and fell instantly into a deep sleep, without feeling my head hit the pillow.

I woke up screaming, disoriented and drenched in sweat. I had been dreaming about being on that cold steel table again, only this time I could move my head. I saw someone else on the table next to me—a girl. *It was Deena!*

As I watched, three little gray, manlike creatures were inserting what looked like surgical instruments into her. She was screaming, *No! Please stop! Please stop, it hurts!* she pleaded.

The creatures didn't seem to care she was in pain, and they didn't stop. I furiously tried to break free of my restraints, attracting one of the little gray men's attention. It produced a wand from the sleeve of its floor-length tunic. Closer came the glowing tip, my terror building the nearer it got—until it pressed the now-red glowing tip to my forehead, and blackness instantly took me.

My brother and Mom both burst into my room at the same time, yelling, "What's wrong?"

I started to tell them about my dream, but the knot sent a sharp pain ripping through my skull. "I just had a bad dream. I'm sorry I woke you both," I answered, stuttering from the pain.

Mom gave me a stern look and said firmly, "Get up and get showered and dressed. We have to talk."

As I swung my legs off the bed and stood up, the pain hit me like a living thing, knocking the wind out of me and causing me to slump to the floor. Gasping for breath, I tried to remember what happened. The spinning darkness took me—thankfully ending the pain.

I woke up in a strange bed, in a hospital gown. I tried to move my arms, but they had fallen asleep at an odd angle. Then I realized that my arms and legs were strapped to the bed. *What the fuck is going on?* I furiously pulled at the straps, getting madder by the second. Slowly, I realized I was not on the steel table.

My struggles alerted someone. A very large man in a white uniform poked his head inside the windowless room and said, "Relax. The doctor will see you soon." Then he closed the door, and I heard the click of a deadbolt.

It wasn't long before a young man, wearing a rumpled and stained doctor's smock, his hair uncombed and wild, his five o'clock shadow very dark, came to see me. "My name is Dr. Merkquack. May I call you Bon?" he asked. I just glared at him, angrier than I had ever been in my life.

"Come now, what harm will it do to answer me?" he said, his face pinched in a strange, unsettling attempt at a smile.

I realized that the more I fought, the longer I would be strapped to this bed. I swallowed my anger and my pride and answered, "Yes, you can call me Bon."

"Now that's better. The sooner you cooperate, the sooner we can take off those nasty restraints. So let's be a good boy, shall we?" Dr. Merkquack said in his most soothing, professional manner. "Do you know where you are, Bon?"

"No, Sir. I don't," I answered.

"Well, Bon, you are in St. John's Sanitarium. You were brought here three days ago, unconscious and badly bruised, by someone or something unknown. Would you like to talk about it now?"

"I don't know what happened," I answered as shame swept over me.

"You have no memory of what happened to you?" he asked.

"No, Sir, I don't," I repeated firmly, anger creeping into my voice.

"Okay, Bon, there is no need to get upset. I'm here to help you," he said as he scribbled in his notebook.

"I see here that your toxin screens all came back clean. So what have you been using to get high? Something the screen doesn't check for, I would imagine," Dr. Merkquack said, pausing in his scribbling.

"I don't get high on anything," I said quietly.

"Interesting," he said, scribbling again. "Then how do you explain your being here?"

"The last thing I remember is waking up screaming and then passing out from the pain. Then I woke up here," I answered carefully, desperate not to trigger the knot on the back of my head.

"What do you remember about what happened after you left the emergency room to go get your car?" he asked.

"I took my girl for a ride and fell asleep parked in the place I go to when I get upset," I answered knowing that if I thought about it anymore the pain would come quick and hard.

"How do you explain the severe genital bruising?" he asked. "Your mom said you broke up with your girlfriend recently."

"I can't remember. When I try to remember, the pain comes," I explained.

"Interesting," he said as he scribbled furiously. "What pain? And what girl did you take for a ride?" he asked.

"I call my car my girl. The pain is from the knot on the back of my head," I said, relieved my secret was finally out in the open.

"Interesting. Show me where this knot is," Dr. Merkquack said, closing his notebook.

"It's right here," I said, instinctively touching the now tingling knot.

As Dr. Merkquack gently felt the back of my head, he said, "I don't feel anything unusual. In fact, I feel no knot at all. Are you sure this is the right spot, Bon?"

"Yes sir, it's right here. Why can't you feel it?" I said, getting angry again.

"Okay, Bon, I believe you. I'm going to order a CT scan to see if there's something I'm missing. We'll know more after the scan. That's enough for now. I'll check in on you later," Dr. Merkquack said reassuringly.

I was on the steel table again, naked and shivering from the cold. There were no eyes watching me this time, and I could move my head. I turned it to the right and saw Deena lying on her right side, facing the wall, her back to me, naked and either sleeping or unconscious.

I tried to call her name, but my mouth was full of cotton and my throat was sore and dry. All I could manage was a hoarse croak. "Deena." She didn't move. I tried again, croaking louder, still no response. Mustering all my strength, I finally managed a shout, "DEENA!"—but still nothing.

Then I heard a noise that sent chills down my spine—the sound of the metal door rolling open! They were coming! I broke out in a cold sweat as I struggled to get free. Suddenly I couldn't move my head anymore, and a pair of huge black eyes looked down at me.

It was one of the gray creatures! I heard someone screaming in terror in the distance. I watched frozen as a red-tipped wand approached my face. When it touched my forehead, blackness took me.

Dr. Merkquack was slapping my face—trying to wake me—as I lurched violently back into this reality, my mind spinning. I was strapped in the hospital bed—no metal table, no huge eyes staring down at me. Slowly, I unclenched, realizing I was safe from the little gray men.

Gradually I regained control, noticing my bed sheets were soaked with sweat and my nose was bloody. "That must have been some nightmare, Bon. Care to tell me about it while it's still fresh in your mind?" Dr. Merkquack asked, scribbling on his ever-present notebook.

"You wouldn't believe me if I told you," I said sullenly.

"Don't be so sure, Bon. I've heard many strange nightmares here at St. John's," he answered, attempting a compassionate smile.

"I can't remember, and if I could, it would bring the pain," I retorted.

"Ah yes, the pain from the knot on the back of your head," said Dr. Merkquack. "What if I told you there is no knot on the back of your head Bon? The CT scan showed nothing unusual. I think you're suffering from an intense psychotic delusion. I'm not sure what has caused it, but I'll find out, I promise you," he said quite confidently. He stood, closed his notebook, and motioned for the guard to unlock the door.

"The nurse will give you a sedative to help you sleep with no more nightmares. I'll check in on you in the morning. Perhaps then we can discuss the knot on your head. Until then, I am ordering that you remain in restraints. Good night, Bon," he said as the nurse entered the room with a large hypodermic.

"Just relax, Bon. If you fight me, it'll only hurt worse, I promise you," the nurse said with a firm yet wary smile as she bared my right buttock. As I looked away, I couldn't help but notice, she seemed to be enjoying my pain.

I tried to relax as I felt the sting of the hypodermic. Within seconds, my eyelids felt heavy, and I faintly heard her say, "That's a good boy, Bon. Don't fight me, and we'll get along *just* fine," before darkness took me.

It was early the next morning, before breakfast, when the orderly came for me and wheeled me, still strapped to the bed, out the door and down the hall, past a wing full of patients. I had never been to this side of the hospital. All the patients in this wing were locked in their rooms.

Some were having conversations with themselves; some were moaning with absolute despair; others were pounding on their doors, screaming in terror. I had no idea what was in store for me. The orderly paused outside a procedure room—waiting.

After a couple of minutes, the lights dimmed, and the screams from inside the room stopped. The deadbolt's snick announced an impending departure. That meant my turn was next. I trembled as the door opened and another orderly wheeled out an unconscious patient, also strapped to a bed. As my orderly wheeled me in, I realized why the other patient had been screaming: this was the electrical shock treatment room, and it was time for my first treatment.

As the orderly strapped electrodes onto my head, I promised myself that if I ever got out of here, I would make Dr. Merkquack pay. That thought steadied me a little.

"Open your mouth and let me put this in. It will keep you from breaking your teeth during therapy. Bite me, and I'll up the dosage of your treatment. That could cause cardiac arrest, and you would die. I'll bring you back only to kill you again if you try to bite me. Remember that when it is time for your next treatment. You only get two chances. I won't bring you back a third time. You'll be just another patient who died during treatment," snarled the orderly with a sadistic glint in his eyes.

I opened my mouth and let him shove the rope in, none too gently. He joined the growing list of people I would hunt down if I ever got out of here. That was my last thought before the current hit, sending my body into convulsions of agony. I barely held on to reality as the second shock struck, worse than the first, and then blackness swallowed me.

I woke in terror, my breath ragged, soaked in sweat—back in my room. No more shocks would come. Then the knot on my head burned with a pain that made light flash behind my eyes, and I screamed in agony. "Please, just kill me!" I pleaded to the empty room, tears streaming down my face as I clawed frantically at the restraints. No one came. No one cared. Here, my fear, my pain, my desperation meant nothing.

∽o∾

It had been six months since my last pain attack when Dr. Merkquack said I could go home. I didn't know what to expect. I had no money, no place to go, no idea where my car was, or if anyone would be waiting for me on the other side of the front door.

None of that mattered. I was getting the hell out of this place. Nothing was going to stop me. I would take the rest one day at a time. Maybe now I could start a new life—one not controlled by what Dr. Merkquack called an "imaginary pain."

As I walked out the front door of St. John's Sanitarium, home for the mentally ill, I had no idea who, if anyone, would be waiting for me. While I was at St. John's, Mom had married a wealthy Australian she met while out man-trolling. She, along with my brother and sister, were moving to Australia and would send for me once I got out. After they left for the airport, her letters stopped. At first, I thought it was a postal issue. By the third week of silence, I confronted Dr. Merkquack.

"I was waiting until you were fully recovered from electrotherapy before telling you," he said. "The plane your family was on was lost at sea. Their plane exploded—an assassination of your new father-in-law over a business deal gone wrong. I'm sorry I waited so long to tell you, but I didn't think you were up to the pain of such a loss. I can order a sedative if you need one," he said, placing his hand on my shoulder with his vile, attempted compassionate smile.

"I'm okay, doc. I knew… I don't know how, but I already knew. If you don't mind, I'd like to stay here on the balcony and watch the moon rise until lights out. I need to say my goodbyes," I said, tears streaming down my face as grief slowly washed over me.

I walked out the front door a free man. As the huge door swung shut behind me, I froze, shocked by who was waiting. It was Deena—and she was driving my girl!

With a squeal of excitement, Deena launched herself at me, grabbing me in a fierce bear hug and plastering my face with kisses. Finally, she slowed down and locked me in a deep kiss of pure passion. The world faded as I returned her kiss, losing myself to her passion, forgetting everything else.

When we finally came up for air, Deena said, "Let's get you home and feed you some good food."

"Where is home?" I asked.

"I have an apartment here in town we can use until we decide where we want to go," she answered, handing me the keys to my girl. "No more questions until we get home," she said firmly.

I slid behind my girl's steering wheel with a huge grin and bumped the ignition. My girl roared to life then settled into her perfect, lumpy idle. For the first time in an eternity, I smiled in anticipation of letting my girl run off the leash again.

As I swung onto the deserted highway leading from St. John's, I stomped on the accelerator and my girl howled, exploding down the highway, rear tires smoking.

"Woohoo!!!!" screamed Deena as I speed-shifted into second, breaking the rear tires loose and flicking my girl's tail out for a second time.

I was so caught up in the thrill that when I glanced down at the speedometer, it read 138. I immediately hit the brakes—we were approaching the interstate, and this was a 40-mph speed zone.

☙✇❧

The male Nenich slave approached the private chamber of the Skreei mission commander with dread. He had been unable to reestablish contact with the male test subject. Their entire scientific mission hinged on that genetically compatible male and his female.

If the slave had lost control of the subject, he knew he and his family would be executed once the ship returned to the Skreei homeworld for his failure. With a shaking hand, the gray slave rang the door chime and announced his arrival.

"Enter," bid a stern, high-pitched command from behind the door.

The slave waited, kneeling, waiting to be acknowledged by his master, who was finishing her daily cleansing ritual.

When the Skreei commander finally emerged from her bathing chamber, the slave nearly fainted from anxiety.

"Have you been able to reacquire the male subject?" she asked.

"No, mistress. I have not. We have lost the female as well," the terrified slave answered from his formal submission position, neck exposed, hoping the Skreei commander would not slash his throat with her killing claw and instead spare his life despite his failures.

The Skreei commander, her killing claws twitching involuntarily in her displeasure, stared at the obviously terrified slave. *What should I do? Tradition demands I execute this slave immediately for its failure. The only thing stopping me is the fact that this slave is the best science tech I have on this mission. Its loss would cause my genetic research mission to fail. If I fail, I will never again receive government funds or permission to continue my research for the cure of the scourge virus that is slowly killing my mate and all of the Elder males this far from the homeworld. I am illegally conducting research on an invasive species on one of the forbidden garden planets.*

"Make ready to move forward one star rotation into this planet's future, then attempt to reacquire the test subjects. If you do not, I will execute you and your family when we return to Skreei. Now go and carry out my orders," she said, dismissing the trembling and weeping slave.

"Yes, mistress," said the gray slave as it slunk out of its master's quarters.

∞o∞

Once we arrived at Deena's apartment and parked my girl in the garage, she began making my favorite supper—fried chicken.

"I saw you on the steel table next to me. What did they do to you?" I asked.

"I will explain after we eat—and not until then," Deena said firmly. I had no choice but to wait.

After supper, we relaxed, cuddling on a sofa built for two, sipping a very nice sweet California Riesling. She whispered in my ear, startling me: "Those dreams about the steel table... they're real. And I have them too."

I had spent the last six months trying to convince Dr. Merkquack, the other doctors at St. John's—and, most importantly, myself—that the steel table and the little gray men were nothing more than figments of my imagination.

"Only I see you on a table next to me. I haven't had the pain in over six months. I also have something to show you. Children, come out—it's time to meet your father," she said.

I froze, stunned by what Deena had just said. As I first laid eyes on the twins, tears of joy filled my eyes. I had a family!

"Hello, Father," they said in unison, their voices oddly flat and unemotional.

"Now go to your room and work on your equations. Daddy and I need to talk in private," Deena urged.

"Yes, Mother," they answered in unison, the same lack of emotion, filing out the door perfectly in sync.

Once we were alone, Deena said, "Don't get attached. They are hybrids, and they'll be leaving for their other genetic half's home planet very soon."

"How could this have happened? Those kids are at least ten years old!" I said, in disbelief.

"They're only six months old. I found out I was pregnant just before I kicked you out. I got scared. I'm sorry," said Deena, tears moistening her eyes.

"I tried to see you while I was pregnant, to explain," she continued softly, holding me tightly, her head buried in my chest, "but Dr. Merkquack wouldn't let me. By the time I realized what our children might be, they were born and started growing so fast I knew I had to keep them hidden from everyone, especially the military. I moved to West Palm Beach under a different name to have the babies. No one knew me there. Once they were born, I moved back to town. By then, the twins were old enough to care for themselves during the day while

I worked to build a bankroll so we could start over somewhere where no one knows us."

"The twins told me they are the last hope of reviving the genetic structure of the Skreei race," she explained. "All males on the Skreei homeworld are born sterile, and the few fertile males left are slowly dying from a disease called the scourge. That makes these two extremely valuable to the Skreei Queen. She will stop at nothing to obtain the twins. They will attack Earth, destroying anything that gets in their way of getting the twins. To keep this from happening, the twins have agreed to go with the Skreei if Earth is left unharmed. They leave tomorrow night to meet the Skreei ship."

"Do you think they'll keep their word?" I asked, my head spinning.

"I hope so," Deena whispered, "Cause there ain't nothing we can do to stop'm, cause we are no match for their technology."

The next morning, Deena and I woke to find the twins already gone. Deena cried for the rest of the day.

∞o∞

"Mistress," reported the Nenich slave, "as you ordered, the hybrids are aboard and in complete hibernation."

"Prepare the probes to find another breeding pair," ordered the mission commander, "one that matches the higher genetic profile. The Royals will want a hybrid from a purer bloodline."

"But Mistress, you agreed to leave this planet once we had the hybrids," gasped her slave. "A Skreei cannot break a contract. It is forbidden!"

"Mind your place, Nenich scum," screeched the mission commander, flying into a full-blown rage, her killing claws held high in a striking position. *How dare a mere Nenich slave lecture me on Skreei law of intergalactic commerce!* "This planet is far too valuable to abandon over a promise to a primitive," she screeched, sheathing her killing claws.

"Once word of our success spreads to the outer colonies," she explained, calming herself, "they will destroy this planet in their greed for a longer life. I will not have broken a contract. I will simply retire and collect the bounty of my discovery from my new estate on the homeworld."

"Now terminate the current breeding pair before the authorities find them," she ordered. "Reset your probes to find a match for the purer genetic profile. The Royals will want their own bloodline. We must act quickly so we can leave this planet before the other colony scientists arrive—or before Hoan, King of the Galaxy, finds out and sanitizes this planet in retaliation for our participation in the fight for an independent Galactic Alliance, free from his royal right to rule. You are dismissed, slave."

"As you wish, mistress," answered the Nenich slave, slinking out of his master's quarters to carry out her orders, thankful to be still alive and without concern for the impending extinction of the two billion helpless beings on the planet below.

Those beings were not citizens of the Galactic Alliance and were therefore unprotected by galactic law and of no further concern. They had fulfilled their part in the Nenich Queen's plan to free her people from the yoke of slavery across the galaxy—by pitting the Skreei Empire against the throne of Hoan and watching patiently as they weakened each other enough for the Nenich to strike the killing blow on both, winning the freedom they had fought so hard for in secret.

Because his brother was the mission pilot, the slave knew something his mistress would never know until their return: Hoan, King of the Galaxy, had already ordered this garden planet to be sanitized and re-terraformed. When the Skreei returned, they would find the Tiggerian Nymppooh and death for their homeworld.

With the blue majesty of a water planet slowly filling the forward view screen of his spacecraft, Mlloog forced himself to focus on his instruments, trying hard not to notice the planet's incredible beauty.

Mlloog had been given the morally repugnant task of sterilizing one of Hoan the Gorn, King of the Galaxy's, prized yellow-sun planet gardens by King Hoan himself.

The fact that billions of sentient beings would perish at the whim of the KoG was evil and morally corrupt, fumed Mlloog. He began the scans anyway, his stomach churning with revulsion—he had no choice.

Mlloog frantically preened the fine hairs along his sensing knoggs to calm his agitation, his third arms shaking badly and weak from the anxiety of what he was about to do. Yet he must—his entire family line would be forfeit if he failed. He dosed himself with the medication he had been given by the flight surgeon before launch. It calmed him instantly, and he began his planned descent into the planet's atmosphere.

No one defied the KoG and lived. King Hoan's penalty for failing a royal mission came straight from Gorn tradition: the offender was forced to watch as his entire family was devoured—before becoming the King's next meal.

A preponderance of galactic bureaucracy ensured the KoG stayed in power for another thousand-year reign. The Royals and the rich elite enslaved the civilized planets through fear of the brutal and ruthlessly efficient Royal Fleet.

Mlloog's preliminary scans showed severe environmental damage within the planetary water bodies' ecosystem, confirming his long-distance scout probe's data. The entire aquatic food chain teetered on the brink of collapse, poisoned by radioactive isotopes leaking from a damaged nuclear power facility.

Repair estimates of 100 solar rotations were in place to restore the Emperor's beloved yellow-sun garden to the pristine condition he so prized.

"Beginning planetary scans to assess the damage caused by the humanoid infestation. Humanoids appear to be remnants of an unknown A'nai refugee colony. Technology failure appears to have perpetuated a downward social spiral; no evidence of known A'nai technology," Mlloog spoke into the mission recorder.

"Visual scans confirm a massive infestation of a primitive A'nai colony is causing the environmental damage. Planetary water bodies are being poisoned by leaking radioactive isotopes from a destroyed nuclear power generation facility built on an island of volcanic peaks. Scans complete. Beginning deployment of sterilizing agent #2 in aerial form," Mlloog reported.

Sterilizing agent #2 came from one of King Hoan's prized specimens—the only surviving specimen of the Tiggerian Nymppooh left within the KoG's vast domain. Its successful eradication and control had secured 6,000 years of Hoan's reign as King of the Galaxy. Its release here furthered Hoan's plans for this entire quadrant of the galaxy. The homeworlds of three of the most powerful opposing senators in the Galactic Senate were in this quadrant.

"Let this be a lesson to those who defy me," was the King's message to the opposing senators. Only King Hoan possessed the technology to destroy a Tiggerian Nymppooh once it sprouted.

Hundreds of billions would die if even one of the Tiggerian Nymppooh's spaceborne spores reached a neighboring populated system. Billions of seed pods were propelled into space in an enormous methane gas release after the entire food source was consumed—seed pods that would drift dormant for thousands of years.

As the second equatorial orbit reached twenty percent completion, a red light alerted Mlloog to a problem with the primary dispersal nozzle.

"Switching to secondary external nozzle," Mlloog said into the mission recorder.

Once the green board confirmed functionality, Mlloog adjusted course to begin a polar orbit for maximum dispersion.

Without warning, the starboard rear-quarter proximity alarm sounded, immediately followed by the port side. Something was flanking his ship. Sensors indicated humanoid atmospheric craft had successfully evaded his sensors and were now in attack position, weapons locked on his vessel.

Their aerial technology is far more advanced than the probes reported, Mlloog grimaced.

Bering Sea, 10 miles west of Hooper Bay, Alaska

"Base, this is Eagle 1: I have a visual on an unidentified aircraft. Still no response to visual or radio signals. Be advised, the craft is leaking some sort of vapor from a protrusion on the belly of the craft."

"Base to Eagle 1: You are authorized to fire. That craft cannot—I repeat cannot—reach the mainland."

"Roger, Base I: Confirming weapons are hot. I have a lock… firing missiles 1 and 2."

"Base, this is Eagle 1: Target destroyed. I repeat, target destroyed. Wreckage landing ten clicks offshore. Launching marker beacon… beginning sample collection of the vapor."

"Base to Eagle 1: Acknowledged. Target destroyed, nice shooting, Eagle 1. Return to base. Stage 3 decon protocol is in effect. Proceed to runway Alpha 1."

"Roger, Base. Eagle 1 returning to base, runway Alpha 1 for decon."

Bleary-eyed, awakened from too-short a nap, the President answered the emergency line. "What is it?!" he snapped into the phone. *Probably another one of the generals overreacting again—they always think the barbarians are at the gates,* he thought.

"Mr. President, there has been an Area 51 event off the coast of Alaska. An unidentified aircraft entered the atmosphere and began leaking some sort of vapor on its second planetary rotation. It has been successfully shot down in the Bering Sea, ten miles west of Hooper Bay, Alaska. Recovery ships will be on site in five hours," the voice reported.

"All state and local police are responding and have cordoned off a ten-mile stretch of coastline, and EMS has every available unit on standby," continued the voice.

"How do you recommend we proceed, Admiral?" the President asked the head of the Joint Chiefs of Staff.

"Sir, I recommend a full media blackout until we ascertain the nature of the vapor and whether it is harmful. I suggest sealing off the area with level-3 bio-containment for Hooper Bay and Fairbanks."

"Admiral, are you sure it was an alien craft and not just some falling space junk?" demanded the President.

"Sir, NORAD confirms this object entered our atmosphere, decelerated, then changed course to begin an equatorial orbit before leaking the vapor. It then altered course to a polar orbit before we intercepted. The craft appeared undamaged and resembles the same design of previous Area 51 crash wreckage. It could be a prelude to an attack," the Admiral answered.

"Bring us to DEFCON 2. Deploy containment units for a possible quarantine, and shut off all news in and out. Is that clear, Admiral?!"

"YES SIR, Mr. President!" shouted the Admiral. Instantly, dozens of generals grabbed phones and barked out orders to execute the President's instructions.

Contact + 24 hours

"Admiral, tell me you have some good news," said the President wearily, exhausted not only by the long night but also by his recent election campaign and the rigors of his first 100 days in office.

"Mr. President, I do have good news. The analysis of the vapor found no pathogens; it appears to have been a liquid leak, sir."

"What kind of liquid, Admiral? What are you not telling me?" demanded the President.

"It appears to have been organic waste and water, Mr. President," said the red-faced Admiral.

"You mean to tell me you kept the leaders of several countries up for the last 24 hours because one of our F22s shot down an alien RV dumping its waste tank in our atmosphere while taking a few pictures of the primitives on the surface, Admiral?!" screamed the President.

"Stand down immediately! This is going to be a public relations disaster! We will be the laughing stock of the world! If anyone's head has to roll, it will be yours, Admiral! Tell the press it was an extreme training exercise in extraterrestrial contagion control. Those two pilots must never reveal what they shot down," ordered the President. "This will blow over in a few days. If it gains any traction in the media, we will proceed with operations against the ISIS training bases in Florida as planned and leak it as a distraction. Report in 24 hours and only to me, Admiral."

"Yes, Mr. President," said the Admiral into a dead phone.

"Dr. Collins, they've ordered all samples of this project to be destroyed immediately. That comes straight from the Admiral himself!" gasped lab assistant Jerry, out of breath from his dash to get there first.

"Jerry, do you understand what this is?" Dr. Collins asked excitedly. "It's living, alien, organic matter! It could change everything we believe about everything. For the good of humanity, we cannot let the Neanderthals destroy something so important."

"Barnibus, the MPs are on their way to collect the samples. You better think of something fast, and I don't want to know what," Jerry said worriedly, edging toward the nearest door, knowing he was going to regret getting involved, fearing the frat brother oath would be invoked.

"I can't do this alone, Jerry. You have to distract them while I hide a sample," explained Dr. Collins. "Come on: Delta Tau Chi! It will be just like college, only a lot more fun!"

"If we get caught, Barnibus, I'm blaming you all the way!" Jerry retorted with a groan. The oath had just been invoked. "Go! They're already at the first airlock. I'll stall them as long as I can," he said, heading for the second airlock to cut them off.

USAF Major Nelson, designated Eagle 1, followed the signal man into the decontamination hangar and waited calmly as the decontamination gases spewed over his F22 Raptor. There was no sign of Eagle 2's Raptor.

Major Nelson was anxious to debrief and get home. *It was his tenth anniversary. If the debriefing went quickly, he might still make the dinner his wife had planned to celebrate.*

Routine decontamination complete, Major Nelson was ordered to stand by before exiting his Raptor. That was four hours ago, and he was trying not to think about his bladder's urgent call.

"Base, this is Eagle 1. How much longer? My reservoir is past full!"

"We understand, Eagle 1. The report on the organic sample has just arrived. We have a green board. You may exit your craft."

"Roger, Base. Just clear a path and all will be forgiven."

As I climbed down to the hangar floor, I was shocked to see a gelatinous slime dripping from my Raptor's nosecone sensor array all the way back to the rear landing gear. At least a dozen troops in full biohazard protective gear surrounded the F22, with flamethrowers lit.

"Major, this way on the double, Sir!" shouted the MP sergeant sent to escort me, motioning me forward with the barrel of his M-4. There was no sign of my wingman Major Healy or his Raptor—just a trail of burned slime extending out the decon hangar.

I was now certain I would miss my special dinner; they might just try and make me and Major Healy disappear to cover up what I shot down. *I'm not going down for this just so the brass—or worse, some politician—can cover their own asses*, I resolved, and I began to plan my escape. My wife Alice and I would have to disappear—we had practiced for just this kind of situation.

When you flew one of the most advanced stealth fighters in the world for a black ops squadron, you learned to take precautions—if you wanted to live long. It was all too easy to become a liability, a witness to things those in power preferred buried. A "training accident," wrapped in the blanket of national security and shielded by the Patriot Act, could make you disappear without a trace.

I just have to signal Alice. I will make my move in the locker room when I am getting out of my flight suit and the guards are relaxed and looking the other way. I might even know them, and then I can make that phone call easily, I thought, laying out my plan of escape.

After a thorough hosing and gassing, I was finally able to exit my flight suit and helmet and answer nature's call. *I shouldn't still be under armed guard. I don't know any of the guards, and I don't recognize unit insignia. And what have they done with Major Healy? We are always debriefed together after a mission like this. Something is up and it looks like I'm in the shit again.*

"Boy, that's a relief," I said as I buttoned my uniform pants and secured my gig line. Now was not the time for a sloppy uniform, the head of the Joint Chiefs waited for me down the hall.

"You guys mind if I call my wife to tell her I am going to be late? It's our tenth anniversary," I asked as I held up my cell phone.

"No calls!" barked the MP sergeant as he motioned to the nearest MP to take my phone. I let him have it. I had already palmed my burner phone in the locker room and activated the emergency signal to Alice while I was in the stall. She was at this moment grabbing our emergency passports and money and loading up our go-bags in the Jeep.

In minutes, she would be headed to pick me up at our designated safe place, then a twenty-minute drive by Jeep to a private airfield ten miles north of Anchorage. There my Lear 23 was being fueled for takeoff just like we planned. Now I just had to get free.

"Sergeant, I am not feeling well. That dog food they gave me for chow is rebelling. Please give the Admiral my apologies for making him wait," I said as I hurried toward the stall farthest from the door. The MP nearest me moved to block the way, M-4 at the ready.

"Let him through. The Admiral is not ready for him yet," ordered the MP sergeant. "He is not a prisoner, so give him some privacy."

"Thank you, Sergeant," I said gratefully from behind the closed stall door.

Once the MPs had filed out into the hallway to guard the door, I wasted no time opening the false bottom of the last stall, dropping down into the escape tunnel underneath, then closing myself in.

This tunnel was a relic of the cold war for the pilots to escape the attention of Russian spy planes. The entrance to the command center had been sealed off years ago and forgotten, but not the one that led to what was once a top-secret hangar that had been recommissioned as the base mess hall.

I found it after searching the base's pre-cold-war designs, which were declassified after a major renovation to Elmendorf Air Force Base to accommodate our F22 Raptors and the B2 squadrons.

We—the founding pilots of the Black Knights, 1st Raptor Squadron, 3rd Fighter Wing—had dug the escape tunnel past the fence to the ravine. We made a pact to keep the tunnel secret, in case one of us was caught in just such a situation.

We all knew the risks inherent with missions such as ours. My wingman Major Healy and I were the only two founding pilots still alive. Black ops combat and experimental aircraft had killed all of the others.

I splashed my way through the slimy ice-cold water toward the end of the tunnel. As soon as I had a signal, I sent a text to Alice with my ETA to the ravine that bordered the southern end of the base. This tunnel ended in the ravine twenty meters past the base perimeter fence: I had about fifty meters to go.

The tunnel's end was supposed to be an easy 10-foot drop into a shallow creek. I had forgotten about the recent spring thunderstorms. They had swollen all of the local creeks, turning them into instant raging rivers. When I reached the end of the tunnel and found churning water, I remembered.

Damn it! I have got to head downstream to get to the bridge where Alice will be waiting with a change of clothes, my go-bag, and weapons. The creek is too swollen to walk in the cover of the ravine. I will be visible to infrared sensors if I cut across dry land. Looks like I'm going to get wet. My mission was a clean escape and start-over in a country with no extradition treaty with the U.S.

After I climbed down from the tunnel's end, I made my way along the swollen creek's edge toward a large tree branch that had become lodged in the rocks after the flash flood waters had retreated from their peak.

With a herculean effort I managed to dislodge the massive branch. Then, using it as a raft, I slipped into the creek's raging middle, gasping from the shock of the frigid water, my legs pointed downstream to fend off the many large boulders as I started racing downstream.

It wasn't long before my legs were so numb from the cold that I couldn't feel them as I bounced off another boulder. I was only halfway to the bridge. Time stretched into eternity as the cold burrowed deeper into my body—my fingers frozen in a death grip around my makeshift raft.

The current slowed as it rounded the wide final bend before the bridge where Alice waited. Warmth and safety were only minutes away. Prying my frozen fingers off the branch, I crawled through the shallows on all fours. The bank felt impossibly far, my body so heavy, my eyelids drooping with cold and exhaustion. No sign of Alice. No sign of our heavily modified Jeep Wrangler.

As I slowly crept toward the bank using just my arms, I was afraid I was going to freeze to death here in this stream—after all I had lived through. My body was numb below my waist.

Alice, where are you... ran through my mind over and over. Determined not to quit I summoned the last dregs of my strength and dragged myself forward with just my arms, now numb and nearly unresponsive. A light appeared on the shore. *ALICE!* "Over here", I croaked, now paralyzed by the icy water as sleep gently took me.

I woke to find myself wrapped in a thermal blanket—naked, with an also naked, sleeping Alice curled up around me.

"You have hypothermia. We have at least twenty more minutes before you will be warm enough to fly," she murmured, wakened by my movements. "Consider yourself lucky you didn't lose anything important to severe frost bite," she said with a sleepy giggle as she lifted her head off my chest.

"Where are we?" I asked urgently.

"Safe is where we are. We are on board the jet. I filed a flight plan—we're scheduled for takeoff in fifty minutes and our flight path has already been approved," she said, checking my watch. "Now lie back down and rest. Your core temperature is still too low," she added drowsily after she swiped my forehead with a digital thermometer.

I didn't protest. My legs and arms were beginning to warm—the tingling was quite painful and getting warmer was the only way to stop it. So I snuggled back up to Alice and waited for the pins and needles to stop. Not until then would I be ready to fly us out of here. When I was finally warmed up, I dressed and made my way to the plane's cockpit.

"Jet 5779 to tower, we are in position and asking for clearance." I said into the comms.

"Jet 5779 please hold your position. You have two ahead of you." answered the control tower.

"Roger, tower—two ahead of us." I looked at my wife, concerned about the delay.

"Do you think they have found us?" she asked. "I don't see any other jets lining up for takeoff."

"Maybe," I answered. "The delay to warm me up might have given them time to find us, but I doubt it. They are probably still searching the base for me."

"Jet 5779 you are cleared for takeoff from runway 2."

"Roger, tower—cleared for takeoff from runway 2." I said with a huge sigh of relief.

Contact + 10 days

Yet unnoticed in the midst of toxic wastelands around the world, new life was emerging. Inexplicably, plants sprouted where none should grow. From the deepest deserts to the densest rainforests, a new species took root, unseen.

Staying small on the surface was the Tiggerian Nymppooh's primary camouflage when so young. Unseen, its roots would quickly circumnavigate the planet, and none would be the wiser until it was far too late to stop the infestation.

King Hoan's favorite pet fed ravenously on any source of solar energy until it was time to bloom. The maturing blooms became filled with larvae, ready to consume every sentient life form on the planet.

The Tiggerian Nymppooh bloom's fragrance was irresistible to any sentient life form, drawing its prey into its enormous clumps of tiny, sticky blooms. Willingly, blindly answering their master's call came its prey, releasing its ravenous, growing larvae with each flower's kiss. When the planet's sentient beings took notice of the pretty flowers blooming everywhere, it would already be too late.

It took three news cycles before pundits—both foreign and domestic—and the media shifted attention away from the costly and absurd military mobilization and the new President's involvement.

The new headline was the phenomenon of a strange plant species thriving in deserts and toxic wastelands worldwide, relegating the presidential blunder to the back page. Reports of these bizarre plants spreading, coupled with the sudden mass disappearances of entire villages in rural India and China, consumed global headlines.

It was as if Elvis had returned to Las Vegas as the opening act for the Second Coming. Believers flocked to the world's wildernesses, leaving all of their worldly possessions behind, to see the flowers, believing them to be a miracle from God—never to be heard from again.

Contact + 23 days

Under our new identities, Alice and I were hiding on a remote, private estate, on the Mekong River in Vietnam when the reports of the mass disappearances began pouring in from every country. I was stunned as news of the worldwide phenomenon—new growth in the most toxic and inhospitable places on Earth—broke across international news outlets.

I knew that ship I shot down was the cause of all of this. *It's that green slime I brought back on my plane! Oh my God what have I done! I have destroyed everything!* The thought consumed me, and I curled up on the floor, numb to the world around me.

What is that smell? It was the most beautiful scent I had ever experienced. *Where was it coming from?* I had to find out. The voices began softly singing in my mind, drawing me out of darkness, urging me toward joy. I stood. I felt like *me naked* Tarzan as I followed my now naked Jane into the jungle, hand in hand, driven by ardent desire.

As we walked, still hand in hand, I was suddenly overwhelmed by my love for Alice—never before had I loved so intensely as now. As I held her close, my lips pressed against hers, our breathing hot and fast, her scent set me on fire and our passions flared uncontrollably. Suddenly, a new awareness swept through us: we would soon be one with the beautiful voices singing in our heads. Our embrace shattered with a single thought, our passion forgotten: *Please help us! We urgently need your help! Come to us now!*

Each tiny bloom's kiss was ecstasy. Soon, a bright light illuminated all, heralding the end of mankind's reign on Earth.

THE ELEVATOR GAME

By

Samara Hanachi

Power and money. That's all they need to stomp on the poor and live a comfortable life where their lies and mistakes are covered up. They become so accustomed to this life that they forget all morals and act on greed alone. My parents tried to protect me from the evil of this world, but they weren't even able to protect themselves. Some people are good, but most are always looking for a way to manipulate you—and who am I? A mere ant in a world full of snakes that only care about money and power.

Sometimes greed can make you do awful things, like leave your friends—or even your sister—in a dangerous world with more questions than answers. Now, I know there are so many other worlds out there with secrets of their own.

"Come on! It'll be fun! I have all of the instructions here," Sam pleads, shaking a piece of paper in our faces.

We were all standing in front of the elevator of Winston Corp., where each of us had received an internship—but not by choice. Sam had sent us an emergency message making us think that he was in danger. But no—all he wanted was to get us together so we could play the elevator game with him.

"We don't even know if this game is safe. What if something happens to us?" Mason questions Sam with his usual worried tone.

He has always been concerned for our safety, acting as if he is the big brother of our group. It's strange, though, that he has never told us anything about his past. All he ever said was that things happened and that he's changed now.

"Someone at the front desk gave it to me and told me it was a fun game that I should try. I don't know who it was—I mean, there are so many employees working under my dad. How am I supposed to remember his name?" Sam replies. His father is the head of the company, and he has always gotten what he wanted because of how rich his family is.

I turn to Ira, and she looks at me while shrugging her shoulders. I sigh. "Fine, explain what we have to do."

Sam gives me a wide smile, "Okay, first let's get into the elevator, and I'll explain everything there."

He steps in first as the doors open and looks at us expectantly. Reed and Ira, who are always along for the ride, enter without hesitation.

"We shouldn't be here when the building is closed like this. What if someone finds us messing with the elevator? Or worse, what if someone gets hurt and there is no one to help?" Mason says, pacing the dimly lit hallway.

I pat his shoulder reassuringly, giving him a slight grin. Then I step into the elevator. Mason bites his lip hesitantly before following me in. Sam's smile widens as each of us step into the elevator.

"Now," he says, "we will go to the fourth floor, the second floor, the sixth floor, then back to the second floor, the tenth floor, and finally the fifth floor—in that specific order. When we reach the fifth floor, a young woman will enter the elevator, but she is not an ordinary woman. You should not look at her no matter what—even if she begs for help."

That's when Reed, probably thinking this was a harmless game, bombards Sam with questions. "Umm, what exactly is this game? Why shouldn't we look at her? Who is she?"

"Nobody knows who she is exactly," Sam replies, lowering his voice for a spooky effect, "but some say a demon or a ghost. If you interact with her, she will kill you in an instant, or worse—drag you straight to hell," Sam says.

Reed's eyes get bigger, but I remain unbothered as Sam continues with the instructions.

"Next, we have to press the button to the first floor. If the elevator goes down to the first floor, then we must all exit immediately without looking back. But, if the elevator starts going up and reaches the tenth floor, then we've been allowed into the other world—otherwise known as the young woman's dimension—where everything is dark, cold, and horrifying."

I act surprised by Sam's explanation, even though I've heard all of this before. "Why would the elevator start going up?" I ask critically, not paying too much attention to Sam's answer.

"I don't know. But supposedly, it looks just like our world," Sam explains, turning towards me. "We have two choices: we can either choose to get out of the elevator and ignore the woman's attempts to stop us, or we can keep pressing the first-floor button to go back to our world."

Ira laughs suddenly, and we all jump, startled after the long silence that followed Sam's speech. "This is clearly not real. Do you guys actually believe this stuff? Nothing is going to happen. There isn't going to be some strange woman, and the elevator won't go up unless we make it." Ira—practically a skeptic—doesn't believe things quite so easily.

"Well, we won't know until we try, right?" Sam challenges, looking at all of us before pressing the close door button.

Ira gently shakes Reed, who was visibly trembling, to come back to his senses.

"Wait, why do you need all of us to play?" Mason asks, suspicious.

"Oh yes, I almost forgot—five people need to play the game for it to work," Sam explains, slipping the paper instructions into his pocket.

I glance around the elevator nervously and try to mentally prepare myself for the other world I'll have to encounter again. I've been waiting for this moment, after all—but now that it's finally here, and I have enough people to play with, my mind drifts back to how I left the last time. Regret and sadness well inside me, though I fight to keep them hidden.

Reed stands in the corner of the elevator, closing his eyes tightly before reopening them. As if new confidence has risen within him, he stands up straight and takes Ira's hand. "It's okay, Ira, I'll protect you if anything happens," he says, putting on a weary smile. He has always been protective of Ira—ever since the fire. Even if he's scared himself, he would never let his little sister do anything alone.

Ira looks at him solemnly, eventually smiling back, comforted by her brother's sudden warmth.

"Ok, now let's begin," Sam says ominously, tapping his fingers together with a grin and pressing the button for the fourth floor.

The elevator door opens, and—as expected—no one is there. I see the room that holds all the employee and client files.

Sam presses the second-floor button. Again no one is there as the elevator doors open. This is there the technical support team works. Before the elevator doors slide shut again, I see some equipment that they must have forgotten to put away.

He then presses the next button leading us to the sixth floor. The door opens, and—like before—no one is outside of the elevator.

Suddenly, the lights inside of the elevator start to flicker. I watch as everyone stands still, terrified, holding their breath.

We are getting closer...

The elevator returns to the second floor. Once again, nothing. A sudden gust of cold air sends shivers down my spine. I see Reed and Ira huddled close together to keep warm.

The elevator reaches the tenth floor with the same result. However, I look closer and notice gooey, black patches on the walls outside. They almost seem to reach out to us, beckoning.

Mason moves closer to me, and even Sam trembles as he presses the button that will lead us to the fifth floor.

"T-this is it, g-guys," he says, barely making out each word.

The elevator shudders slightly as it descends, but we all remain silent. The door opens, and I can feel my heart hammering inside my chest as the pale, young woman creeps into the elevator.

Everyone's face showed disbelief—we all knew there was nobody else inside the building. Sam had told us that he made sure the front door was locked before we started. We quickly avert our eyes, remembering the instructions of the game. Sam trembles as he presses the button to the first floor.

We wait—but to everyone's horror, the elevator starts going up.

The elevator shakes violently as it ascends, and the woman starts to sob as she begs, "Please, help me! I'm so scared!" No one dares to respond. We all keep our eyes fixed away from her, ignoring her pleas. "Why won't you help me? Please—look at me!"

I'm terrified as she continues pleading. Her voice gradually gets deeper and more aggressive as the elevator comes to an abrupt halt on the tenth floor. Her head turns slowly, the sound of it crackling echoes throughout the elevator. I can feel her eyes, if she even has eyes, latch onto me.

"Weren't you here before?" she rasps, an inhuman noise rippling from her throat. I don't answer her, hoping she will remain silent and leave me alone. "You are making a mistake coming here again! Where are your other friends?" She says, laughing grimly.

The elevator doors open to the regular tenth floor—the one we're used to seeing every day—but there were slight differences. It was dead silent—like the whole world came to a stop. I can feel the dull frigid air and the darkness coming from it.

I can hear Sam pressing the first-floor button repeatedly, but the elevator doesn't move.

Suddenly, we are all pushed out of the elevator as the woman calls after us, "This isn't where you belong!"

We don't turn back to look at her as she continues to laugh demonically.

The door shuts behind us with a loud screech, and a heavy silence falls—except for the echo of her laugh, lingering in the shadows.

"I'm sorry guys," Ira whispers, "I had to push us out because that thing was about to kill you."

"How did you know?" I say, hardly moving my body to look at her.

"From the corner of my eyes, I saw her lifting her hand towards you, so I assumed she would hurt you. Plus the elevator wasn't budging anyway."

"Well, at least we didn't have to stay in the elevator with that creature," Sam says, his voice low. Reed creases his eyebrows as if still trying to process what just happened.

We all were.

"I knew this wasn't a good idea," Mason says, giving Sam an angry stare. "And now, not only do we have no information about this world, but we also have no clue how to get back."

"Of course I know how to get out of here! I just didn't expect this would be real!" Sam exclaims.

"Yuna," Reed says, turning to me, "why did that woman say you were here before? What is she talking about?"

"She was obviously lying—just trying to get into our heads. Probably wanted to provoke us to speak," I say, trying to eliminate any suspicions about me.

Before anyone can question me further, soft footsteps approach.

Everyone freezes in fear.

Ira silently gestures toward the conference room—or where the conference room *should* be. We all rush inside, and I shut the door behind us, careful not to make a sound.

The room falls silent as the footsteps draw closer.

"I told you they were here. I could sense them as soon as they entered our world," a voice says outside the door.

I tilt my head in confusion. *Why does he sound like Mason?*

"Okay, then where are they? And why would they come here to begin with? I mean, it's not like they were summoned," another voice responds—one that sounds almost identical to Sam's.

"I don't know where they are now, but they're definitely here. We must find them in order to leave this wretched place," the one who sounds like Mason says. I can hear the disgust in his voice as he hisses each word.

"Should we tell the others that their humans are here?" Sam's voice asks.

"I'm sure they've sensed their humans and are already making a plan to capture them. Let's work together: if you find my human first, I'll help you find yours—and vice versa. Then, we'll kill them and take their bodies to enter the human world," Mason replies with confidence.

"That's a great idea!" Sam exclaims.

Their footsteps grow fainter. One of them hums as he skips down the hall. No one in our group speaks until the humming fades completely.

"What the hell?" I whisper-yell, turning to everybody, baffled.

"Why did they sound like you and Mason?" Ira asks, directing the question at Sam. He was the one who made us play this game, after all, and I don't remember anyone else being around.

"The game never mentioned anything about this! I mean—those people, or whatever they are—want to kill us!"

"What we need to know," Reed cuts in, his voice trembling slightly, "is why they sound like you guys in the first place!"

Sam doesn't respond. He looks like he's thinking deeply, lips pressed into a tight line.

"Look, guys," Mason says, "I don't know why those people have the same voices as Sam and me. But you can't blame Sam for not knowing everything. I knew this game wasn't safe, but we're here now, and we need to make a plan to get out before they find us."

I realize I'm smiling at Mason unknowingly and quickly catch myself before anyone notices.

"Sam…" Mason says, gently shaking him out of his thoughts. "You said you knew how to get us out of here, right?"

Sam looks at Mason with an expression I've never seen before—a mix of sadness, guilt, and regret.

"We're supposed to go back with the same elevator and press the same buttons," he mumbles. "Then we can exit on the first floor."

"Okay, that's simple enough. We're already close to the elevator, so let's go—quietly," Mason says.

I open the door slowly, peeking through to see if anyone is nearby. When I'm sure the coast is clear, I wave everyone forward.

Cautiously, we step out of the room one by one.

Ira makes sure to close the door softly after everyone, and we all walk down the hall toward where we came from. I stop in my tracks when I look up to where the elevator should be. My heart skips a beat, and my eyes go wide as I blink, trying to will it back into place.

"Umm… where is the elevator?" Reed whispers, unsettled.

With my feet frozen in place, I try to comprehend why the elevator isn't there anymore. Wasn't it there the last time I escaped? Is this what my other friends saw?

"What!? The game instructions never said that the elevator would just disappear after coming here," Sam claims as we all continue to stare at the blank wall in front of us.

"Well, well, well, what do we have here?"

Everyone turns toward the voice, and I gasp when I see another Mason standing in front of us—with a disturbing smile on his face.

He's wearing the same blue jeans and black T-shirt as *our* Mason, but the look in his eyes is completely different: desperate, angry… and maybe even a little sad.

Our Mason always has a soothing, protective, and caring look in his eyes.

Another Sam skips toward Mason, and they both look at us with hungry smiles.

"That was fast! I guess we won't have to look for them. Your plan worked after all," Sam exclaims.

"Yes, it did. And now we can kill them quickly," Mason says menacingly, stepping closer.

"Why do you want to kill us?" I blurt out, trying to defuse the situation.

Sam laughs as Mason hisses, "Why? Because you humans are filthy creatures who don't care about the lives of others. You only know how to take power for yourselves—all in the name of greed. You always try to take what doesn't belong to you."

I freeze.

He—or *it*—is right. Humans *are* selfish at heart. I had to learn that the hard way. Even my friends and I have some kind of darkness within us, just waiting to come out when the opportunity strikes. But not all humans unleash their bad side for greed. Some can control it— use it only when necessary to protect the ones they love. My parents worked for horrible people and only brought out their darker sides to protect me. People with morals, people who understand the weight of life—they can keep their darkness at bay.

"You're right," I say, keeping my voice steady despite the trembling in my hands. "Some people really do care only about themselves and their power. But not every human is like that. Some use their strength to protect the ones they love."

The other Sam stares at me in disbelief.

"The humans we've seen are far from good. I doubt you're any different," he mutters.

"Why do you look like Sam?" Ira speaks up.

"Don't you know?" he replies. "You humans created us. Every person creates a doppelgänger—born from the worst thing they've ever done. Those other selves live here, in this dark hell of a world."

We all exchange glances, trying to process what he's just said.

"We don't have control over our thoughts or actions," Mason adds. "As soon as you feel, think, or *do* something awful, *we* are the ones affected. We feel the urge to kill cruelly because of that.

We're connected to you. We know everything that's happened in our respective humans' lives."

How does that even work?

Before I can respond, Ira and Reed appeared in front of us with disgusted looks on their faces.

"Looks like you guys found the humans," Reed says, glaring straight past me.

I turn around to see *our* Reed staring at him—in disbelief.

"Why don't you tell her what really happened?" the doppelgänger taunts, his gaze fixed.

Reed doesn't respond, but instead hovers in front of Ira, eyes locked on his double.

"What is he talking about, Ree-Ree?" Ira asks, trying to make him focus on her, but he doesn't move.

"Oh, this should be fun," the doppelgänger Reed says, his voice loud and clear for everyone to hear.

Ira's doppelgänger smirks. "You're always so good at everything, aren't you, Ira? Did you ever tell them how you passed that entrance exam—or should I?"

Ira looks down at her feet.

"I-I have no idea what you're talking about," she says, her voice trembling.

Everyone looks at her—confused by the doppelgänger's words, and even more shocked by Ira's reaction. She's always been confident under pressure. So why is she breaking down now?

"Come on, tell them, Ira. Tell them how you cheated on the test," her double urges.

Cheated on a test? Ira would never do that…right?

Ira hesitates, then whispers, "Sh-she's right. I cheated on the test—after breaking into my teacher's office to find the answer sheet. I didn't study and was so worried I'd fail everything."

Appalled, we all stare at her as she fidgets with the zipper on her jacket.

Reed and Ira—the doppelgängers—laugh at our reactions.

"How about you tell us about the fire, Reed?" Reed's doppelgänger says, making an explosive gesture with his hands.

"I—I'm not going to talk about the fire," Reed mutters.

"Well, of course. It's up to you," his double replies, starting to pace slowly across the hallway. "I mean, it's not like *you* started it to begin with…"

Ira shakes her head. "You didn't start the fire, Reed. Don't listen to him. Nobody died because of you."

Reed shifts his gaze toward her, and his other self smiles with satisfaction.

"H-he's right, Ira. I started the fire in our house—the one that killed our sister. I couldn't save her. It's all my fault," he says, his voice breaking.

Ira steps away from him. "What? How? Why?" she stammers, each word a blow.

"I'm sorry. I made a mistake," Reed murmurs, his voice cracking.

"Oooo, I like this game!" doppelgänger Sam says, clapping his hands together.

I hear *our* Sam gulp beside me.

"The rich kid who always gets what he wants and never takes responsibility for his actions. You know exactly where I'm going with this, don't you?" Sam's double sneers, eyes fixed on him.

Sam bites his lip but doesn't answer.

"I d-dealt drugs a wh-while ago," he finally says, forcing the words out. "And I gave some to my b-buddy because he asked for it. I d-didn't imagine he'd use it to overdose…and kill himself. There w-was evidence against me, and I would've been convicted—if my dad h-hadn't covered it up."

I can hardly believe what I'm hearing. But then again…*am I any better than them? I've done things I'm not proud of too. I left my sister. My friends. I just—left.*

"What do *you* have to say for yourself?" Mason's doppelgänger asks, lifting his chin toward Mason.

Mason steps forward. "I'll confess before you say anything," he says, clenching his fists.

"Maybe if all of us confess the worst thing we've done, it'll give *us* and *you* some kind of relief," he continues, giving me a quick, almost hopeful glance.

"I—I went to jail because I was hanging out with the wrong people. When they turned on me, I got revenge by giving the police everything I knew. My testimony put them away for life."

He doesn't look anyone in the eye.

My vision blurs as I stare at his back. *Is this really the same Mason I knew?*

Before I can react, I *feel* something behind me.

I can't move. I can't speak.

I try to look—but in a flash, I'm somewhere else entirely.

Something is definitely in front of me, but why is it staying in the shadows? *How did I end up in the storage room?*

"Hello, Yuna," the figure says—and I gasp.

Her voice. *Is that… my other self?*

"You must be wondering why and how I brought you here," she says, stepping out from the shadows. "But all you need to know is that I'll kill you for making my life so miserable."

She walks closer, and I shrink back in fear. But then I realize—of course she hates me.

I created her.

My doppelgänger exists because of what I did. Who she is now… that's on me. My expression changes to that of sympathy and guilt.

"Why are you looking at me like that? Don't give me your pity!" Yuna screams, suddenly thrusting a knife to my throat.

"I'm sorry," I say, forcing myself to maintain eye contact, though my legs are trembling.

"You were created from something I did to my friends," I continue, my voice steadying. "You never asked to be born like this. I can't imagine what it's like—to live in a dark, cold world, your actions and thoughts not your own. You must crave the freedom to choose, to be yourself, to act on your own terms."

I search her eyes. Behind the mask of rage, I see it—pain. Helplessness.

The knife is still at my neck, but her grip loosens slightly.

"Kill me if you want," I say. "You should kill me. But maybe... maybe there's a way out of this world for both of us. I want to help you. Please—trust me."

"How can I trust you?" she spits. "You made me like this. I just want a life of my own."

She slams me harder against the wall, tightening her grip.

"You're right," I whisper. "I can't ask you to trust me. But maybe I can earn it. Maybe I can show you that I'm serious about finding a way out—for both of us."

Looking at her is like looking in a mirror of shattered regrets.

She steps back slowly, still gripping the knife tightly as she watches me.

"How do I know you don't just want to die right now?"

"You don't know," I say. "But if I fail to earn your trust... then you can do whatever you want to me. I won't stop you."

She narrows her eyes suspiciously, but her grip on the blade loosens. And then—she exhales, a long, uneven sigh.

"Why did you leave them?"

I look at her in confusion.

"Why did you leave your other friends here?" she asks, crossing her arms, waiting for a proper explanation.

I swallow the bile in my throat and try to stand up straighter. "I... I didn't want to leave them. They told me to leave and get out of this place. You weren't even here when I came last time—how did you know about it?"

"Of course I know! I was created because of that. How could you leave your friends, even if they told you to?" she snaps.

I hesitate but still manage to gather my voice. "You were created because of that? That's why I could get out of here without having to do anything! My friends pushed me into the elevator so I could survive—but I wasn't planning to just forget about them. I needed four other people, and…" I lift my chin so the tears won't fall. "I wouldn't leave behind my little sister."

"Well, you did!" Yuna bites back.

My vision blurs as tears well in my eyes, and I shut them tightly, letting go of the tears. For a while, the room is silent—only the soft sound of my tears hitting the floor breaks it.

Yuna grips my shoulder lightly, nodding, her voice hesitant. "Fine. Let's go back."

Suddenly, we're back on the tenth floor—but no one is there. I turn to her in fear. "Please help me look for them." *What if Sam and Mason did something to them?*

Yuna rolls her eyes in annoyance and looks down at her feet, clearly debating whether to help me. When she looks up, I give her my most pleading expression.

"If you don't stop making those puppy eyes," she says flatly, "I'll scoop them out myself."

I immediately stop.

"Where should we look first?" I ask, scanning the room as if my friends might just appear.

"I know Sam and Mason well. They'll have your friends in their secret place. The only question is—why bring all of them there? *Your* Sam and Mason are all they need to get out of this place," Yuna explains.

"Well, there's only one way to find out," I say, determined.

She approaches, and I brace myself for that strange sensation that always comes when she teleports us.

Before I even blink, we're in front of a door. I read the words posted at the top: *Meeting Room 405*. This place was always reserved for the company's usual guests. I glance at the side of the door and spot the familiar infinity symbol scratched into the frame.

The inside of the room—the curving walls and the little door in the corner I never knew the purpose of—make it unique.

Yuna walks up and presses the infinity symbol.

My expression shifts from uncertainty to astonishment as the wall opens, revealing a long hallway. She motions for me to follow. I move slowly through the opening, turning around once to confirm that yes—the wall really did just open. I wonder if this feature exists in my world too… and if that little door inside the room is another entrance.

As we walk down the hallway, I hesitantly ask, "Have you seen my sister in this place at all?"

Yuna turns to look at me for a long moment before responding. "I've been here long enough to know that your sister and the friends you came with last time aren't in this building."

I look down—not wanting to meet my own eyes.

"But who knows? They could still be out there somewhere, even though there isn't much—"

Before I can question her further, we reach the end of the hallway, which opens into a large room. At first, I don't see anything—until I turn to the side.

Reed, Ira, Mason, and Sam sit against the wall, their faces drawn with terror and worry. The doppelgängers are nowhere in sight. When they see me, their eyes light up—but the joy vanishes the moment they spot Yuna behind me.

"Don't worry, guys. She's not here to hurt anyone," I reassure them, walking cautiously, wary of a trap.

After hugging everyone tightly, Mason blurts, "I thought something awful had happened to you. We were so confused—except for the others."

"Speaking of which, where are they?" I ask.

"They brought us here and then left without saying a word. How did you find us?"

I glance toward Yuna, who stands a few paces away. "It's a long story, but Yuna's going to help us all get out of here," I say, smiling softly at the soul I created. She rolls her eyes, but there's a flicker of amusement.

Reed reaches to put a hand on Ira's shoulder, but she turns away, clearly irritated.

"Guys, we need to help them. You heard what Sam and Mason said—our doubles were created from our worst deeds. We should work together to escape this place," I say intently, the thought of saving everyone filling my mind.

Before anyone can respond, footsteps echo in the hallway. We huddle together—except for Yuna, who turns to face the sound calmly. Each step reverberates against the floor until Sam and Mason emerge… along with Reed's and Ira's doppelgängers.

"Well, well. Look who joined the party," Mason says, smirking at Yuna. "Didn't expect you here."

"I'm not here to join anything," Yuna asserts, arms crossed.

"What do you mean? We're all here to kill our humans so we can leave," Sam says, baffled.

Ira stares at her double, then clings to my shirt. I instinctively step in front of her.

"Maybe there's a way for all of us to escape," Yuna says. I grin at her—she's giving us a chance.

"What are you talking about? Why would we want to escape *with* our humans? They're the reason we suffer!" Reed shouts, irritated at Yuna's suggestion.

"You're right. They are the reason. But it's not their fault that their thoughts and feelings affect us so deeply. Aren't you tired of killing?" Yuna asks.

"Why don't they just stop thinking horrible things?!" Ira exclaims.

"It's in our nature to have bad thoughts—even if we don't mean them," I say, stepping forward. "I'm sorry you go through so much pain because of us. But if we work together to leave, maybe that pain will stop."

"The only way out is to kill our humans," Mason says flatly. "That's what makes the elevator reappear. So even if we wanted to get out together, there would be no other way"

"I know who to ask about that," Yuna replies with certainty.

I look at her, bewildered.

"I've been through a lot," she adds. "We can summon a demon. It'll know another way. But it'll come with a price."

"A demon?" Reed yells. "There are demons in this place too?"

Yuna nods.

"Let's say we do consider this," Sam says. "What would we even do in the human world?"

"Maybe you'll be our long-lost twins," Ira jokes, her tone softening.

They exchange uncertain glances. Yuna wastes no time, grabbing some candles from a nearby table.

"How are you going to light them?" I ask.

"Like this," Yuna replies. Her finger suddenly lights on fire, but it doesn't spread to the rest of her body. She lights each candle, muttering a few unrecognizable chants before placing each one on the floor in front of her.

We wait in silence. Seconds pass. Then minutes.

I start to speak—but before I can, a man—or something like a man—appears.

"What do you want?" the demon grumbles, clearly annoyed.

"What took you so long?" Yuna snaps, hands on her hips.

"I was taking a shower," he mutters, rolling his eyes and mimicking her posture.

"I want you to tell me how we all get out of here without having to kill anyone," she says, keeping a serious tone.

"You know I can't tell you anything without a price."

"Yes, I know. So name your price and tell us everything," Yuna replies, unphased.

The demon grins. "Each of you gives me a sample of your blood. That's generous compared to asking for a heart."

Yuna tilts her head. "What's so special about our blood?"

"Combined with your humans' blood, it can do wonders," he says eagerly.

"Fine. But the information you give us better work," Yuna says firmly.

"It will. It's simple. You must all accept each other—no matter what you've done. You've already begun by confessing. But some of you aren't there yet."

"Seriously? That's it? That's all we had to do?" Mason exclaims.

"I don't make the rules," the demon shrugs. "Now, for the blood."

Two vials appear out of thin air. Yuna and I step forward to give ours.

Mason touches my shoulder. "Are you sure this is safe?"

"Don't worry. It'll be fine," I say, with an encouraging nod.

The demon collects our blood, then I ask, "Who still hasn't accepted themselves?"

He points to Ira and Reed.

"I almost forgot," he says, "each of you must say: *I accept myself and the self I've created, no matter what I've done.*' But it has to come from the heart—or it won't work."

The demon vanishes before we can ask anything else.

I sigh, the weight of my mission returning—my friends and my sister are still out there. What if something happened to them? I really hope they're okay. I searched everywhere in the building with Yuna before coming here, but they were nowhere to be found.

Yuna turns to the group. "You heard him. Ira and Reed still have to accept themselves and each other, no matter their faults."

Ira and Reed look away from each other. Ira hugs herself tightly for comfort.

"Are we really doing this?" Sam whispers to Mason.

"Isn't this what we've always wanted? If there's another way, why kill our humans? It's not their fault they created us," Mason whispers back.

Reed's double steps forward, head lowered. "I'm sorry for forcing you to confess."

Reed smiles. "Don't worry about it. It was my fault anyway."

Ira glances at her brother, tears welling, then looks away again. Reed approaches gently.

"Look, Ira, I'm sorry I never told you. And I'll never forgive myself for starting that fire—"

"Don't say that," Ira interrupts, struggling. "You *have* to forgive yourself. I know you didn't mean to start the fire. And you've always been there for me."

Reed smiles and hugs her tightly—a long, forgiving hug—then turns to the rest of us.

"Guys," I say suddenly, "I need to stay here to find my sister."

"Your sister? What are you talking about?" Sam asks, confused.

"That's not happening," Mason says. "You can't stay here alone!"

"I know... even so I have to find her, and I don't want anyone to have to stay here because of me," I explain.

"We can come back after we escape and bring food, water, whatever we need," Mason says, trying to convince me otherwise.

I know Mason would stay here for me. But would the others want to come back? I doubt it.

"Yuna, listen to Mason," Ira says looking around at everyone expectantly. "We will all come back here with you. Friends always stick together."

Everyone nods. I smile.

"Okay. Let's say what the demon told us."

Starting from me, we go around, each carefully reciting: *"I accept myself and the self I've created, no matter what I've done."*

A few moments pass. Nothing happens.

Then—

"Look, Yuna!" I gasp. Her hands and legs begin to fade. She looks at her hands in astonishment.

The others begin to fade as well—limb by limb—until their bodies vanish. We watch, captivated by the scene.

"Thank you," I whisper, tears streaming down my face.

She smiles, nodding. "You'll find your other friends and your sister."

Then—she disappeared completely.

The others say heartfelt goodbyes before their doppelgängers vanished into thin air. Then silence.

The room shifts—and suddenly we're back in the hallway in front of the elevator. I jump excitedly thinking we made it out—not realizing that no one is next to me until I stop.

The hallway dissolves into an open white space before my eyes.

Why is this happening?

Didn't we do everything right...?

I'LL TAKE THAT BET

By

Kirk Forseth

Johnny Crawford, Jason Emmerick, Eric Lindell, and Pete Howard were four college friends at the University of St. Francis in Illinois. They had met on campus and hit it off right away. They shared several of the same classes, all of which were designed for students studying to become robotics engineers. The quartet studied and worked on projects together, and, while they studied hard, they partied even harder. They were notorious for it. Drinking was involved in most of their shenanigans, but what set them apart from other university students was their penchant for placing bets. They were so close that they rented a townhome together so they wouldn't have to apply to any of the fraternities.

The winter semester had been brutal, and they couldn't wait for spring break. While most of the kids at the university were heading to Florida or Mexico, they were going on a tour of the Old West. All four were fanatics when it came to old Westerns, country music, and the whole theme of the outlaw. Of the four, three came from money and didn't need student loans. Jason, Eric, and Pete were set financially, while Johnny was the odd man out.

Three weeks before the trip, Johnny broke the news that he couldn't go. His parents wouldn't co-sign for a motorcycle, which was how the group planned to get around the Old West. He'd had his heart set on going, but his parents couldn't afford the payments. They tried their best, reworking the budget as much as possible, but the outcome was always the same. They were robbing Peter to pay Paul.

The trio tried to hide their excitement for the trip while Johnny moped about, feeling like he'd let his friends down. While they'd be on spring break, he'd be stuck at home.

Then came a Saturday night, two weeks before the trip. The guys were playing beer pong and kept raising the stakes with each round. The game went to a best-of-seven series and finally came down to Johnny and Eric.

There were five hundred dollars at stake, and Johnny—exceptionally gifted at beer pong—was about to win. Then, to his surprise, Eric claimed he didn't have the money on him. Johnny was heartbroken, but then Eric said he had something worth more than five hundred bucks. He pulled a manila envelope from his book bag and held it up high, a smirk on his face. Shaking it, Johnny didn't know what to make of it. Eric insisted the envelope was worth more than the bet. Johnny tried to read his friend's expression, to see if he was bluffing—something wasn't right.

"You scared?" Eric asked, grinning.

"No," Johnny said, hesitant. "I just don't know if what's in there is actually worth it."

Eric raised an eyebrow. "So, you don't trust me?"

"I do," Johnny said quickly.

"Then let's finish the game. You'll find out what's inside when you win."

Johnny pressed for more details, but Eric wouldn't budge. "You gotta play to find out," he said. When Johnny hesitated further, Eric added, "There's only one condition: if you win, you can't give it back—no matter what's inside."

Johnny froze. "This isn't another date with Ugly Fiona again, is it?" He put the ping pong ball down. "Because I'm not going through that again. I barely survived the first one. She's still calling me."

Eric laughed. "Nah, man. It's nothing like that. It's worth way more than five hundred."

Johnny looked at Jason and Pete, who were cheering him on—a beer in one hand and fist pumps in the other. He had never questioned his friend before—except in the case of the Ugly Fiona situation. But something didn't feel right about this bet. He knew it deep down. If he lost, he'd lose the $500 he worked so hard for. To fund the trip, he'd taken on odd jobs here and there to earn enough. But then again, he wasn't going on the trip anymore. *What was the point?* Wiping the sides of his mouth, he contemplated whether this was even worth it.

Finally, he said the notorious phrase his friends had grown to love—"I'll take that bet!"

Eric and the rest of the guys grinned. Eric made the shot look legit, but he missed intentionally. He knew his friend's pride wouldn't have accepted the prize outright. Johnny stepped up and sank the last ball into the cup. He downed the drink—victorious. He had beaten his partner in crime. Placing his $500 back in his pocket, he reached for the envelope and opened it.

Inside, he found a set of keys. He looked at them, confused. There was still weight to the envelope, and he looked inside again. He pulled out a motorcycle title—registered in his name.

Stunned, his gaze turned to his friends. Eric, Pete, and Jason beamed at Johnny as they folded their arms proudly.

"I can't accept this."

"You got to, Bruh. You won the bet."

"You missed intentionally, didn't you?"

"Did I?"

"Dude, we can't go on the trip to the Old West if you're not there," Jason told him.

"Yeah. We all chipped in and got you a graduation present," Pete told him.

"But…"

"You're Beer Squad. No man gets left behind."

"Thank you. I don't know what to say."

"Just say you're coming with us, and we'll be fine."

"Hell, yeah, I'm coming."

When the time finally came, the Beer Squad packed up their motorcycles with everything they needed and hit the road. Each of them had passed all their finals, including gender studies—barely. This wasn't just a spring break trip. It was a celebration as the next term would be double the workload. They roared out of the city into the great unknown. After many hours on the road and stops for the washroom, they finally reached their first destination—the infamous Deadman's Gulch in Colorado. Their ultimate goal was to visit Lincoln County to see where Billy the Kid became famous.

Hiking the trail was an ego breaker. The quartet thought they could walk the whole trail, but the group made it only halfway before turning back. The Beer Squad wasn't designed for long hikes. They decided to go to the nearest tavern and order some beers.

Making it to town, they found an authentic-looking saloon. They pushed through the double-swinging doors and headed straight to the bar—just like the old cowboys used to when running rampant in the area. As they drank, they made bets as they usually did—each one more ridiculous than the next.

In the middle of one of their dares, the saloon doors swung open. A tall man entered. He wore dark gray pants, a matching vest, a white shirt, and a long black duster. A black hat rested low on his brow, hiding his eyes. He had a bushy mustache, and his unshaven face was framed with a thick layer of stubble. Upon reaching the bar, he ordered a whiskey and drank it faster than it was set down.

The Beer Squad gave him a passing glance and then returned to their bets. The latest bet? Johnny had to hit on the fiery redhead who was bartending. She was dressed in period clothing and was gorgeous.

Kim, the bartender, looked to be about the same age as the twenty-two-year-olds. She was buxom, and that was all the college student needed as motivation. Johnny was the one who had always had his way with the girls. He was known as Mr. Hookup. Not only would he get the girl, but he could also go into any restaurant with a few dollars and come out with a feast. How he did it baffled his friends. He just had that way about him. He was a kind-hearted individual who had a way of connecting with people.

After making the bet, Johnny was preparing to make his move on Kim when the Beer Squad had to change gears. As they were getting louder and rowdier, the bartender asked them to move to the tables.

The stranger at the bar didn't react as they took their banter to the nearby table.

Once seated, the bets continued. The stakes became higher and higher—just like the alcohol content in their beverages, as they moved from beer to the hard stuff. Then it came time for them to start drinking the *really* hard stuff. The four men were already buzzed when they ordered the 100-proof whiskey from Kim. With four shots before them, their bets started flying as usual. It was all fun and games, as it usually was, until Jason opened his mouth.

"I bet I can outdrink everyone here!"

"Oh, you think so, do you?" Pete asked him.

"I know I can."

"I bet you a hundred bucks you can't." Eric started the betting process.

"That's chicken feed!" Jason blustered.

"I raise it to two hundred," Johnny said, feeling lucky.

"No," Jason said, "let's make the stakes higher."

"Like what?" Pete asked.

"I say, I can outdrink everyone here! I'm quite certain that I can... I'm willing to bet my soul on it." Jason slurred.

"Oh... yeah? I bet my soul, too!" Eric replied.

"What about you two?"

"I'll take that bet," the tall stranger said, slamming his upturned shot glass on the counter.

"You don't want to take his bet." The fiery redhead warned them.

"And why is that?" Jason asked.

"That's Coydog Bill McGraw. He can't be trusted."

"Coydog?" Pete snickered.

"You got a problem with my name, BOY?" Coydog growled, stepping toward him.

"No… no… no, Sir." Pete stumbled over his words when he saw the blackness in the man's eyes.

"Then, I'll take that bet!" the stranger said, grabbing a chair from another table and taking a seat.

"I'm sorry, Mr. Coydog, Sir. But we only make bets amongst ourselves." Jason told him.

"What the hell's wrong with you, boy? I said, I'LL TAKE THAT BET!"

"We were just messing about. No harm, no foul. You understand, right?" Johnny said, trying to use his power of persuasion.

"You all made an offer on a bet, and I claimed it. Are you yellow or something?"

"We're not yellow, Sir. We do it as a joke between us. We didn't mean it." Eric informed him.

"Then you shouldn't have said it. He said he could outdrink everyone here, and I've come to collect. You bet your lives. I want to claim them."

"Mr. Coydog, I don't think you understand…" Pete went to explain.

"Are you calling me stupid, boy?"

"No… no, Sir."

"Then I suggest that you ante up on that bet."

"This is ridiculous! Kim?" Jason called over to her.

"Hiding behind a woman's skirt, huh, BOY?"

"I am NOT!"

"Then ante up!"

"Fine! Pete, Eric, Johnny, you in?"

Pete and Eric joined in right away, but Johnny hesitated. He didn't like the fact that this stranger was trying to "claim their souls." Something didn't feel right about him, and that something was setting off all his alarms. He tried warning the others to walk away.

"Chicken liver, yellow-bellied, tenderfoots," Coydog muttered.

The Beer Squad wasn't taking that lightly and encouraged the cautious Johnny to join them—he was their ace in the hole.

"And what do we get out of this?" Johnny asked him.

"You keep yer souls."

"We already own them."

Coydog reached into his long coat, pulled out a small sack, and tossed it onto the table. It was a five-pound bag bursting at the seams. They looked at each other, baffled. The cowboy placed a toothpick into his mouth and shifted it from side to side—waiting.

Not knowing what Coydog was offering as his stake, Johnny picked up the bag and looked inside. Gold dust. Five pounds of pure gold dust.

He paused, dumbfounded, as the Beer Squad inquired about the contents. There was enough gold there to ensure that the four of them would be on easy street for the foreseeable future. Eric, who dabbled in gold and silver, did the math quickly. That bag was worth about half a million dollars. He leaned over to the squad and whispered the good news. They all started seeing dollar signs before their eyes. They were used to playing high stakes, but this was taking it to the extreme. Their chief concern was that it wasn't pyrite, also known as fool's gold.

"Is this…" He started to ask.

"It is."

"Do you know how much this is worth?"

"A lot," Coydog said coldly.

"Is it real?" Pete asked.

"It's five pounds of pure gold dust."

"HOLY SHIT!" Jason proclaimed.

"So… you boys in?"

"We're in!" Eric proclaimed. "What do we have to do?"

"Wait…"

"As you said, you could out-drink me… now prove it!"

Jason called Kim and asked her to bring them several bottles of 100-proof whiskey. She warned them—Coydog never loses, and liquor doesn't even faze him. But it all fell on greed's deaf ears, except Johnny's. Still, although hesitant, Johnny was part of the Beer Squad, and no man was left behind. Plus, they had all seen the gold and wanted it.

Jason poured the first round and then the second. The five men started slamming down the whiskey as if it were water. Four became five, and then six. Then, they started feeling the effects of alcohol. At least Pete did.

"How are you hanging, Pete?" Eric asked him.

"I feel pretty…"

"What?"

That was when Pete broke into song. He started singing "I Feel Pretty" in such a horrific way that the other drinkers had to cower. Pete was singing off-key and very loudly. Kim was grateful she had no other customers, or they would have been chased away from the establishment. They downed their seventh shot. Pete stopped singing, shook his head, and all the color went from his cheeks. The other men watched as he swayed back and forth, his eyes nearly rolling back into his head. Then, without a second gesture, he plopped onto the table.

They were used to this—Pete was a lightweight. He was their weakest member when it came to drinking. The three friends stared at him because he didn't look right. Sitting beside him, Jason lifted Pete's arm and let go—it came crashing back down. He did this three times, and each time, the result was the same. He was dead to the world. The three friends looked up at Coydog, who barely seemed inebriated and was smiling at them. His cheeks were a little more pigmented than when he first sat down.

The eighth and ninth shots came next, and it was Eric's turn to start turning colors. Instead of pale, he looked green—very green. Johnny called for a bucket in case his friend threw up. Johnny didn't want the fiery redhead to have to clean up the mess. That wouldn't be fair to her. The tenth shot came next. The sickly friend did his best to keep it down, but then he vomited into the bucket. Lifting his head, he looked so dehydrated. Jason was about to call for a glass of water when Coydog stopped him. The rules were to outdrink him in whiskey, not water.

Eric's shoulders slumped as there was nothing left in the tank for him. He then fell forward, his head down in the bucket. Jason didn't want to lift him, so Johnny did. Looking at his friend, Johnny could see that something was wrong with him. He then looked at Pete—he was the same. They weren't breathing.

With two squad members dead, Johnny sobered up right then and there. Two of his three best friends were now deader than a doornail, and their drinking host was looking more alive than ever. Coydog had removed his long-brimmed hat, revealing his eyes.

"What the hell is going on here?" Johnny asked.

"What we said we'd do—we're playing for your lives," Coydog said with a sinister smile.

"That was just a figure of speech."

"Was it?"

"You're killing them?"

"No. Not at all. The liquor is doing that. I'm just collecting on the bet."

"Who are you?"

"The kind bartender told you I'm Coydog Bill McGraw."

"What the hell are you two talking about? We have a contest to win!" Jason said with heavily slurred speech.

"Jason, we can't win this round," Johnny said, as he tried to convey that they weren't playing with some Schmoe off the street.

"Like hell we can't." He replied, trying to focus on his friend.

"That's the spirit, boy!" Coydog encouraged him.

"Now, let's drink!"

Jason struggled to pour the next round. He, like the other two, was fading fast.

Coydog barely looked like he'd taken a shot. Why should he? There was something not right with him. What if he actually *was* claiming the souls of his friends? That meant he wasn't human. If he weren't human, he could easily outdrink them.

Coydog pounded the next shot down as Jason tried to mimic him. No sooner had he banged the shot glass on the table than he belched and looked at his friend. Johnny had no other choice but to drink his as well, or else it would be a forfeiture.

"Come on, Johnny—bottoms up?" Coydog said with a smile.

Johnny was as inebriated as his friends, but fortunately, he'd hit the proverbial wall. Ever since he realized that his friends were dead and that Coydog was claiming their souls, he sobered up. He wouldn't feel its effects no matter how much more he drank. Now, he was in dangerous territory, as he could die from alcohol poisoning. What good would it do his friends if he died?

Jason fell off the horse fast.

The black eyes that Coydog came in with were now crystal blue. Johnny was worried. The cowboy was getting stronger and more vibrant with each drink they took. There had to be a way out of this fiasco.

"Shooting for twelve!" Jason said as he poured the next round, getting more on the table than in the glass.

"I think you'd better let me pour from here on out," Coydog told him.

"Let's go, lucky thirteen!"

Jason was losing all the color in his face. He wouldn't make it past this round if he did at all. He and Coydog held up their glasses and waited for Johnny to do the same. Reluctantly, he did, and the two booze hounds pounded back the next round.

Jason smiled as his eyes glazed over—nothing was left in the tank for him.

Coydog was getting stronger as his opponents were getting weaker. Johnny watched as his friend slowly faded away.

The soul taker poured another round, and they raised their glasses. This time, right after the cheers, Jason passed out. His chin smacked the table, and he fell to the floor.

Johnny checked—there was no pulse, just like with Eric. All three were fast asleep.

Johnny looked at the soul taker and received a smile in return. He took pride in his work.

This wasn't what the humans had signed up for. It was supposed to be just another stupid bet of the Beer Squad. They had all been under the impression that this was a regular drinking game, not some way for them to die. Then he looked at Kim—she was as white as a ghost. She… wasn't even real. She was a specter. Looking back at Coydog, he watched as the "man" put a cigarette in his mouth and lit it with a match.

"I don't have all day, boy!"

"So, you can claim my soul, too?"

"Aw, you want points because you figured it out. It's a damned shame you did. I like it better when the souls I take don't. It makes their hellish aftermath that much sweeter."

"This is ridiculous."

"No, this is what I do for a living. I claim souls of the stupid."

"I'm not stupid."

"No, you're the one who figured it out."

"I'll make a bet with you!"

"Oh…" Coydog chuckled. "And what's that?"

"I bet that I can beat you at poker!"

"In exchange for what?"

"My friends back."

"Oh, I'm afraid it doesn't work that way," he said, chuckling again.

"What? Are you yellow?"

"I'm far from being yellow, you gutless little turd."

"Then prove it. One hand. That's all I need."

"And what do I gain if you lose?"

Johnny started thinking about it and offered his brand-new motorcycle. The soul taker declined the offer as he was trapped inside the town's confines.

Johnny asked, "What do you want?"

Coydog responded, "Souls."

If the last member of the Beer Squad lost, he would have to bring a thousand souls. Knowing that was a bit much, they started negotiating back and forth until they reached an agreement upon a hundred souls, plus Johnny's. The human started thinking about how on Earth he could get that many souls for Coydog Bill McGraw.

Coydog looked at him, sat back, and folded his arms. This was better than he could have ever imagined. Most people didn't want to visit the Old West anymore, and souls were getting harder to come by—especially gullible ones who would risk their souls.

Coydog wiped the sides of his mouth and finished off his cigarette. It'd been some time since he'd been able to smoke one. It'd be a damned shame if he couldn't do it again by losing the bet.

They shook on the deal, with the last Beer Squad member proclaiming, "I'll take that bet!"

Johnny ran his fingers through his hair and sighed. He knew that this could be the end of him. He took a few deep breaths and looked at Coydog, who was smiling away.

Johnny asked the barmaid if she had a deck of cards, but the quick gunslinger produced one.

Taking the cards out of the box, he started shuffling. Even inebriated, Johnny could tell that the dealer was a skilled card player. Fortunately, Johnny was an expert and knew the slights used by the soul taker. He observed that the soul taker was stacking the deck—maneuvering select cards to the top. That's when he offered to cut the deck. The squad member performed the cut and then watched the stranger deal from the top and the bottom, where the select cards had landed. The card swindler was so good that you had to be a professional card player—or magician—to see the technique.

The two men sat there, staring at each other. It was as if they were playing chess—but without the pieces. Johnny was feeling sick. He wanted to throw up. He lowered his head and regained his composure.

Looking at the blurred cards, he saw that he had two aces, a jack, a five, and a nine. The aces were welcome, but he had to keep a straight face for the rest. Coydog spread his cards out, as if he had to, and smiled. There was the ace, king, queen, and ten of spades. His lips tightened, sliding slightly to one side—just enough to make the Beer Squad member think something was off.

They sat there for what seemed to be forever. Then Coydog shifted in his seat and said, "Make your move."

"If I win, I get my friends back, correct?"

"I already said that you would."

"I'll take two."

Coydog smirked, knowing he had the kid right where he wanted him. Taking two cards, Johnny looked at his hand, and it was just what he needed. He lucked out, or so he thought. Unconsciously, he let out a slow sigh. This didn't go unnoticed by the card hustler.

Coydog said he would take just one card.

Discarding his odd card, he took the one he knew he needed. The card shark left the card face down and gave Johnny a cocky smile.

The tension between the two was growing. That was the only exchange they could make, and the Beer Squad member was hoping that what he had was enough for the win. This was going to be a go-big-or-go-to-hell situation.

"Time's up!" Coydog told him.

"Let them go!" Johnny said as he sat there, still fighting the urge to throw up.

"Show your hand!"

Johnny laid down his cards—two aces and three jacks. One of which was the Jack of Spades.

When Coydog saw that the card that should have been face down in front of him was in the kid's hand, he flipped his card over. It was the two of hearts. Coydog slammed his fist onto the table. He wasn't supposed to get that card. It was meant for the kid in front of him. That card should have been in his hand. He stared at the intoxicated kid—furious. He'd lost the souls he had just claimed.

Coydog snapped his fingers, and the inebriated friends woke up, looking at each other. They knew that they'd lost, but worst of all, they were going to have one hell of a hangover the next day.

The color left the soul taker's face and eyes. He was back to the same way he'd first come into the saloon. Johnny picked up the bag of gold and tossed it to the soul taker. The creature looked at him curiously.

"Take it. You'll need it for the next group of suckers." Johnny told him.

"You won it, fair and square. I will not let it be known I don't honor my bets."

Before Johnny could reply, Coydog and Kim were gone. They sat in a full saloon with three bartenders swamped with customers. Jason, Eric, and Pete looked around—their heads still swirling. The victor stood up, told his friends he'd be right back, and took the sack of gold with him.

Stuffing the five-pound bag into his duster, he went to the bathroom. It was a relief to use the bathroom finally. After he threw up, he sighed. That was a close one. No matter what he did now, he would not make any more stupid bets. As for the other three, that'd go without saying. He was surprised the card shark didn't see him switch the cards out. Johnny was glad he was an amateur magician and had studied magic since he was five.

Returning to his friends, they agreed to cut their trip short, pack up, and leave.

The three got to experience, for a time, what it would be like when they were stripped of their bodies. The hellfire and brimstone stories were all true.

It took a few minutes for their bodies to adjust, but soon they were as sober as their savior. Each shook Johnny's hand, knowing that he had saved them. The debt of buying him the motorcycle now felt repaid a dozen times over. With a new lease on life, none of them intended to waste it again.

They had had enough of the Old West. They hopped on their choppers and started the long drive home.

LIANA AND THE SEVENTH SPIN

By
Roberta Azzopardi

She had always known that house on the small crest by the sea—the one the sea teases playfully, waves lapping at the very foot of the stairs that led to its blue door. A natural stone breakwater jutted over the water a few hundred metres away, enclosing the small cove like a one-armed embrace. The house gazed placidly, four windows for four eyes and a small wrought-iron balcony that sat like a frown between them. Vines had crept up one of its walls, leaves brushing each other, lifting and falling with the currents of the wind, a clingy lover that fawned in worship. It seemed to her a stoic dwelling—cynical, arrogant almost—in the way it stood erect. It existed outside of everything, outside of space, outside of time. Permanent. Out of place. Odd. A bit like her.

"That place is cursed. Don't go near." Her mother would frown, wrap the shawl tighter about her and give the house a fleeting, ugly look—as if she were afraid to rest her eyes on it for too long.

"Don't go near. I'm warning you." Her father pointed an accusing finger at her, as if she had already done what he was warning her against. She looked away as he sighed, wiped his sweaty forehead with a dirt-streaked sleeve, stopping to lean on the rake he held. She crouched and dropped a few seeds in the trench he had dug out, watching as he rolled the soil over them, burying them. Around her, father, son, mother, daughter repeated the same act over and over, season after season, until the young were young no more and crossed the trench to take the rake—until death claimed them too.

Sometimes, it felt to her that death had already claimed her.

She existed with the seasons and unlike the house, she existed *inside* them too, with the planting and the harvest, with fine lines deepening on her mother's face, and hair whitening on her father's head. Nothing else changed. Nothing else happened. It was stifling.

Don't go near. Don't go near. Don't go near.

The house held her only fascination. It too never changed, even when it should. Even when no one tended the garden, or painted the door, or repaired the roof, which should have had holes sometimes, like everyone else's. Even when no one went in or came out, when no light came on at night, the house never changed—like a fly in an amber stone.

And it was perhaps this atemporality—this existence beyond anything that was natural—that scared the superstitious village. When a group of curious boys once got close enough to peek inside a back window, they claimed an ivy branch had wrapped itself around their ankles in warning. They ran, leaving the house in peace.

Whenever the sun or moon hit that small window at the top, and the house looked like a cyclops, she bit down on the urge to stand up, walk down the path that led to the cove, climb up the tendrils she knew would never hurt her, and peer inside. Instead, she would go to her bed, face the other way, curl up and let sleep carry her off.

She never remembered her dreams—except that one time she felt, rather than remembered, that she had fallen from tremendous heights. She woke suddenly, her heart racing. Sitting up, auburn hair tumbling over her shoulders, she stared at her reflection in the mirror. Her eyes were wide, like they had seen something she was desperately trying to recall—but couldn't. The memory slipped from her fingers like silk thread. Gradually, her heartbeat slowed, returning to the dull throb she was more accustomed to.

What adventure had she been on at night?

"Liana! I made your favourite breakfast! Don't let it get cold!"

It was Liana's eighteenth birthday—no longer a child, though the thought did not excite her. Already the boys had started looking at her differently, having apparently forgotten little, odd Liana. She avoided their gazes, afraid they would interpret her glance as interest—where there was none.

No one shared her curiosity, her desire to truly *live*—in the way she would sometimes run down a hill just to feel her heart pounding in her chest like it wanted to burst free, just to prove to herself that she was alive.

It was no one's fault. She had always been the strange one.

With age, something else had started to happen—alongside the curves she had unwillingly developed, the dull ache at the base of her back. A mounting desperation at what she imagined the rest of her life would look like. The girls had already practiced it, when their first bleeding arrived and they were no longer just children. But even then, they were still allowed their ribbons and toys. It was different now, and the sensation was akin to something falling to the pit of her stomach. A tangible dread.

"Li-ANA!"

"I'm coming."

She jumped out of bed, wriggled out of her cotton nightdress and into her blue one—a faded coarse thing with a white hem at the bottom. The smell of eggs and pancakes rose to meet her as she descended the stairs.

A quick peck on the cheek from Mother and Father, coffee brought to the table as opposed to her customary brewing responsibility, and a plate with thin slices of pancakes loaded with syrup—the only variations in an otherwise normal day.

As she licked her spoon clean, eyes closed, her father opened the door.

"Let's go."

✂o✄

The sun was relentless. Liana shielded her eyes and squinted. Already, her dress clung to her back with sweat, her fingers grimy.

She looked down.

At her feet, just as she was about to step over it, something shiny caught her eye. She scooped it up and held it in front of her eyes, between her thumb and index finger. It was round and cold to the touch—like it had not had time to absorb the heat yet. It was a metal of some sort, though it had a pearly finish she had never seen before. One side was smooth and slightly rounded while the other side was pierced by a small serrated hole. Liana frowned as she turned it around in her hand and tried to guess its use. The hole seemed to have been designed to fit around something—like a knob.

"Liana! Why are you stopping?"

Liana slipped her small treasure into her pocket and moved on, dropping seeds into the trench, her mind distracted.

✂o✄

Later, she'd say she had been *called* to her window.

She sat there now, her hair framing her soft face, the object lying cold in the palm of her hand—called there to see a blinding white light flicker twice from the topmost window in the attic of the house by the sea. She recalled the shock, the way her mouth formed a perfect O of surprise, like the suddenness of the moment needed a way out.

But just as quickly, it was gone—like lightning on a clear day.

Liana stood up, backed away a couple of steps. The pearly knob throbbed in her closed palm like it had acquired a life of its own, and it matched, beat for beat, her own racing heart.

She grabbed her cloak, threw it on over her white cotton nightdress and silently made her way out. She paused in front of the path that led to the house.

How often had she lingered here, toeing the dirt trail she never dared to take? Had she been afraid of her parents, the villagers? Or was she scared she would be disappointed? That the house would turn out to be nothing but an abandoned dwelling that time was kind to?

All her hopes of something *happening* in her life had been pinned on this house. If it turned out to be nothing, then her very life, she felt, would turn out to be the same.

Liana tucked her hair behind her ear. Twice. And stepped forward.

The house felt larger than it looked. The vines were both soft and strong beneath her touch as she started making her way up the wall. They were a few layers deep, providing a secure foothold.

She turned her face against the crisp wind so it could brush her hair away from her eyes, until she was finally there, at the edge of the crescent window. She breathed deeply, stepped up and peered inside.

The room was largely empty. The wooden ceiling slanted like the roof outside. The floor was littered with scraps of paper, and a tall, gilded mirror leaned against the beams directly opposite the window. A table formed an angle beneath the slop of the roof, empty but for some loose paper—and a strange circular object that spilled its metal contents before the woman who sat in front of it.

Liana's eyes widened as she held the vines tighter, her knuckles turning white.

The woman's back was straight, her hair gathered in a soft chignon at the nape of her long neck. She wore a loose dress with a wide neckline and flowing sleeves, secured just below her chest with a thin rope-like belt. The colour was like nothing Liana had ever seen anyone wearing in Soverleen, a deep ruby red, like the setting sun, with wide pleats at the bottom.

She was writing on the papers, stopping occasionally to fiddle with the object in front of her.

There was something familiar in her fluid movements—in the way she held her arm as she wrote. Without looking, Liana knew the writing would be slanted like the ceiling overhead, though she did not know how she knew.

She waited with bated breath, following the woman's gestures until the moment she stood up and, still with her back to Liana, walked to the mirror.

With one last look at the papers and the object she left on the table, she stepped into the mirror—which rippled like water, swallowing her whole in a blinding flash.

Then, like a curtain at the village's small theatre, the entire room went dark.

Liana felt her feet slipping, like the vines couldn't be bothered to provide a hold anymore. She hastened to get down, nearly falling as the branches went limp and soft. She jumped, breathing hard, her hands against the wall, eyes to the ground.

What she had just witnessed went beyond reason—and yet, she never, for one second, doubted what she had seen.

Hesitantly, she walked around the house—which stood indifferently, as it always had—and tried the front door.

Locked.

When she returned to stand in front of the window again at the back of the house, the moon had turned it white, like the pearly surface of the knob that was still in her pocket. She gazed hard, her heart dancing in her chest with the same thrill and uncontained happiness the first explorers of unknown lands must have felt.

And so it was that for the next few days, as the same white light flashed twice from the window—heralding the woman's arrival—Liana ran to watch a similar scene unfold before her.

That it was the same woman every time was not immediately clear.

On the second day, a woman dressed in a long white dress, a gold belt secured below her chest and a thick necklace of a blue stone Liana had never seen before, sat at the desk—shuffling through papers, writing notes of her own, assembling and disassembling the mystery object before her. At first, with her golden skin tone and straight jet-black hair brushing her shoulders, Liana was sure it could not be the same woman with the soft chignon—until, in a gesture that looked more like despair, the woman leaned against her chair and pulled at her hair, revealing the same—though much shorter—soft, curling, dark auburn hair from the day before.

A wig!

She placed the deceiving item on the table and, arms glittering with gold bracelets, she set about adjusting the small items before her, consulting her papers, taking something out and placing another back inside. The items, too small to make out, somehow seemed to fit inside the larger circular object. But when the woman got up with the same slow movements Liana felt like she knew intimately, the object still had its entrails spilled about it. She picked up the wig, placed it back on her head, and after one long sigh, walked to the mirror. Her feet slapped against the hard stone in her golden sandals, and she disappeared again.

This time, Liana slid back down with more ease.

The door, and every other window in the house, however, were still locked—a secret now forthcoming, now barring.

Knowing there was a pattern to the madness, Liana anticipated the next arrival.

Although it was doubly hard to get to the high window with vines that had turned unforgivingly dewy and slippery, she made it on the third day—just in time to see the woman step out of the mirror.

Liana peered carefully, catching a glimpse of the face: slightly rounded at the cheekbones, getting sharper at the chin in a heart shape, the movements too quick for her to notice the features clearly. She was wearing a long skirt made of animal hide and a small band that wound around her breasts, covering little else. Her hair was long and straight, a dark brown that caught the moonlight as it swayed with her movements to sit down. In one hand, she held a spear; from her other closed palm, three shiny items tumbled out, which she placed next to the ones she herself had left behind the day before. She placed the spear gently against the table, pulled the papers toward her and started the now familiar process of reading, writing and assembling (for now Liana was sure that that was indeed what she was trying to do) the item in front of her.

Every night continued to be the same.

As the seasons rolled naturally, so did the woman step out of and back inside the mirror without fail.

She wore thick furry jackets, a hood that enlarged her head four times over, boots still flecked with snow, her face ruddy from the cold—in her hand a small wheel, a thin needle-like item.

She wore a long, satin dress in bold colours, decorated with small pink flowers that wrapped around her tightly, forcing her to take small steps. Her face was deadly pale. In her hair, two sticks held a bun, and in her hand, five little balls made a tinkling sound as she laid them on the table.

She wore a beautiful velvet gown with a pearl netting in her hair and a small pouch around her waist, from which she procured two crown-like instruments. She tucked a stray lock of hair behind her ear—twice.

She wore bonnets, hats, crowns and scarves, long dresses and short dresses with frills and tassels. She wore trousers like a man, aprons, gold and diamonds. She had clean hands and a dirty face. She had long hair and short hair—but always the same colour. And always—always—bearing items.

Liana watched, her heart in her throat as the item on the table grew smaller and then bigger, smaller and bigger again until the contents all but vanished—each lodged meticulously inside.

Every day she wondered at the woman—who she was, what she was doing, where she was going.

Something stirred inside her when she once had a clearer look at the woman's face. It troubled her—the way she felt she knew that face and yet had never seen her before. The determination with which she stepped in and out of fate. She longed to be her—or at least to step inside that room to talk to her. But she did not dare tap against the window. Whatever the woman was doing seemed to be of extreme importance, and Liana was afraid she would upset the equilibrium which seemed to hold everything perfectly balanced.

Like the house that suffered nothing, she too did not wish to cause any trouble.

And yet...

And yet, that little pearly knob she had found all those days ago—exactly on the first day of the woman's appearance—was that not tied to this event?

Could it not also be part of the mysterious object the woman was building?

Surely, if that were the case, the house would let her in?

And yet, even the vines made it clear she was not welcome once the woman disappeared. She was unwanted... at least, Liana thought as she made her slow way back home one night. At least for now.

But she had not been the only one to witness the strange light flashing every night from the little window shaped like a moon.

At first, little Sally believed it to be the moon and thought nothing of it. But when it was repeated two, three, four times, she started fearing monsters lurking beneath her bed—brought forth from the terrible house by the sea. When she told her mother, it took the sensible woman a couple more days to stay up at night and see for herself what her daughter was harping about every single morning.

What she saw terrified her.

Very soon, the entire village knew of the strange happenings, and much to Liana's dismay, the elders decided that "something must be done." Though what that something was remained uncertain.

"Surely it's just a prank from one of Garrett's boys," Liana said one day as she wiped the dishes with her mother.

Her father was smoking his pipe, gazing intently into the fire like he could see something no one else could. Her mother shivered.

"I always knew something was wrong with that house. We should have burned it down long ago."

"Burn it?" Liana stopped, hand hovering over the little china plate with a chink at the top.

It was her father who answered with a grunt.

"They're thinking of burning it down with the full moon. The priest said it would be auspicious."

"But that's... that's tonight." Liana hadn't realised she had gripped the plate—the one with the chink at the top and little flowers forming a garland around the edge. When it shattered on the tiles at her feet, the flowers scattered—the chain broken.

"Oh look what you've done, Liana!" Her mother bent forward to collect the larger pieces.

But Liana was still staring at her father, who turned in his seat, craning his neck to look at his daughter.

"So it is," he said, taking a puff from his pipe as he surveyed the scene, his eyes finally resting on her. "You'll stay put, let the men handle this." And he shifted his gaze away—as if that settled matters.

That day, the first flashes of light came earlier, when the sun had not yet set—like it knew something had gone very wrong.

Liana left through her bedroom window and ran, hoping no one had seen the flashes so early in the day. But when she climbed the tendrils—each leaf pushing against the soles of her feet—and peered inside the room, there was no one there. Liana stared at the still mirror, at the object on the table that now looked complete, though she still could not figure out what it was, and at the papers waiting for the woman to rifle through.

But no woman came, even though the room remained as clear as day and the vines sturdy and secure.

Liana climbed back down and rushed to the front door just as the sun completely set and dusk stretched its dark fingers across the sky. Already the moon hung pale and full—a patient marker, an omen of the end. Liana stood in front of the door and tucked her hair twice behind her ear. Her heart had lodged itself somewhere, making an awful racket against her ribcage in the dead silence.

The door was ajar.

The lapping sound of the waves disappeared the moment she stepped inside, as if she had travelled somewhere far with just one stride. The house was empty but clean; no coat of dust covered the floors, the mantelpiece, or the wooden balustrade. Dark outlines marked where portraits once hung.

The silence was absolute.

The air smelled of wax and honey somehow, lavender, strange spices, sandalwood. She followed the strange scents that mingled and took her far away—to places she had never been but somehow still knew. *Patchouli and musk.* With every step, her gait grew more confident. *Jasmine and rosewater.* She had been here before, many times.

She climbed the stairs to reach the attic and paused inside the room. There stood the mirror, there the moon shaped window and there the table with paper and… the object.

She walked toward it first and leaned forward so she could look at it at eye level. It was as big as the span of her hand and four fingers thick. On one side, it had the face of an unfamiliar clock. There were no numbers, but strange symbols, a completely different alphabet. Instead of hands, the sun, the moon and other bodies which could sometimes be observed in the night sky were scattered across its face, still and dull. At the top of the strange clock, an abrupt and jagged nail with a flat head pierced the implement and stood out like a button waiting to be pressed.

Liana touched it but it was too hard to bend or be pushed back. The back was plain and unadorned, a little dent at the top marked the spot where it could be opened.

She turned now to the papers scattered on the table. Slowly, like a sacred ritual she was initiating, she sat down and started reading.

Rome, AD 1497. First Spin.

The two items were retrieved from the tomb of Saint Peter in a little hole in the wall indicated by the Seeker. Beware of the Borgia Pope. He has seen you and has taken a liking to you. He must in no way get close to you.

I have taken the first of the crowns and placed it right beneath Mercury, where it lodged on its own, seemingly attracted like a magnet. The second I placed directly above, at an angle, like so.

Next to the words, a little diagram of the inside of the clock was drawn, with arrows and instructions. Liana blinked, grabbed another page, unsure what it was she had just read, hoping that the more she read, the more the picture would come together.

Kyoto, AD 1600. Third Spin.

The orbs were still located at Fushimi-Inari Taisha, but moved marginally due to the Earth's differently tilted axis. The trip was, thankfully, uneventful but remember, if you see the horse bolt, you must stop it, or it will kill Date Masamune. The Guide has told you of the samurai's importance in years to come.

The five orbs I have placed descending, not ascending in size this time, starting from Mercury, and ending with Jupiter.

Liana shook her head. With shaking fingers she turned the pages over scanning the familiar swirls in the words, breathing in the scent of ink and old papers.

Tulum, AD 1132. Fourth Spin.

Persepolis, BC 500. Second Spin.

Kansas, AD 1962. Sixth Spin.

Pompei, BC 50. First Spin.

And again.

Tulum, Rome, Persepolis, Granada, Nairobi, Melbourne, São Paolo.

First Spin, Second, Third up until the Sixth.

Her eyes grew wider with each affirmation, with each variation in instructions, with each dated adventure that seemed to be repeated and only slightly different every time.

Six times she visited every location on the same year, points that spanned the entire globe, places Liana had never heard about in the limited schooling she had received—places that did not exist yet.

Six times she had retrieved the same items and attempted to build this... this celestial clock.

With her fingers she trailed the name at the end of every entry—a signature of sorts. With it, memories she never knew she had stored, were freed.

Elena. אֱלִיעָנָה. *Helen. Liane. Ηλιάνα. Elienah.* اليانا. *Illeana. Liana.*

Whispers in her head, from people who had long gone or who were still to come. All the names she had been called by across time and space.

Relief flooded her as the caged feeling she had suffered her whole life lifted, the sweetest moment of her entire life. *Finally.*

Outside, someone shouted and a rock was thrown, breaking the glass in the moon window.

Liana turned, narrowed her eyes. *It was time.* She stood up, took the little pearly knob from her pocket and hesitated. Downstairs, the fire had already started raging, swallowing the house.

Her hand hovered over the Course Corrector, feeling its energy radiating. Would this time be the one? Would she carry it to the safety of the White Haven? She chewed the inside of her mouth, but the smoke had already started slipping through the crack under the door. So she held the powerful instrument in her arms like a precious bundle, pushed the knob down and turned it sharply anticlockwise. The world bended on itself and merged in one straight hole through which she fell and fell and fell...

∽o∾

Liana opened her eyes, hugged herself and cursed.

"Damn it."

"Indeed. Seventh time lucky?"

She accepted the hand that was offered her and got up, brushing her skirt and tucking her hair behind her ear. Twice. The Guide was looking at her with a lopsided grin, his face as timeless as himself.

"That's what you said the third time."

"And the fourth, fifth, sixth."

They started walking away from the little circular pad she had landed on, down a white path and between white walls. Above them, the roof was open to a limpid blue sky. Two large moons hung above them—one white, one blue.

"What was it this time, do you know?" Liana asked stretching her neck this way and that.

The Guide shook his head. He was not much taller than her, but it always felt like he was—a towering, warm presence.

"It could be any slight variation in the gears or oscillator. You need to figure it out Eleyna."

She groaned softly, pinching the bridge of her nose. "I'm starting to think there's a missing piece."

The Guide looked at her, though not in surprise. "What makes you think that?"

Eleyna gestured with her hands, feeling the ghost of the Course Corrector in her arms. She shrugged.

"I've started feeling when a piece is in its proper place. The Corrector sucks it in and it vibrates, just a little." She shook her head. "I was sure I had it this time."

The Guide smiled at her. "Then perhaps you need to find that missing piece by yourself."

"But it could be anywhere, any century… How can I find it if even the Seeker wasn't able to?"

They had arrived at a little patch of garden on top of a gently sloping hill. A familiar olive tree, its trunk thick and old and carved by millennia, stood at the top, the same olive tree from which the dove broke off a branch to give to Noah after the flood.

The Guide had stopped, placed a reverential hand on the bark. "You're not looking hard enough where it matters," he said, slowly.

Eleyna bit her lip. "I don't understand."

"Why are you so quick to dismiss the one that brought you here?"

"Liana?" Eleyna's eyes went wide, as the Guide smiled.

"Your true self, the one who braved the house against all odds. The one who yearned for bigger things, the one who had dreams, who paved the way for you. Here." He paused, cocking his head to one side. "Or have you forgotten?"

She hadn't. Shame rose to her cheeks as she realized how Liana had taken on the weakest shade in her colourful lives—how her life started mattering less and less, even when she knew she owed all her lives to her.

"I thought there could only be that one last piece. But you're right."

He grinned. "I am always right. Helps to know everything and be everywhere at once I suppose, but still. It takes work."

"Sure." But she too grinned in return, squaring her shoulders and turning to face him. "I'm ready."

"You know the rules."

Eleyna rolled her eyes. "Don't alter the course of history. Changing the fabric of time is why the Course Corrector is needed in the first place." She said in a sing-song voice. She coughed at the look from the Guide. "Time is relative," she continued soberly. "Liana will experience day-to-day changes, but in the mirror's parallel worlds, time is infinite."

"Good. And?"

"Only Liana's memories are erased every time she—and I—wake up on her eighteenth birthday."

"Thus closing the loop. Good."

He looked at her, his face softening. "Godspeed."

He leaned forward and touched her forehead.

When she opened her eyes, she found herself in a lavender meadow.

Provence, AD 1254. Hélène sighed and closed her eyes again. He had been right. Time had found Liana for a reason, and she needed to enter that shade of her life with more faith in her true self. Liana might have no memories, but ideas can linger much, much longer, and she needed to implant the right kind in herself first. The kind that whispered—*I believe in you.*

She stood up between rows of swaying lavender.

"Le septième, c'est la bonne."

The Seventh Spin had begun.

DREAMLAND

By

John D. McArthur, Jr.

Within six months of its release, an unprecedented eighty percent of the population had installed the Dreamland app. It seemed as if everyone wanted to control their dreams, and every morning, social media overflowed with glowing reports about the nicest dreams users had ever had in their lives.

Not everyone thought the Dreamland app was wonderful. A group called Nightmare loudly protested its use, claiming it was bad for the soul and warning that users' private information was at risk, as government officials and others could access the chip used to make dreams.

Dreamland assured the public all their information was securely protected, and since Nightmare had been successfully painted as a lunatic fringe, their protests were easily ignored.

Using Dreamland was simple. After paying a membership fee and setting up automatic withdrawals for the monthly usage fee, users would receive the Dream Maker—a small postage-stamp-sized chip to place on their forehead and sync with the app. They could then choose from a selection of preplanned dreams on the app. After clicking on the icon for the desired dream, a small red light would appear on the Dream Maker device, and the chip would activate to control your dream.

With over 1,000 titles to choose from, dream packages included stories of adventure, action, comedy, and music as well as love and romance. (If you were over eighteen, you could also access more graphic adult stories.) There were also dreams featuring peaceful pastoral scenes and sounds.

There was another option users liked—especially after they had been using the app for a while—where they could build their own story. There was an additional cost for this option, but many claimed it was the best thing about Dreamland.

Joseph and Catherine had purchased Dreamland and enjoyed telling each other about their dreams over breakfast. One day, they decided to try dreaming the same dream on the same night.

They had both reached the skill level that allowed them to write their own dreams, so they sat down before they went to bed and outlined the dream they wanted. The story would be of the two of them, going on a cross-country road trip. They chose the places they wanted to see (Yellowstone, the Grand Canyon, and the beaches of Hawaii), how they would travel (in a convertible), what the weather would be like (sunny, mid-70s, low humidity), and where they would stop for the night along the way (camping in the mountains and a nice hotel in Hawaii). The best part was they could enjoy this entire trip in a single night—without ever leaving home.

When they woke up the next morning, they were surprised to find that although they had programmed the exact same dream, it played out differently for each of them. Jacob loved the beauty of Yellowstone, but Catherine couldn't enjoy the scenery, because she kept seeing bears and rattlesnakes along the trails. Catherine loved the beauty of the Grand Canyon and hiking down into the gorge, but Joseph kept slipping and falling off the narrow path that led to the bottom of the canyon. Fortunately, when he fell, the patch would catch the disruption and return him to the trail. Catherine also could not figure out how to drive to Hawaii and imagined Joseph repeatedly trying to drive the car into the ocean—only to sink. In Joseph's dream, he simply saw the ocean, and suddenly he was on the island. Neither of them enjoyed the Hawaii part of their dream. Catherine found herself on a beach so crowded she could not move, while Joseph could not find his way out of the hotel to even get to the beach.

They both laughed over breakfast at the differences in their dreams. Over the course of the next few nights, they managed to fix the discrepancies and experience the exact same dream. Still, Joseph and Catherine felt something was missing. Holding hands and laughing together wasn't the same in a dream as it was in real life.

One day, Catherine was telling her friend Linda about the emptiness of the dream.

Linda said, "You feel empty because you aren't really together. What you need to do is use his chip. That way you will feel his emotions and it will be like he is there."

"Have you tried that with Jack?" Catherine asked.

"Yes, and it is wonderful. But you need to wear both his and your patch."

"Why?"

"Because if you just wear his patch, you will be him, not you. The computer chip will respond like Joseph—not you—it will show his experiences and emotions, not yours."

A little skeptical, Catherine responded, "If I did that, Joseph wouldn't be able to dream."

"Actually, he can if he is lying close to you," Linda said and then whispered as if what she was suggesting was illegal. "And I mean within a foot of your head. Otherwise it won't work."

"Let's give it a shot," Joseph said when Catherine told him about the conversation. "This could be fun. I'll let you wear my patch tonight and maybe tomorrow, I can wear yours."

Catherine smiled, not really sure about the idea, but they sat down to plan out the storyline they wanted. They decided they would be the first settlers on Mars.

"Are you sure you want to do this?" Catherine asked. "Maybe we should just do the cross-country road trip. We know that story."

"What could go wrong?" Joseph replied. "We will be together, and if it goes bad, we can wake each other up, right?"

∽o∾

Catherine put the two chips on her forehead and Joseph snuggled up next to her, his head touching her forehead.

"Goodnight, sweetheart," he said.

"Goodnight honey. Don't let go, ok?" Catherine pleaded.

Joseph gave her a kiss, and within a few minutes, they were asleep.

Joseph found himself—without a spacesuit—on the surface of Mars, alone. There was a small cabin in the distance with smoke curling from its chimney. He somehow knew that was where they lived. The landscape was barren and a faded red. Even the sky had a faint red tint.

"Joseph…" came a very weak and uncertain voice.

Joseph turned and saw Catherine in a space suit.

"You don't need the suit," Joseph said smiling.

"Okay," Catherine replied, but she made no attempt to remove it, and her voice remained distant and faint.

"I can't hear you very well," Joseph said loudly as he stood next to her.

"I can hear you just fine," Catherine said. "No need to shout."

"Sorry. Let's go check out the cabin, okay?"

Catherine and Joseph took each other's hands and started toward the cabin. Joseph saw something out of the corner of his eye and turned to see what it was. Suddenly, he was gone.

"Joseph! Joseph!" Catherine shouted.

Suddenly, Joseph was back. "That was weird," he said.

"Don't leave me like that!" Catherine shouted. Joseph could feel her breathing on him, even though she was wearing a mask.

Joseph looked up. "What the—" he began and suddenly disappeared again.

"Joseph!" Catherine screamed as she woke up.

She was trembling in bed while Joseph said soothingly, "It's all right. It's all right."

Once she calmed down, Joseph told her, "I think when I turned away in real life, I left the dream. And that may be why I had trouble hearing you—because the patch was on your head, not mine. You said I had to be very close to you for it to work. Shall we try it again?"

"Not tonight," said Catherine, still trembling. "Let's just put our own patches on and program one of the pastoral scenes for the rest of the night."

∾o∾

At work, Catherine told Linda what happened, and Linda laughed. "I told you to stay close—within a foot. I forgot to mention what happens if one of you turns away. Jack and I use rope and tie ourselves together."

Catherine looked at Linda incredulously. "Joseph and I aren't into stuff like that."

Linda laughed and walked away.

Later that afternoon, Linda came up to Catherine and, with a serious tone, said, "You know there is an abort button on the app? If you get scared—especially if you cannot get Joseph back— use it."

Catherine didn't respond and Linda added, "I'm serious. If Joseph disappears for too long, abort the dream."

∾o∾

That evening, Joseph and Catherine decided to choose a simpler and safer dream: they would go on a picnic in a city park. Catherine told Joseph about the abort button, and after a few minutes, they found it.

To use the abort option, you had to set a password. To activate the abort, the user would need to repeat the password three times in a row while in the dream. They decided on "abort"—an easy to remember word and not one they would normally say. After entering the password, they set up the dream they wanted and got ready for bed.

"How about if I wear the patches tonight?" Joseph asked.

⚜

Once again, Joseph entered the dream first, and he smiled at the familiar scene before him. The dream was set in a park where they had often picnicked, and all the memories there were very pleasant.

Catherine arrived and she looked lovely. She wore a flowered sundress and a big, floppy hat. She was carrying a picnic basket— although one already sat on the picnic table. The dream corrected the error, and Catherine opened her basket which contained fresh fruit, a variety of sandwiches, fried chicken, a whole cake, and drinks.

As they set things down, Catherine looked away—and suddenly disappeared.

At first Joseph was confused and a little scared, not knowing where Catherine had gone. He could vaguely remember that disappearances could happen, but he could not remember why—or even how he knew. Somehow, though, he felt he shouldn't worry, so he finished setting the table and called out, "Catherine, come here," and she appeared again.

Catherine appeared confused at first but quickly picked up the storyline and acted as if nothing had happened. They ate their meal together, and then Catherine stood up and said, "I need to go"—and disappeared again.

⚜

Catherine woke up, got up to go to the bathroom, then returned to bed and fell asleep—turned away from Joseph.

Her dreams, without the patch, were disjointed. One moment she would be on a road trip with Joseph and the next, she was deep-sea diving. Then she found herself having a picnic—not with Joseph, but with a bear. Later, she saw herself taking a walk with Joseph. Throughout these dream sequences, she could hear someone mumbling something she couldn't understand. Suddenly, everything started to go dark.

With a start, she woke up and turned back toward Joseph, snuggled up to him, and fell asleep. She found herself back with Joseph at the picnic.

The next morning, the big news story was about the terrorist group Nightmare. Apparently, they had hacked into Dreamland's computers with the intent of shutting the app down. Dreamland officials assured everyone that the company had a very secure system and safety protocol in place to prevent any virus from entering the program. The feeble attempt by this radical mob had been shut down, and the FBI was searching for those responsible.

There were a couple other news stories which were largely ignored and dismissed. One was from the CDC, reporting an increase in people dying in their sleep. The other was a warning about the economy's free fall, due in large part to the revenue losses of the movie, TV, and cable/satellite industries. The report also noted a lack of productivity across all companies and industries. Although statistics were not available to explain why or what was happening, business owners pointed to an increase in people calling in sick, arriving late, leaving early, and even sleeping on the job.

That night, Catherine told Joseph she was very tired and wanted to use one of the pastoral scenes, by herself, so she could sleep. Joseph agreed and after they entered the information on the app, he opened the box where they stored their Dream Maker chips.

"Oh, darn it," sighed Joseph. "The chips are stuck together."

"Can you get them apart?" Asked Catherine.

"I think so," he answered as he started to pry them apart. "Man, they are really stuck."

"Be careful," advised Catherine. But it was too late—Joseph pulled too hard, and one of the chips ripped in half.

"Oh my," exclaimed Catherine. "What are we going to do?"

"It's okay," said Joseph. "It's my chip. I'll sleep without it and place a rush order on a replacement so it will be here tomorrow."

Without the chip, Joseph started to dream the picnic story again, but the scene was dark. He thought he heard Catherine crying somewhere, and in the distance, he could see his other dreams swirling around in a vortex as everything turned black. He heard a voice shouting at him in the distance, but he couldn't make out what it was saying. He felt like he was falling, but unlike most dreams—where falling causes you to wake up—Joseph just kept falling. His heartbeat increased, and he began to sweat. He wanted to shout but couldn't. Suddenly, there was a flash of light, and he woke up.

Joseph looked over at Catherine, who was sleeping peacefully. But Joseph was trembling and he couldn't slow his racing heart. He got up and went to the living room, where he spent the rest of the night restlessly in his recliner.

∽०∾

Joseph called in sick to work. Several times throughout the day, he drifted off—and each time, he found himself in the black vortex. But now, there were no glimpses of other dreams—just darkness. The voice was still there, shouting at him, but he still couldn't understand what it was saying. Occasionally, he thought he could pick out words like *stop*, *dream*, *worth*, or *life*.

Catherine had disturbing news when she came home from work. Linda's husband, Jack, had died in his sleep. A ghoulish rumor had spread through the office that Linda and Jack had attempted some very strenuous sexual activities and Jack's heart had given out. However, when Catherine called Linda to tell her how sorry she was, Linda told a very different story.

Jack had actually set his Dream Maker to a pastoral setting—to sit in an open field of sunflowers.

"But the thing is," Linda confessed, "and I did not tell the doctors or police this—in my dream, which was also a pastoral dream of me sitting by a waterfall, Jack came running up and said, 'Don't do it, don't do it, don't do it.' Then he collapsed, and I woke up and saw Jack wasn't breathing."

A few days later, Dreamland released an important press statement. The terrorist group Nightmare had indeed infiltrated Dreamland's computer systems and installed a virus designed to transform users' dreams into nightmares.

Dreamland identified three major glitches the virus was known to cause.

First, the virus made it extremely difficult—if not impossible— for users to wake up from their dreams. Dreamland believed this was the cause of several deaths during sleep. As a result, in addition to filing charges of computer hacking and terrorism against Nightmare, Dreamland was also seeking murder charges.

Second, the virus had the capacity to embed itself in a person's subconscious, allowing it to appear in dreams even without the use of the Dream Maker chip. Although Dreamland stated it had successfully removed the virus from its app, the company admitted it could not eliminate versions already buried in users' minds. Dreamland expressed hope that an antidote would be available within a few months.

Third, there were growing reports of people "jumping" out of their own dreams and into someone else's. Dreamland believed this "jumping" only occurred when users had shared their chip with another person. This practice, they warned, was strongly discouraged. The full consequences of unauthorized chip sharing remained unknown.

In response, Dreamland's legal department was pushing for new laws that would allow restraining orders and breaking-and-entering statutes to apply to dream invasions. Technicians were also developing a system update to block unwanted guests from entering dreams. In the meantime, Dreamland recommended that anyone experiencing repeated intrusions to purchase a new chip, which would reset their dream history—similar to changing a password.

∽o∾

However, even with the new chip Joseph had ordered, Catherine still "jumped" into his dream. At first, he didn't mind—she greeted him with a warm hug and seemed genuinely happy to see him. But suddenly, her eyes darkened, and she began to laugh—a guttural laugh, unlike any sound he'd heard before. Then she began to tell him how awful he was—how he wouldn't amount to anything and how she didn't know why she put up with him.

With a start, Joseph sat up in bed. Catherine wasn't next to him. He noticed the bathroom light was on, and he could hear her crying. Gently, he opened the door.

Catherine screamed and shrank into a corner. "Stay away from me! Stay away from me!" she cried hysterically.

"What's wrong? What happened?" Joseph asked.

She looked up at him, breathing hard, eyes wide. "My dream. You entered my dream and you were awful. You walked in with an old girlfriend hanging all over you. You came right up to me and said, 'This is what a real woman looks like.' Then she spit on me. I called your name—and you slapped me."

"Catherine," Joseph said calmly as he knelt beside her. "It's okay. It was just a dream. I wasn't there. I didn't hit you."

"Then how do you explain this?" Catherine asked as she turned the side of her face toward him. On her cheek was a large red mark—the clear outline of a hand.

∽o∾

Dreamland did not return Joseph's emails describing the dream. They were both afraid to go to sleep that evening. If they did not wear the patch, they would have the horrible black vortex dream. If they did wear the patch, they did not know what would happen.

They decided to use the abort option if either one appeared in their dream. "Remember," Joseph said before they fell asleep. "I love you, and I would never hurt you."

"Promise?" Catherine asked as she snuggled close to Joseph.

He gently kissed her on her forehead and drifted off to sleep.

Joseph dreamed he was in a large open field, talking with someone about buying the property and building a house there. As the house began to take shape in the dream, Catherine suddenly appeared and lunged at him with a butcher knife.

"Abort, abort, abort" Joseph said. He jolted awake—but could still feel the cold steel of the knife against his chest. He felt his chest. No wound. No blood.

He looked over at Catherine. She was on her back with her hands stretched out above her head as if she was getting ready to lunge at someone with a knife. But she was motionless—as if someone had paused a movie.

Unable to wake her up or even move her arms, Joseph called 911. When the EMT's arrived, they knew exactly what had happened and what to do.

"You used the abort option, didn't you?"

Joseph nodded his head.

"Worst option ever. We have seen cases like this. We had two other calls earlier tonight. One person aborts—and the other person freezes."

"But we weren't sharing our patches."

"Doesn't matter. Ever since that virus hit, if another person enters your dream and you abort, they freeze—doing whatever they were doing when you aborted. Looks like she was coming at you with something. Probably a knife, right?"

"But we weren't mad at each other."

"That doesn't matter either. This virus does funny things. We need to take her to the hospital. County General is setting up a special unit for these cases."

"Will she be okay?"

"To be honest I don't know. She's still alive. All her vitals are still strong but her body will not work. Doctors are trying to figure out a cure.

He paused.

"If you pray—pray a lot."

∽o∾

Later, when Joseph finally returned home from the hospital, he looked at his chip and declared, "I'm done with this" and tore the patch in half.

That night, as he drifted off to sleep, the black vortex returned.

The first time it appeared, Joseph woke up in a panic—but told himself, *It's only a dream. I can't let it scare me.*

Over the next few hours, Joseph fell asleep and woke again—each time the vortex returned. But with every return, he managed to stay in the dream a little bit longer, and it became a little less scary for him.

The next night the vortex dream changed. He no longer felt like he was falling. Instead, it was just black—with no noise whatsoever.

The night after that, it wasn't as black, and he could see himself.

The following night it was light, but he saw nothing. Everything was empty and blank.

On the fifth night, Joseph did not dream at all, and he had his first good night's sleep in months.

Nightmare released a statement defending their actions.

The founder of Nightmare had been an app developer at Dreamland. Around the time the app was released, he raised concerns about the dangers of the program, but his supervisor, the CEO, and the board of directors ignored his protests and called for more testing.

"Although it is true we hacked Dreamland's system and installed a virus," the statement began, "the one virus we planted has not caused all the glitches in the app.

"The only thing our bug can do is disrupt a dream by making it a nightmare. We apologize for any distress the nightmares may have caused, but we stand by our decision to plant the virus because of the dangers Dreamland presents to individuals—and to society at large.

"Dreamland has been infecting people's brains—manipulating users' sleep patterns—effectively making them dependent on the app. More usage means more profit.

"The only way people cannot wake up from a dream is if they use the abort option. The abort option is hidden to keep people from using it, and should only be used as a last resort. The person who activates the abort will wake up, but anyone who has jumped into the dream is suspended in time.

"We believe it is only a temporary condition, and our hope is that the one suspended will eventually wake up. If you have a loved one in suspended animation, please call our hotline…"

It took Joseph a few hours to reach someone at the Nightmare hotline. When he got through, they took his name, phone number, email, and mailing address. Then she asked him to verbally agree not to sue or hold Nightmare responsible for any grief or loss due to the suspended animation.

"But you are the ones who infected the program," Joseph said.

"Yes sir," the operator acknowledged, "but our virus was made worse through Dreamland's program. We will reimburse you for any hospital costs and expenses, but we ask you not to sue us for damages."

Joseph sensed Nightmare was only trying to protect themselves and did not care about Catherine, but at this point he felt he had no other choice.

"We are sorry Catherine is in this temporary condition," the operator continued after Joseph agreed not to sue. "We at Nightmare are working day and night trying to find a cure. We ultimately hope individuals like Catherine will come out of this condition in 30 to 60 days, but we do not have enough data to confirm this. In the meantime, we encourage you to stay at Catherine's side as much as possible and talk to her. Our expert opinion is that Catherine is floating around in her mind in limbo, and she can hear and feel what is going on outside. Something as simple as holding her hand will be a great comfort and may even speed up her recovery."

"That's it?" Asked Joseph. "There is nothing more I can do? There is nothing that you can do but hope? There has to be something. Anything. Please."

There was a pause from the operator and Joseph heard a click. "I turned off the machine recording our conversation," she whispered. "This is off the record. If you say anything, we will deny it, but early research suggests if you enter her subconscious through a dream you can bring her out. You would need to use both chips and simply program in her name. No scenario or dream story."

Joseph heard a clicking noise again and the operation continued in her normal voice, "I'm sorry but we will update you as soon as we have more information. Thank you for calling Nightmare and know our thoughts and prayers go with you."

It took almost a week for Joseph to get a replacement chip.

Since the initial report of a virus infecting the app, Dreamland's revenues had plummeted. The development team was frantically trying to roll out new, safer versions of the app, but they were running out of time. One-day delivery had been suspended, and nearly three-quarters of the staff had been laid off. Bankruptcy seemed inevitable. Joseph held his breath, hoping the chip would arrive before Dreamland shuttered for good.

When the chip arrived, Joseph entered "Find Catherine" in the scenario line. Then he retrieved her chip from the drawer where it had sat since she was hospitalized. Into hers, he entered "Find Joseph."

Without wasting a moment, he rushed over to the hospital.

Sleep would be hard to come by during visiting hours, but since he had permission to stay overnight, he waited. All evening, he sat by her side, gently stroking her hair, whispering to her, telling her stories. More than once, tears came to his eyes as he thought about losing her, or worse—of what might happen when he found her. After all, the last time he saw her in the dream world, she was attacking him with a knife. What would happen if she succeeded this time and killed him in their sleep?

About an hour after visiting hours were over, the floor became quiet and the lights were turned off or down.

Joseph pulled the two chips out of his pocket and placed them both on his forehead. He opened up the app on his phone and sat it on the table next to the bed and quietly said, "I'm coming for you Catherine. Don't hurt me. I love you."

It took Joseph about half an hour to fall asleep. But when he finally reached REM stage, he found himself floating in a pure white void. There was no sound. He saw nothing. After floating for a while, he said, "Where are you Catherine? I'm looking for you."

There was a low moan. Joseph looked up—and there she was.

Catherine.

She was in the distance floating toward him. She was still frozen with her hands above her head. In her hands—still gripped tightly—was the butcher knife. As she drifted closer he noticed her clothes and hair began to move as if they were being blown by the wind. Then her legs began to move as if she were running toward him. She was trying to scream, but she wasn't able to get the words out.

As she came closer to him, she was no longer in a state of suspended animation at all. They were both on a grassy hill. It was sunny, and behind Catherine, Joseph could see the dream house he wanted to build.

Tears filled Catherine's eyes—and everything went black.

www.ingramcontent.com/pod-product-compliance
Lightning Source LLC
Chambersburg PA
CBHW052030020726
47501CB00004B/1337